THE BLOOD COVENANT

THE BLOOD COVENANT

Chris Nickson

SEVERN
HOUSE

First world edition published in Great Britain in 2021 and the USA in 2022
by Severn House, an imprint of Canongate Books Ltd,
14 High Street, Edinburgh EH1 1TE.

Trade paperback edition first published in Great Britain and the USA in 2023
by Severn House, an imprint of Canongate Books Ltd.

severnhouse.com

British Library Cataloguing-in-Publication Data
A CIP catalogue record for this title is available from the British Library.

ISBN-13: 978-0-7278-5048-5 (cased)
ISBN-13: 978-1-4483-0723-4 (trade paper)
ISBN-13: 978-1-4483-0722-7 (e-book)

All Severn House titles are printed on acid-free paper.

Typeset by Palimpsest Book Production Ltd.,
Falkirk, Stirlingshire, Scotland.
Printed and bound in Great Britain by
TJ Books, Padstow, Cornwall.

The blood of the covenant is thicker than the water of the womb. Ouch hoer ich sagen, das sippe blůt von wazzere niht verdirbet.

Heinrich der Glïchezäre, *Reinhardt Fuchs* c.1180

With gratitude to all the keyworkers who kept going through the pandemic. Health care, social care, teachers, fire and ambulance, police, supermarket and shop workers. We are all in your debt.
Thank you.

And to the memory of Jim Carter, Cricket, 1955-2021
Dead of Covid-19 in Mexico
The ripples of your life will grow wider

ONE

Leeds, October 1823

His footsteps rang and echoed off the walls. Simon Westow stayed in the shadows, losing himself in the night, hands pushed deep in the pockets of his greatcoat. He walked, trying to escape his thoughts. But they weren't likely to grant him the peace he craved.

For three days he'd hunted a servant who'd stolen some of her mistress's money. Yet everywhere he went, somehow she managed to keep a pace ahead of him. Even Jane, the young woman who worked with him, hadn't been able to find her.

They'd finally caught her early on Monday afternoon, tracked her to the ruin of a house out along the Dewsbury Road. The slates were gone, scattered and broken on the floor. A heavy rain was falling; water dripped from the joists and puddled on the floor. The servant had crawled into the one dry corner of an empty room. As soon as they tried to pull her to her feet she began screaming, scratching and gouging, fighting for her life. Well she might; if the constable arrested her, she'd hang.

They'd recovered what she'd taken. Most of the money and all the embroidered lace handkerchiefs, almost five shillings' worth of them. Simon and Jane took it with them, walked away and left her there, still sobbing. The mistress didn't want to prosecute. They were thief-takers, hired to return what had been stolen for a fee. The law wasn't their business.

Simon strode home through the dusk and rubbed his cheek where the girl's nails had raked his skin. He was weary, utterly drained. The rain had tailed off to a light drizzle, but he was sodden from the day, hunched into his coat, boots splashing through the puddles on the cobbled street.

The girl had made them work for their money and she'd possessed the devil's own luck for too long. But they should have found her sooner.

'Westow!' The shout made him stop and turn. A short man was hurrying towards him, shoes with silver buckles tap-tapping on the pavement. Wrapped up warm, wearing a thick coat, leather gloves and a beaver hat with a black silk band. A walking cane helped him keep his balance. Dr Hey, one of the physicians from the hospital. His father had been a founder of the infirmary, a place Leeds had needed for far too long.

Simon stood and waited. The few times they'd met, Hey had always been smiling, full of quips and mischief. Not today, though; his face was grave and disturbed.

'All recovered now?'

'Fighting fit,' he lied. For much of September, Simon had been laid low with a sickness, exhausted, often dizzy, unable to do much more than lie in his bed and doze. Hey had visited, prescribing his tinctures and potions, not that they seemed to make much difference. The diagnosis changed each time he came. He didn't know. None of the doctors did; that was the problem.

For days Simon sweated and stank, trapped in hot, delirious dreams where dying felt like it might bring relief. Then, over the course of a single night, the fever broke. He slept, to wake as weak and helpless as a newborn child.

Whenever he opened his eyes, his wife was there. Rosie fed him beef broth, spooning it into his mouth. Once he was stronger, she prepared simple, nourishing food to build him up again. In the quiet moments he watched her sitting at his bedside, worrying about him, about their future. His twin sons came and curled around him, a reminder of everything that made life worthwhile. His biggest reason to fight and recover.

Clients arrived, wanting to employ him to find this or that. Rosie listened and passed the information to Jane. She did the work, never failing. By the start of October, Simon was back on his feet. Slow at first, unsure on his feet and tiring easily. And still the physicians couldn't agree what he'd had.

It didn't matter, he decided; it was over, he was improving. He walked; short distances to begin, just from the house on Swinegate to Briggate and back. That was enough to exhaust him. A little more each day, impatient and pushing himself. But under it all, he felt a new caution: the illness had taught him how fragile life could be. One small breath of sickness could turn the world upside down.

He was still far from the way he'd been just three months before. Something as simple as chasing down the servant had left him tired out.

'I suppose you look well enough,' the doctor told him. 'But being out in the damp isn't going to help. Actually, I've been hoping to find you for a few days now. You testified to the commission that was in town three years ago, didn't you?'

'Yes.'

Oh, he'd talked to them. Men sent from London, part of an investigation around the country into child labour and abuse. Simon knew all about that; he still carried the scars on his body. He'd agreed to give evidence. As he spoke, seeing them sitting safe behind their polished table, he relived all the punishments and torture he'd received as a boy, at the mill, as an inmate of the workhouse. Year after year of it, from the time he was four until he turned thirteen, when he could take no more and walked away, knowing that even death would be better. Just the memory made the skin of his hands turn clammy and his heart beat faster. He'd talked. But he didn't believe they'd ever really listened.

'What made you think about that?' Simon asked.

'A pair of deaths I had to examine recently.' Hey pulled some papers from the inside pocket of his coat. 'I made a few notes I wanted you to see. Read them and come to see me when you have the chance.'

Back in the old stone house on Swinegate, wearing warm, dry clothes, Simon read as he ate supper, then spent the evening quietly brooding. For once he scarcely paid attention to Richard and Amos, the twins. Little else existed beyond the thoughts in his head.

'What is it?' Rosie asked after she'd put the boys to bed. She had a flicker of fear in her voice. 'You're not starting to sicken again, are you?'

She sat across from him at the table in the kitchen. Until the boys were born, she'd worked with him as a thief-taker. Now she mostly kept the house and looked after the books. And she could still be dangerous, when he and Jane needed help.

'No, it's nothing like that. No need to worry.' Simon took a deep breath and told her about Hey. 'He made a copy of what he'd written when he saw the children's bodies. The older boy was ten. He'd lost two fingers on his left hand when he was younger. He was covered in bruises, it looked like he'd been beaten with a stick or a strap. It was much the same with the younger one. He was just eight.'

'Who did it?' Rosie asked. Her fists were bunched, fingernails digging into her palms.

'A mill overseer,' he replied.

'Which mill?'

Simon shook his head. 'He didn't put that in there.'

Now he was out here, walking as he tried to stay ahead of his memories and pain. All too often lately, weariness overwhelmed him as soon as he settled under the blankets. Tonight, though, he couldn't sleep. The moment his eyes closed, they sprang open again. After an hour he'd given up, slid out of bed and dressed.

The sky had cleared. It was colder now; his breath bloomed in front of his face. The remnants of rain dripped slowly from gutters. The stink of the manufactories had returned to fill the air.

Simon walked.

Damn Hey. He'd released the past from its cage. Now it was hounding him, snapping and snarling at his heels. All these years and still it wouldn't leave him alone. But better for Simon to be doing something than be restless and wakeful at home.

He'd gone from Sheepscar across to Holbeck, along the river all the way to the ferry landing as he tried to exhaust his mind. He'd sensed Leeds grow silent around him as people gave up on the last dregs of night. He was tired, his legs ached and his feet were sore. But he knew he'd be out here for a long time yet. Bloody Hey.

Simon made his way past the warehouses on the Calls. Bone-weary, needing to sleep. But the images, the history, the pain kept raging through his head. He was just a few yards from the river, heard the water lapping and smelled the low, thin perfume of decay.

A sound cut through, the creak of oars in their rowlocks. Late to be out. Maybe someone was stealing from the barges moored at the wharves. Never mind, he decided; it wasn't his business. Not until someone paid him to retrieve what might be taken.

'Grab him under the arms. Get him out of there.'

The night watch, taking care of some drunk who'd fallen in the river. It happened at least once a month. A man would grow fuddled, lose his way and walk into the water. Some jumped, dragged down by despair. A very few were lucky; they were pulled out and survived. Most drowned, found bobbing downstream when morning came.

'He weighs a bloody ton.'

'You don't need to be gentle, he's already dead. Just grab him. Oh Christ, his throat's been cut. The constable's going to want to see this one.'

Simon felt a chill rise through his body, colder than the night. This was more than another drowning. He started towards the voices, then forced himself to stop. He dealt with stolen things. Not with corpses or death.

Three paces and he understood he couldn't fool himself. He wanted to know.

The men were on Pitfall, only a few yards downriver from Leeds Bridge. Two of them, standing and stretching their backs. Between them, lying on the stones, a shape that had once been a man. Simon could make out the jacket and the trousers, soaked and stained by the water. The men from the watch turned at his footsteps, surprised to find another living soul out at this hour.

'Can I see him?'

One of the men shook his head. 'You don't want to do that,' he said. 'The dead are never pretty, mister.'

'I know,' Simon told him. 'I've seen my share.'

A short silence. In the glow from a pair of lanterns, he caught the two men glancing at each other. A penny for each of them helped make up their minds.

The light caught the corpse's face. Simon knelt, brushing away some dirt and a piece of cloth that was caught in the man's hair. He lifted the chin. A straight, deep gash across the neck. Clean and quick. But definitely no accident. Murdered and tossed into the river. He hadn't been dead long, either; it couldn't be more than an hour or two. Nothing had nibbled at his eyes yet, the flesh was still intact and fresh.

He didn't recognize the face. The best he could judge, the man had been about thirty, with dark, wiry hair, a thick face and a stocky body. His shoes had gone, and one foot was bare. His clothes looked reasonable. Nothing expensive, but hardly rags. Middling.

One of the men coughed.

'There's something else, sir.' He raised the lantern. 'You see? Down there.'

The right hand was missing. Severed at the wrist. It looked like a single, swift blow had gone through the bone. For the love of God. Before or after he was dead?

'The constable will be wondering who you are, sir. He's going to want to know about someone asking to see the body.'

'Tell him it's Simon Westow. The thief-taker. He knows me.'

He gave the corpse a final glance. Who were you? he wondered. What did you do to deserve that?

Simon pushed his hands back into his pockets and began to walk again. Mile upon mile as past and present twisted and plagued his mind. From street to street until he believed he'd covered every single inch of Leeds. His legs were like lead and his head ached. He turned east, heading towards daylight, a faint, blurred band on the eastern horizon that slowly widened.

His heart was heavy, every thought bleak and darkened by shadows. He felt exhaustion all the way to his bones. Sleep was just a taunt, running ahead, out of reach.

People were up, moving through the streets like ghosts. On their way to early shifts at the factory and the forge, the workshop or the mill. Barely dawn and already the chimneys were churning out smoke; he could taste the soot on his tongue.

At the coffee cart outside the Bull and Mouth Inn, Simon put down his ha'penny. It was a good place to hear gossip, to eat bread and dripping and fill his belly. Maybe the hot drink would revive him. News of the dead man had already spread to become part of the currency of speech. Everyone had their ideas and their questions. The word that his hand had gone had spread, a common horror now. But nobody seemed able to give him a name.

A few shops were opening, boys sweeping the pavements, clerks and apprentices polishing the windows as he passed.

On the far side of the Head Row, he pushed at the door of

Mudie's Printing Works. George Mudie was tinkering with his press, tightening a screw here, loosening another there, then running a sheet through before examining the broadside ballad that emerged.

Until the owners found him impossible, he'd been the editor of one of the Leeds newspapers. After they sacked him, he tried publishing a news sheet of his own, but discovered it was no trade for a man with short pockets. Now he made a living as a jobbing printer, with his own shop and creaking press. But the newspaperman remained, curious, eager for a good story, with an agile mind and plenty of questions.

'Any gossip about the body they found?' Simon asked. Rumours always seemed to fly to Mudie and he was the sort who relished knowing them.

'Gruesome, that's what people are saying.'

'That part's certainly true.'

The man stopped and stared at him. 'You saw him?'

'Right after they pulled his corpse out of the river.' He described it all, and Mudie narrowed his eyes as he listened. 'No one seems to know who he was, though.'

He shrugged. 'It'll all come out. Someone will claim him. Either that or they'll tip him in a pauper's grave.'

'Whoever killed him knows exactly who he is.'

Mudie snorted. 'They're hardly likely to say, though, are they, Simon?'

TWO

'Make sure you grind those seeds very fine, child,' Mrs Shields said, then coughed again, a thick, liquid sound that came up from her lungs.

Jane pressed down with the pestle, working it around and around the mortar until the mustard was a brown powder, so pale it looked golden in the light from the window.

'Now just a tiny touch of the oil from that bottle.' The old woman pointed. 'Not much, you want it to be a paste.'

Late October dampness clung in the air. The wet autumn weather had settled on Mrs Shields's chest, all too often leaving her hacking and gasping for breath. Sometimes her face was tight with fear of the next bout.

But she was older now. This year, each month seemed to show on her face. It left her a little weaker, more bent and fragile.

The changes worried Jane. Mrs Shields had taken her in. For the first time since she was a young girl, she felt as if somewhere was home.

'That's enough. Now put it on that cloth.'

She did, fingers moving deftly as the woman removed her dress and the linen underneath. Her chest was small, bony, breasts pale and withered, hanging down. With a gentle touch, Jane spread the poultice over the skin, lightly pressing it down and covering it with a clean cloth.

Mrs Shields closed her eyes, sighing as she felt the warmth, relishing it as she lay back in the bed.

'Why don't you try to sleep?' Jane said.

Earlier, she'd placed a warming pan between the sheets; the mattress was warm and welcoming. She gathered another heavy woollen blanket that had been hanging by the fire and laid it on top of the woman's scrawny body.

'Does it help?'

'Yes, child.' She sighed with relief. 'Thank you.' A calm smile. 'You were such a wild little thing when you came here. Look at you now.'

Jane squeezed her hand and stood close until the woman began to doze.

In the kitchen, she cleaned everything. Yes, look at her now. A year before, she could never have imagined doing this. She'd have been more likely to kill than heal. But times changed.

Her fingertips traced the ladders of scars on her forearms. All those cuts she'd made to ease the pain of living. Yet she'd only felt the need of it a few times since she came to this house; none at all since spring, she realized with astonishment.

Work had kept her busy while Simon was ill. Small jobs for the most part; things easily resolved, nothing to tax her too much. He was back now, trying to act as if everything was the way it had been. But she could see the difference. His face had grown thinner, more careworn, carrying its fears just below the skin. He moved a little more slowly, not quite as quick to react as before. That alarmed her; for a thief-taker, speed could mean life or death.

Jane knew Simon valued her talent, her skills. She could follow without being seen. Raise the shawl over her hair and she could vanish into the scenery on an empty street. With the knife in her hand, she was deadly.

Assisting him had saved her from the world. For a long time, that had been enough. These days, though, caring for Mrs Shields was more important. It filled her soul and left her content. The money she made hardly mattered. She and Simon split everything they earned. Jane had plenty hidden away. More than enough to last her a full, long life, even if she chose to live well.

Simon returned to the river. Down the few yards of Pitfall to stand looking at the water. It was dirty and sluggish, reeking from chemicals and disease. Dead animals drifted by – a dog, a cat – followed by branches that moved in slow circles in the current.

The body was long gone, taken to the mortuary at the infirmary. But he wanted to see the area once more in daylight. Maybe it would help him understand and stop him drowning in all the history that swirled around him.

Simon turned as he heard the footsteps on the cobbles. A man with long, dark hair that spilled from a low-crowned hat. His eyes were filled with sadness. In his early forties, most probably, with weatherbeaten skin that left deep lines around his eyes and mouth. It was the face of a man who'd seen a great deal in his life. His clothes had a cut that Simon didn't recognize, the coat heavier than any he'd seen in Leeds before, made for a harsher winter than a person would find in England.

'Are you Mr Westow?'

'Simon Westow, yes. You'll have to forgive me, I don't know you.'

'My name's Charles Ramsey, sir. It was my brother Sebastian they brought out of the river here last night.'

At least the body had a name now.

'My condolences,' Simon said and the man nodded his acknowledgement. 'But how do you know me?'

'I talked to the constable. He told me you saw my brother. I was just up the street and someone pointed you out.' Ramsey spoke with a curious accent, clipped and wounded by grief.

'He was already dead by the time I saw him.' Simon stared at the cobbles. 'I'm sorry for your loss, Mr Ramsey.'

'I don't know who'd want to do something like that to Sebastian.' Ramsey took off his hat, twisting it between his hands. 'I've been gone from here for twenty-five years. Signed up on a ship when I was young. I only returned a few weeks ago, so I didn't know him too well. Sebastian's younger than me. Was,' he corrected himself. As he spoke, his accent became more pronounced. The vowels grew sharper, with a drawl to the words.

'Where did you go?'

'America, sir. Boston, in the Commonwealth of Massachusetts. I jumped ship as soon as we docked. It's a fine city, plenty of opportunities for a resourceful man.' For a moment, his face cleared and he began to smile. Then he seemed to hear his words and stopped.

'What did your brother do?'

'He was a clerk. Nothing dangerous. Nothing illegal. There was no reason for anyone to hurt him.'

'He didn't know any criminals?'

'I don't believe so.' The man shook his head. 'I've only been back here for a month. No, I'm sure he didn't. Sebastian was a very straightforward fellow.'

'Then I'm sorry.'

'The constable told me that you're a thief-taker.'

'That's right.'

Ramsey hesitated for a moment.

'I'd like to hire you to find out what happened to him. Who killed him and . . .' Cut off his hand, Simon thought. Words the man couldn't bring himself to say. But who could?

Simon sighed. 'You need to understand, Mr Ramsey: I find things that have been taken. Objects. Money. I don't hunt people. Murder's a business for the constable and his men. Not someone like me.'

Ramsey nodded. 'Perhaps he'll find whoever did it. But I'd rather have someone else searching, too. I can pay, if you're worried about that. I've done quite well for myself in America.

I came back to persuade my brother to move over there and work with me.'

'I'm sorry. You need to see what the constable can do.'

'What if it's not enough?' Ramsey sighed and raised his eyes, looking around as if he was seeing everything for the first time. 'I don't know Leeds now. It's a long time since I lived here. It seems like I don't remember it at all. It's changed.'

'It keeps changing,' Simon said. 'Every single day. I hope you can find the man who killed him.'

As he dragged himself home, Simon tried to understand why he'd turned the man down. He hadn't told Ramsey the truth; he'd hunted people before. Plenty of times. He'd found killers. But a tiny voice inside had whispered no, warning him to keep clear of it all. Maybe it was time he learned to follow those instincts.

By the time he reached Swinegate, his shoulders were sagging. He hung up his coat and ambled through to the warmth of the kitchen, craving nothing more than something to drink, then bed and hours of sweet, dreamless sleep.

In the doorway he stopped short. Rosie was sitting at the table. Across from her, with his back to him, was a figure with broad shoulders and unkempt dark hair.

'My husband,' she said as the man turned.

THREE

He knew the face. But there were plenty in Leeds who would recognize Thomas Arden.

He was one of the wealthiest men in town. That was what he claimed, and maybe he was. If the stories were true, he'd first made his money by crime, beginning with a year or two as a highwayman on the turnpike road near York. Over time it had become a part of Arden's myth; why would he deny something like that?

He'd certainly arrived in Leeds with enough in his pockets to buy land and start building and selling houses. It had been a shrewd move; people were flooding into the town for jobs at the manufactories and the demand for places to live was insatiable.

That made him wealthy.

Then he started erecting factories and taking shares in the businesses that filled them.

That brought him more money than he could ever spend, a fortune that turned him almost respectable.

The years had smoothed some of his rough edges, but he was still quick to anger, with a voice that rose into a bellow when his temper flared.

He was the last person Simon wanted to see. He needed his bed, to fall away from the world for a few hours.

Still, he managed a genial smile. It was always good business to be polite to the rich.

'Mr Arden. What can I do for you?'

The man stood. He was large enough to be menacing, with wide shoulders, a bull neck and a crooked, broken nose. But good living was changing him. Under the expensive waistcoat, his belly was running to fat and his thighs strained hard against the seams of his pale trousers.

'You're a thief-taker.' A gruff voice, eyes boring into Simon's face.

'I am. Has something been stolen from you?'

'Not from me. My son.'

Arden had three children. His two daughters had made good marriages into county families; they were rarely seen in Leeds. Franklin was the son, the youngest, in his early twenties, content to live off the family name and spend his father's money.

Thomas Arden's wife had killed herself when the boy was twelve. After that, Franklin had run riot, and his father had done nothing to curb him. He grew, he gambled, he whored, he fought. He sired bastards and had a reputation for hurting the girls he found. Every time, his father reached into his purse and paid them off. Arden owned the house on the Head Row where his son lived, gave him an allowance, and took care of the night watch and the magistrates whenever he was arrested. No charges ever came to court.

'What was taken?'

'A pair of silver candlesticks,' Arden said. 'They weren't

particularly valuable, but they'd belonged to his mother. A gift from her parents.'

A curious choice of words, Simon thought. *His mother*, not *my wife*.

The man described them, took a notebook from his pocket and sketched the hallmark.

'There's good money in it if you bring them back and tell me who did it,' Arden said.

'When were they taken?' Simon asked. 'Does your son have any idea who's responsible?'

Arden reddened and looked down at the flagstones on the kitchen floor.

'He came home drunk Sunday night and passed out in his bedroom. Left the front door unlocked. Someone walked in, helped himself to the candlesticks and some money that was on the mantel. The first my son knew was yesterday morning. The woman who cleans the house told him.'

Simon nodded. 'I thought you had a bodyguard,' he said. 'Why not get him to ask some questions? They'd probably be returned in a few hours with an apology. He scares people. So does your name.'

Arden snorted. 'Aye, or whoever did it might take to his heels and that would be the last I'd ever know of it. People tell me you're sly.'

That was one word for it, Simon thought.

'You know my fee is based on the value of what was stolen.'

'Like I told you, they're not especially valuable. Not in money. But I'll make it worth your time. I'll pay you well over the odds.'

'Very generous of you.'

'Are we set, then?' Arden took it as given that no one would refuse him. He stood and extended his hand.

'Your son has no idea who might have taken them?'

'No. None at all.' He spoke with a preacher's finality, nodded and left.

Simon heard the door close and turned to Rosie. 'I'd never have expected to find him here.'

She frowned. 'I hope he never comes again. He just sat and glowered until he heard you return. Refused to tell me what he wanted, as if it wasn't a woman's business.' Fire flickered in her eyes. 'There's something about him. Don't trust him, Simon.'

'I won't,' he promised. 'No need to worry about that.'

He rubbed his eyes with the heel of his hand. Bed, he thought, while he could still climb the stairs.

FOUR

Jane watched Simon's face as he told her about the job. It was late afternoon; dusk was merging into night. They sat at the table in the house on Swinegate as the oil lamp cast long shadows into the corners of the kitchen.

He still looked ground down by his illness, she thought. Deep circles under his eyes. Staring down at his hands as he spoke, instead of at the others in the room.

She glanced at Rosie, sitting at the far end, watching her husband with worry and tenderness.

'I'll make a start on talking to the fences,' Jane said.

'Tomorrow will be soon enough,' Simon told her.

She shrugged, stood and left. Tonight was a good time to begin.

The shop was tucked away in a tiny yard off Kirkgate, down a damp ginnel that was barely wide enough for a man to walk. As Jane opened the door, the smell hit her. It caught in her throat, made her want to gag. A cloying taste, so sweet that it was sickly. She forced herself to take a shallow breath, then entered. Ruby Hallam was perched on a tall stool behind the counter, looking older and smaller than ever. She seemed to be wearing every piece of clothing she owned. One shawl over her head. Two more, both thick wool, heaped around her shoulders. Three coats that Jane could see. A grubby white cap was tied over what little remained of her grey hair. Small steel spectacles perched on a fleshy nose.

Ruby's voice was a raw, grating cackle. 'Well, well, if it isn't Simon Westow's little angel. You haven't visited me in a long time, pet. What happened, did you hope I'd died?' A grin that showed a toothless mouth.

'Silver candlesticks,' Jane said. All she wanted was to be out of here as soon as possible.

'What about them?' The woman narrowed her eyes. 'Are you looking for some?'

Jane pounced on the words. 'Do you have any?'

'Maybe.'

Jane studied the face. Ruby tried to give nothing away, but her mouth betrayed her, sour and bitter, turning down at the corners.

'Who offered them to you?'

When she answered, regret coloured every word. 'Someone came in yesterday. A young man. He tried to sell me a pair. Lovely design, very elegant. The real thing, proper hallmark an' all. But he wanted more than I could afford to pay.'

'Who was he?' She took a silver sixpence from her pocket and placed it on the counter between them. Enough to tempt the woman. But she only shook her head.

'Never seen him before. Tall, fair hair.' A pause. Jane brought out a second coin, another sixpence. 'Pox marks on his face. Just enough to notice. He got off light with them, he did.'

'If he comes back, send me a message.' She rubbed her thumb and middle finger together and the light of greed sparked in the old woman's eyes.

Jane gulped down the cold air as she came out. It was foul and harsh, dark on her tongue, but after the taste in the shop it was like balm.

The woman had set her on the trail. Ruby's shop was out of the way; if the seller had gone there, he must have tried others first. That meant it was only a matter of time. She just needed to keep asking questions until she heard the right answers.

Yet after an hour she was no closer. The thief had been here and there, offering the candlesticks, but cautious and skittish, never agreeing a price. What was holding him back?

The question niggled at her as she walked up Vicar Lane, past the lights shimmering behind the windows in the House of Recovery.

From nowhere, she felt a prickle up her spine.

Jane didn't stop, never broke her stride. She turned down Lady Lane, past the houses that had been thrown together for the people arriving in Leeds. She cut through a ginnel and came out on Nelson Street.

The feeling was still there, stronger than ever. Someone was following her.

And then . . . nothing. The sense of a person behind her vanished as suddenly as it arrived. Going back to Green Dragon Yard, as she cut through the gap in the wall to Mrs Shields's house, she began to wonder if she'd imagined it all.

It had felt so real. How could that have been in her head?

'He knew what he had, Mr Westow.' The man fidgeted, hands moving constantly. 'The candlesticks, he realized they were proper quality.'

Walter Knight had been a fence far longer than Simon had been a thief-taker. He possessed an eye for quality, paying as little as possible for stolen items and selling them on at a profit. Most of his goods went down to London; he had excellent contacts and there was always a steady market. Knight had a fair reputation and did good business from his shop on Water Lane.

The man had plenty tucked away, Simon was certain of that. But he never displayed it. In his old clothes, shoes worn down at the heel, a shave once a fortnight, he looked every inch the pauper. Even on a morning when the damp chill seeped through the windows and up through the floor, he never lit the stove. Cheaper to put a second coat over the tattered one that seemed a part of his body.

'Why didn't you buy them?'

'Couldn't have turned much profit at the price he wanted.' Knight sucked on his teeth. 'If I can't do that, what's the point? And he wasn't willing to bargain.' His expression soured. 'I tried, but he wasn't having it. Said he'd go somewhere else.'

'What did he look like?' Simon asked.

'A few pox marks on his cheeks,' the man answered after a little thought. 'He'd have been a good-looking lad without them. Fair hair, long, you know, the way they like it these days. Young, I doubt he was more than twenty-five. Tall, too, about your height.'

Still early and he'd already discovered that the thief had been in one other place trying to sell the candlesticks. It had been the same tale there. He'd demanded too much money.

But no name, and even with the pox scars, the face rang no bells with him. Yet the man knew many of the fences in town.

That meant he was familiar with Leeds. No matter, they'd track him down. They had a sniff of him now.

'It's obvious he's not a stranger,' Rosie agreed when he returned for his dinner at noon. Only a morning's work and already he felt as if he needed a rest. The illness had turned him into an old man, an invalid.

'I certainly don't know him,' Simon said. He turned to Jane; she shook her head. 'You'd think someone would be able to place him from those scars.'

'If wonder if he knows who owns those candlesticks,' Rosie continued. 'Maybe he took a chance and sneaked into the house without a clue who lived there.'

'Very likely,' Simon agreed. No one with a scrap of sense would dare to steal from an Arden.

She cocked her head and smiled. 'So perhaps he doesn't know Leeds *that* well.'

'We'll find him.' Simon stood, just as the boys burst through the door in a storm of noise. He grabbed them, jostling and wrestling, tickling until they were screaming for him to stop.

In the confusion, Jane slipped out, unnoticed. What Rosie said made sense. He wasn't someone who stole regularly, or they'd have come across him before. But he was familiar with people no honest person should know. How?

Jane moved around quietly. No sense of anyone following her today. She asked a boy who performed magic tricks on the streets about a pock-marked man, then two of the young pickpockets trying their hands along Commercial Street. One of them remembered the scars and the flopping, fair hair. But he didn't know any more.

A few she talked to could recall him. But no one had ever talked to him, none had heard his name. Nobody had any idea where he lived.

'There you are,' Kate the pie-seller said. 'Two pieces. Plenty of meat in those. You'll always need fattening up, you will. You're still almost as scrawny as the first time I met you.' Jane handed her two pennies. 'That man you were talking about, I know who you mean. I've noticed him around.'

'You have?' Jane asked. 'When did you see him last?'

'It must have been Saturday.' Kate was a big woman, large and forbidding, with a husband who beat her if she didn't bring home enough money. 'Walked right past without even a look, same as ever. He was with that friend of his.'

Jane's head jerked up. 'What friend? Who?'

'Arden's son. You must know him. The one who reckons the world owes him everything.'

'Franklin Arden?' she asked, scarcely able to believe what she'd heard. 'Are you sure?'

'Of course I am.' She turned her head and spat in disgust. 'He's an evil piece of work, that one. Do you know some of the things he does with girls?'

'Yes.' Jane fumbled another coin from her pocket and put it in Kate's tray. 'That's for the information.'

She hurried away, all her thoughts turned upside down. The thief and Franklin Arden were friends? Simon needed to know this. It changed everything they were doing.

Jane had heard the stories about Franklin Arden. They spread, little by little. How he hurt women simply for the pleasure of giving pain. One hadn't been able to walk properly for a month after being with him.

If he tried with her, she'd kill him. It would be a service. She'd gone after men who raped and hurt. For a while, the need for revenge had felt as if it would consume her. Finally it passed and the blood lust had quietened. But a man like Arden could make it return.

Simon felt the surge through his blood. What in God's name was Arden trying to do? Test them? Play them for fools?

'First, you'd better make sure it's true,' Rosie warned him.

He sighed and stopped himself. His wife was right. Caution was the best plan with someone like Thomas Arden. Present him with facts he couldn't deny. He looked at Jane. She was sitting on the bench, staring down at the table.

'Let's see what we can find. We'll meet back here at dusk.'

It didn't take him long to pry loose a few slivers of information. Enough to finally piece together a picture of the man.

His name was George Collins. He'd been born in Chesterfield and trained as a lawyer at one of the Inns of Court in London; left before he was called to the bar. A little over a year earlier he'd drifted to Leeds. Not one of Franklin Arden's closest friends, but they'd often been seen drinking and gambling together. He survived on family money, it seemed. A little, but it was never ever enough. The kind who didn't want to settle into steady work, preferring an easy lazy life. One that included theft, apparently.

'Tomorrow we'll go and see Thomas Arden,' Simon told Jane. 'First thing.'

'Why not find Collins and return the candlesticks?' she asked. 'He stole them, he doesn't deserve any favours.'

'Maybe not,' Simon agreed with a small nod of his head. 'But this is the Arden family. We'll give them the chance to sort it out themselves, if they want.'

'All right.'

There was someone behind her. No doubt at all. Jane glanced back, but the evening swirled with a heavy, damp mist; it was impossible to see anything clearly. Near the top of Albion Street, the feeling disappeared again. He'd gone. It was like a goad, pushing and prodding at her.

The next time, she'd discover who it was.

FIVE

Arden was breakfasting; that was what the servant said as she showed them into a parlour where the coal fire burned warm and bright. It was a room to impress guests, decorated in the finest taste that money could purchase: a wallpaper of pale, comforting blue and white stripes, an oil painting of a naval battle hanging over the mantel, the long-clock ticking soft and serene in the corner. The chairs were upholstered in deep blue velvet. A plush Turkey rug covered the polished floorboards. It was all understated, a dignified announcement that Arden had arrived, that he was respectably rich these days. It was exactly what people expected from a house in Park Square.

Half an hour later he bustled in as if he'd dashed through to see them.

Jane had been staring out of the window. She turned as he entered. Simon rose from his seat.

'Do you have the candlesticks, Westow?'

'No.'

The man's eyes narrowed. He frowned. 'Why the hell not? Isn't that what I'm paying you to do?'

'We know who's been trying to sell them.'

'Then—'

'The thief is a good friend of your son,' Simon said.

That was enough to silence him for a moment. 'I see,' he said, and drew a breath. 'Do you know his name?'

'George Collins,' Jane answered.

Arden stared, assessing her. 'I suppose I should have guessed. A waste of a man. Doesn't have any real money to his name.' He snorted. 'Always asking Franklin for a little loan to last him until his allowance arrives.'

'Do you still want us to retrieve the candlesticks?' Simon asked. 'Or would you and your son prefer to do it yourselves?'

Arden considered the question for a few seconds.

'Go ahead and take care of it, Westow. That's your job. Bring them here and I'll pay you. Was there anything else?'

He left the room. A servant waited by the door to escort them out.

A misting rain was beginning to fall. Jane raised her shawl over her head. Simon tapped his beaver hat in place and buttoned his greatcoat.

'Do you know where Collins lives?' she asked.

'On Boar Lane,' he replied and glanced up at the sky. 'It's not far. Why don't we pay him an early visit? Better than standing around and getting wet.'

The lock was so flimsy it couldn't have kept a child out. Simon took a set of picks from his waistcoat pocket. A few seconds' work and they were inside Collins's rooms.

The heavy curtains were closed against the day. A stink of stale tobacco clung to the walls. Nothing stirred. He wasn't surprised; Collins was probably the type who caroused until the small hours and woke late. An open door led through to the bedroom. Simon put a finger to his lips and trod carefully, barely making a sound on the floorboards.

Collins was asleep, one hand thrown high above his head on the pillow. The covers were tangled around his shoulders.

With a glance and a nod, Simon directed Jane to the far side of the bed as they drew their weapons. He pushed Collins's shoulder. Gently at first, then another, firmer prod, again and again until he began to stir.

'Time to wake up, George.'

Collins opened his eyes, bleary at first, then suddenly alert, terrified at the sight of a stranger with a blade. He turned his head, looking for an escape. But Jane was there, her expression set, the knife steady in her hand.

'Where are the candlesticks?'

'What?' He looked as if he was desperately trying to make himself smaller, to disappear under the sheets and blankets.

'The candlesticks,' Simon repeated.

'Drawer.' He stammered out the word.

Jane searched, bringing out one, then the second. Simon smiled.

'Very good. Now you just lie here for a while, George. Go back to sleep and pretend this was a dream. It never happened. You didn't see anyone.'

Ten seconds and the place was a memory. Collins would be too petrified to move. He would never dare to raise an alarm. Who could he tell? What would he say – that someone had taken the items he'd stolen?

Two days and the news had spread all over Leeds. Simon Westow had recovered a pair of silver candlesticks that had been stolen from Thomas Arden's son. Simon hadn't told a soul, and he was certain that Collins would never have opened his mouth. That left Thomas Arden.

Why? he wondered.

'Maybe he's pleased with your work,' Rosie said.

They were lying huddled together in bed, the darkness close around them. The weather had turned. The murkiness and damp had vanished, in its place brisk daytime skies, with a nudge of frost and plunging temperatures at night.

Simon shook his head. 'It won't be that.'

Arden wasn't the type to let people know his business unless he had good reason.

'He could be trying to shame his son. He said it only happened because Franklin was careless, coming home drunk and not locking the door.'

'I suppose that's possible.' But it didn't *feel* right. From all he'd heard, the young man lived for his own pleasures and his father indulged him. Nothing was likely to shame him.

Maybe it didn't matter; he'd been paid. When he delivered the candlesticks, Arden had pulled a roll of bank notes from his pocket. True to his word, he'd been generous, no denying it. Simon had walked away satisfied.

'You're Tom Arden's blue-eyed boy now, eh, Simon?' George Mudie said when he called at the printing shop. 'Quite surprising. Usually he spends praise like a miser. If I were you, I'd watch myself.'

'Why?' he asked. 'Why do you think he's doing it?'

'He probably has a plan of some kind. Like it or not, you're a part of it now.'

A tiny cog in whatever machine Arden was building.

'Any idea what it might be?'

Mudie shook his head. 'You'll find out when he's good and ready. But if you have any sense, you'll prepare yourself.'

'For what, though?'

'Anything at all.'

Mrs Shields was improving. Drier weather helped; the cold didn't sap her strength the way the dampness had. Her cough had eased, she had more colour in her cheeks, and she was insistent on doing things in the house for herself.

It was good news. Jane didn't want the old woman to die for a long time yet. They'd barely begun to know each other, just a year so far. She was greedy for more, relishing the sense of having a family once again.

It made up for all those years she'd had to live on the street, after her father raped her and her mother pushed her out and locked the door. She had a home again. A welcome. Who would want to have that snatched away?

Noon had just passed when Jane walked to the market, huddled in her cloak and shawl, a basket hanging from her arm like a servant or a housewife. All the best produce had long since been picked over. Some carrots left, a few potatoes. Enough for the two of them. Then down Briggate and Kirkgate to the butcher with his shop on Timble Bridge.

From the corner of her eye she noticed the children who crept unseen. They took food they could scavenge or steal, trying to keep themselves alive for another day. Not so long since she'd been one of them.

The feeling struck her as she took a short cut through a ginnel off Albion Street. A chill creeping up her spine. Someone was behind her again. No mistake; it was as strong as a blow. Jane switched the basket to her left hand, gripped the hilt of her knife and drew it from the pocket of her dress. Out of sight, but ready. And sharp, carefully honed on the whetstone just the night before.

There were places she could hide. Unless he was better than her, he'd never even suspect she'd seen him. Jane ducked into an opening, then behind a wall. Out of sight, but still able to peer out at whoever passed.

The footsteps seemed loud enough to crack the sky. She pressed back against the stone and twisted the gold ring Mrs Shields had given her to keep her safe. He stopped, pausing to cock his head as if he was listening, turning it just enough for her to make out his features. Not even a moment and he hurried on again, scurrying ahead like an animal.

Jane couldn't move; she felt fixed to the spot. She knew him. She'd always known him. She'd always hate him. The angry eyes, cheeks flushed bright with drink. The thin mouth. She hadn't seen him in years but he was there every night, crawling around the edges of her dreams, staring down into her face.

Her father.

SIX

'Those papers you gave me,' Simon said. 'Why did you want me to see them?'

It was a crisp Monday, balanced on the cusp of autumn and winter. He'd walked up to Dr Hey's house on Albion Place to ask the question that kept nagging at him.

'You were the only person I could think of who might understand,' Hey answered with a sigh and a tight smile. His hands were clean, scrubbed fresh, moving delicately over the papers on his desk.

'I did,' Simon told him. 'I understood all too well. But what do you want me to do about it?'

'Do?' Hey looked puzzled. 'They're dead, Westow. There's nothing we can do for them. Why, what did you think I wanted?'

'I don't know. But it brought back all the memories.' They still flowed through his mind in the night.

'That wasn't my intention. I'm sorry.'

'Too late now. It happened.'

'I had to . . . tell someone. If you want my advice, you'll try to forget it,' Hey told him.

So easy to say, Simon thought. So hard to do. The man had needed to pass on the weight of his knowledge, to take any sense of guilt from his own shoulders.

'What you wrote . . .'

'What about it?' Hey asked

'You described them physically, you gave their injuries, but not *who* they were. You never even wrote down their names.'

'Is it important?'

'To me it is.' Of course it was. They'd suffered. They deserved to be remembered.

The doctor nodded and picked a sheet from the top of the pile, squinting at his own spidery writing. He looked up.

'Very well. Are you sure you want to know?'

'I am,' Simon said.

'The older boy was called Peter Hardy and the younger one was Jacob Easby. We didn't have a chance to save either one of them.' He closed his eyes then opened them again. 'They were weak when they came in, they'd been malnourished all their lives. There wasn't much more to them than skin and bone. God knows how they managed to work at all, let alone survive twelve- or fourteen-hour shifts.'

'Children do. It's been that way since before I was born.'

'That doesn't mean it should happen.' Hey's anger flared for a moment and died. 'I told you the Easby boy looked young. I honestly believed he was six, Westow. He was eight years old. Eight. Neither of them had an ounce of strength left. The slightest sickness would have killed them.'

'What did you list as the cause of death?' Simon asked.

The doctor hesitated. He placed the paper back on his desk, aligning it precisely, and sat back in his chair.

'I said that they died from exhaustion,' he admitted with embarrassment.

'Why did you need to lie?'

'You know the answer as well as I do.'

'Yes,' Simon said. Of course he did. Powerful men owned the mills and factories. Rich men who had the money to build the hospitals and pay the doctors. It wouldn't do to make them guilty of a child's death.

'I'm sorry, but . . .' There was no need for Hey to finish the sentence. It was the way of the world.

'Where did they work?'

The doctor stared at him then shook his head. 'Don't, Westow. Don't ask. There's a mirror on the wall behind you. Turn and take a look at yourself. A proper, honest look. Do you see it? Your face is still thin. Those clothes are hanging off you. You lost weight while you were ill and you haven't gained it back yet. You're still recovering. Doesn't matter whether you admit it or not; it's there.'

He looked; the reflection didn't lie. Hey was right. Simon could feel the small knot of anger in his belly at hearing the truth.

'What about it?'

'Please don't make this into a cause. You're not well enough yet and nothing you do will change a thing. All that will happen is that you'll make some powerful enemies.'

Simon chuckled. 'Sometimes I think I've spent half my life doing that. Whose mill was it?'

He took a slow breath. 'Are you absolutely certain you want the answer to that?'

'It's why I came. You gave me those notes. You made me remember. Now you owe me the whole story.'

'Very well,' Hey said after a long moment. 'It was Seaton's. And never say I told you that.'

'I won't. But I'd like to know everything you have about the children.'

'There isn't much. It's all here.' He tapped the paper with his fingertips. 'Take your time, Westow. I have to go over to the infirmary and examine the new patients. And listen to reason. Please.'

Ebenezer Street, the houses standing in the shadow of the Methodist chapel. When he was young it had been the Baptists who worshipped there. A different heartbeat in the same skin. It was a desperately poor area, a long terrace of badly built back-to-back dwellings that hardly caught any light. All of them grouped around a court where the piss and shit settled ankle deep.

No clean air, everything coated in grime and soot. Some hopeful soul had strung a line across the road to try and hang out their washing. But nothing was ever going to stay clean for more than five minutes around here.

Seaton's mill loomed at the bottom of the slope, by the old mill garth. Blackened brick, windows set high in the walls, smoke churning from a chimney that reached up to the sky. Most of these families probably earned their money there. Not far to go to work. Not far to go to die.

He had no reason to be here. This wasn't his fight. Peter Hardy and Jacob Easby weren't his children. They had their families to mourn them. And Hey had been right – he wasn't well yet. Nowhere close to being who he should be. To whoever he had been.

But he remembered other children who'd died in the mills.

Workhouse children, no more than fading names in ledgers now. If he didn't care, who would?

Simon knocked on the door of number seven. At first he thought nobody was at home. Then he heard an infant's wail, and eventually a girl stood gazing up at him. She looked like flesh stretched over twigs, wearing a patched cotton dress that reached halfway down her calves. No stockings or shoes, only a pair of grubby feet. The girl couldn't have been more than five, but she assessed him with the calm, suspicious eye of an adult.

'I'm looking for Mr Hardy,' he said.

'Me pa's at work,' the girl answered. 'So's me mam and me brother and sisters. It's just me and Caroline here. I look after her.'

Soon enough they'd grow and become more wage earners for the family.

'You had a brother who died.'

'Peter.' She nodded, her expression serious for a moment, then clearing. What was death to her, anyway? How could she really understand it at that age? Simon had been four when sickness took his parents; he'd accepted it without question, even the move to the workhouse. He missed them every day, but it was how life happened when you were young.

'When will your father be home?'

'When his shift's over.'

'Can you tell him a man named Simon Westow called and I'll come again later? It's not bad news, no need for him to worry,' he added with a smile. He took a ha'penny from his pocket and placed it in the girl's fingers before raising his hat.

Nobody answered at number thirty-seven, where Jacob Easby's family lived. No matter. He'd return.

'Child,' Mrs Shields said with a calm smile, 'is something wrong? You've hardly said a word all morning.'

'I'm just thinking, that's all,' Jane replied. Her father's face had ripped away sleep. Each time she turned her head in the night he was there, glimpsed at the very edge of her vision. He was nowhere and everywhere around her. 'When I went to the market yesterday . . .' she began, and stopped.

'Did something happen?'

'Yes.' She forced herself to say the word. All the years she survived on the streets, even when she lived at Simon's, she'd kept her problems inside. Solved them on her own. If nobody knew, they couldn't use the weakness against her. If she failed, she made cuts on her arms. To suffer, to learn from her mistakes.

But now . . . now she lived in a world that wasn't so brutal. That could forgive. She wasn't going to give her father the chance to ruin it. But she needed to tell Mrs Shields. By habit, her fingers strayed to the gold ring, stroking, feeling the smoothness of the metal.

'What was it, child? Sit down and tell me.'

'Oh my,' she said when Jane finished. She frowned. 'I thought he left Leeds years ago with your mother.'

'It was him.' She bristled at the doubt behind the woman's voice. 'Definitely.'

'I believe you.' Gentle, soothing, Catherine Shields stroked Jane's hair. 'I know you'd never forget his face.'

'Why? Why is he here? What does he want? Why is he following me?'

'I can't tell you that, child. But it won't be anything good. You know that as well as I do.'

A devil. That was what she'd thought during the night, with eyes that burned right through her.

'The next time . . .' Jane said.

'What will you do?'

She'd force the knife against his throat and make him beg. Make him kneel and pray for her to forgive him. Too many years she'd dreamed of having him at her mercy. Of making him pay for all those things that had happened to her because of him.

'I'll make him tell me what he wants.'

She'd been too stunned to act. Too slow. To realize he was so close after all these years, to smell his stink . . . everything cascaded over her and then he was gone. She'd failed. Once she arrived home she'd rolled up her sleeve and touched the scars on her arms, the cuts she'd given herself. She'd even taken out the knife and rested it against her flesh. But nothing more. Cutting her skin and drawing her blood wouldn't change anything. It wouldn't bring her redemption.

'After that?' Catherine stared at her with a shrewd eye.

'I don't know.'

It was a lie. She knew, but she couldn't bring herself to tell Mrs Shields the truth. She was going to kill him. No mercy for a man like that. No pardon in the final minute before execution.

'Simon would help you,' the old woman said. 'Why don't you ask him?'

Jane shook her head. This was her battle. Hers alone.

By the middle of the afternoon Simon felt ready to drop; the day had caught up with him. But he forced himself to keep going, spending an hour moving from inn to inn until he found Barnabas Wade. The wind whipped up Briggate, the air growing more raw and bitter by the minute. The outside passengers on the coaches that arrived looked frozen and terrified as they clambered stiffly down to the cobbles.

Wade had settled on a bench beside the hearth in the Talbot, close to the sooty chimney breast. He had a glass of rum in front of him and a newspaper open on the table. But he wasn't reading. Wade was eyeing the newcomers with a predator's gaze.

He was a disbarred lawyer who made a living of sorts selling shares. Most were worthless, but his tongue was glib enough to give them the promise of tickets to fortune. Enough people gave him their money to keep him going, and the contracts he made them sign stopped them going to court after they realized they'd been swindled. So far he'd managed to stave off poverty. He veered between survival and not having quite enough money, constantly trying to keep himself afloat.

He kept his eyes and ears open and he knew some secrets about Leeds that few ever heard.

Simon placed a fresh glass of rum on the table in front of him. 'How's business?'

'Terrible,' Wade replied. He watched as the passengers entered, rubbing their hands at the warmth 'Look at them. They're half-frozen. All they want is some warmth. No chance to talk about stocks. Still,' he added, 'it might pick up if the snow starts and they're stuck here.'

'Snow?' Simon asked. It was too early in the year for that.

'The drivers say there's already a little up north.' He grinned with anticipation. 'Give them a few days stuck here and I'll make some proper money.' He paused. 'From the look on your face, you didn't come to talk about the weather.'

'What do you know about Seaton?'

Wade took a sip of the rum and pushed his lips together.

'The mill owner? I don't think there's much to tell. It must be, what, fifteen years since he built that place down on the old garth?'

'Somewhere around then,' Simon agreed.

Wade shrugged. 'He's not from Leeds. He seems to think he's a farmer. I do know he's never lived in town and only shows his face when there's a problem. I think he was here a few years back when everyone was worried about the machine breakers. He has a place out in one of the villages.' Wade shrugged. 'That's about it.'

'Where did he make his money? Do you know?'

'I've no idea. I didn't see the need. He was never likely to spend any of it with me.'

Simon placed some coins on the table. 'There's more if you can find out.'

The money vanished into Wade's hand. 'Why are you so interested in Seaton? Has he hired you?'

'I'm curious, that's all.'

Wade narrowed his eyes. 'That's not like you, Simon. Usually you need a reason to be curious.'

'His name came up.' It was close enough to the truth.

'I can ask. After all this time I don't know if anyone will remember, though.'

'Money's good at jogging memories. I'll pay.'

Wade took his time. 'If that's what you want.'

'It is.' Simon started to rise, then sat again. 'And whatever you have on Thomas Arden.'

The man laughed. 'A little late for that, isn't it? I hear he's been singing your praises as a thief-taker.'

'He has; I'd like to know why.'

'You must have heard the tales about him.'

'Those never mean much.'

'Maybe not. In his case, though, most of them are true,' Wade said. 'He did a bit of everything illegal. Around York, Malton, up there.'

'What about him being a highwayman?' Simon asked.

'I wouldn't put it past him. He's never denied it, has he? Once he'd made enough, Arden came to Leeds and started buying buildings.' He pursed his lips. 'Mind you, there are folk who claim he used force to make a few of his deals.'

'Did he?'

'I heard of two cases, yes. Why?'

'I just wanted to know.'

'Be careful. He's killed people.'

'That's easy to claim.'

Wade gave a slow shake of his head. 'He has, Simon. Truly. Do you remember a man called Sykes in York?'

'No.' He leaned forward, resting his hands on the table.

'People talked about it for a long time. It all happened before Arden moved here. The way I heard it, Sykes tried to con him out of some money. The next thing anyone knew, his body turned up.'

Simon tried to play devil's advocate. 'That doesn't prove Arden killed him.'

'He told people he did it.'

Simon had never heard of the murder. But York was twenty-five miles away; what happened there had little to do with his life.

'How did this man Sykes die?'

Wade sighed. 'For the love of God, Simon, how should I remember?' Suddenly he sat upright. 'No, wait, I can tell you one thing. It shocked me at the time. His right hand was gone. Sliced off at the wrist.' He stopped and cocked his head. 'Sounds familiar, doesn't it?'

'Like the body they pulled out of the river a few days ago,' Simon said quietly.

'Exactly. I told you, be careful. There's one other thing, too.'

'What?'

'Arden was supposed to have had a partner when he was a criminal. It was never more than gossip. I'm not certain he existed.'

'See what you can find out about Seaton. And Arden.'

'I'll try.' But his attention slipped away as a new group of travellers entered, fresh from the coach that had just pulled into the inn yard.

Knowing Wade, he'd grow distracted and forget. But Simon knew a lawyer in York, someone he'd done business with in the past. A letter and the promise of a guinea to ask some questions . . . It might prove to be a good investment.

SEVEN

'I know it's a tragedy,' Rosie said. 'But those children are dead, Simon. You can't bring them back. What good will it do for you to rake things over?'

'I'm going to ask a few questions, that's all,' he told her. 'Talk to their parents.'

He paced around the kitchen, rested his hands on the range to feel its warmth.

'Why?' Rosie asked.

He stared at her as if he couldn't believe the question. 'You know why. You've seen all those old scars on my body often enough.'

'I don't understand what you think you can achieve.'

'I don't know that I do, either,' he admitted. 'But maybe it'll let me sleep at night.'

It was long past dark. He was beyond tiredness; even the thought of putting one foot in front wearied him. But he'd promised the girl he'd return. The Hardys and the Easbys would have finished their shifts by now.

'I'm Simon Westow. I talked to your daughter. She was looking after your littlest.'

'Billy Hardy.' The man gave a wary nod. He stood with a clay pipe in his mouth. 'What do you want?'

'To say I'm sorry for your loss.' Hardy's face became stone as he listened. 'Your son worked at Seaton's mill, didn't he?'

A gaze like stone. 'I asked you once, mister. What do you want?'

'I know what killed him, the way the overseers used him.'

'What about it?' Simon saw the man clench his fists.

'I'm a thief-taker.'

'Is that right? Come to tell me they committed a crime when they killed my lad, have you?'

'I spent seven years in the mills when I was a child. I learned the hard way.'

'You got out, didn't you?'

Simon nodded. 'I was lucky. Most aren't.' He nodded towards the building at the bottom of the street. 'Do you work there, too?'

'The dye works in Sheepscar.' He held up his hands to show the colours that had become part of his flesh.

'How long have you been there?' Simon asked.

'Ten years. Came here from Ripon. Nowt to be had on the farms up there. Nothing that paid. Someone said there was work down here just for the asking.' Hardy gave a short bark of a laugh. 'Right enough. It's just a different type of slavery, just no fresh air or green.'

'Why not go back?'

'I left because there were no jobs. They haven't grown on the trees since then. I'm married, I've got seven children.'

'Are your family at Seaton's?'

'The younger ones. The last two will be soon enough. We've got to try and earn a living. Seems like it costs you money to breathe in this town.'

'I'd like to give your son some justice.' He hadn't planned the words. But as soon as he spoke them, Simon realized this was why he'd come.

'How?' Hardy puffed on his pipe.

'Change things.'

Hardy snorted. 'What do you plan on doing, Mr Thief-taker? Do you have more money than God? More power?'

'Of course I don't.'

'Then you'd best stop dreaming. His mam has cried herself to sleep every night since our Peter died, and she dun't seem likely to stop. There's no joy in this house. There never will be again. But there's nothing we can do. *Nothing*. Do you know what'll happen if I complain, or threaten, if I say one bloody word?'

'I can guess,' Simon replied.

'No need. I'll tell you. We'll be out on our arses and there won't be another factory owner in Leeds who'll employ us.' He stared at Simon. 'You tell me what choice I have.'

'It was the overseer who was responsible. Give me his name. I'll take care of things.'

Very slowly, Hardy shook his head. His eyes glistened. 'I daren't,' he said quietly. 'They might find out.'

He closed the door and Simon was caught in the night. The man was scared, and who could blame him? Mill owners, factory owners, they were the ones with real power. They had the money. Billy Hardy grieved for his son, but he was powerless and he knew it. Too many children died every year, in the ground before they could enjoy their lives. Disease, accidents, violence. So many killers. Simon thought of his own boys. He wanted Richard and Amos to grow and thrive.

Another door further down Ebenezer Street, another man standing on the step. This one was brawny, the type who might look menacing except for the sorrow filling his eyes.

'Dr Hey told me about your son,' Simon said. 'I'm sorry.'

'Not as much as I am.' The man looked him over. 'My name's Jeb Easby. What do you want?' Simon introduced himself and the man said: 'Whatever you're selling, I don't have the money to buy.'

'I'm not selling anything. I'm a thief-taker. Maybe your son needs some justice.'

'I daresay he does.' He turned his head and spat into the street. 'Him and the Hardy lad, all the others who've gone before and them that's still waiting to be born. It's a grand idea. How do you plan on achieving it?'

'Talk to the overseers, the men who hurt him.'

'What do you think? They'll listen and suddenly realize the error of their ways?' The contempt oozed out of his words. 'If that's what you believe, then you're not half as clever as you look. Who do you reckon backs the overseers, eh?'

'Seaton.'

'Of course he does. They make him money. He's not about to get rid of them.'

'No,' Simon agreed.

'The rest of us, we're expendable. Everybody up and down this street. Wear out one and there are ten more waiting.' His eyes were bright with fury. 'Push us hard, then throw us away when they can't use us any more. Or are you going to tell me you can change Seaton's mind?'

'We both know better than that.' Simon stood, hands pressed into his coat pockets. 'But maybe I can make the overseers see sense.'

Easby shook his head. 'I'll believe that when I see it.'

'Give me their names.'

'No. If Seaton's men found out I'd done something like that, I'd be lucky if they just sacked me. I can't take that chance.'

At least he'd tried. He couldn't blame the men for being fearful. This was their lives, their futures. Simon heard footsteps and turned his head. A pair of men strolled past, coming from the factory, dressed too well to belong anywhere near Ebenezer Street. They eyed Simon and the man on the doorstep with suspicion.

'You said you wanted a sing-song, Mr Westow?' Easby asked. His voice rang out clearly.

'Sing?' The question baffled him.

Easby gave a sharp nod. 'Well, you come to the glee club meeting in the room above the Pack Horse tomorrow night, and we'll make sure you have one. Good songs and a drink or two.'

Now he understood. 'Yes, that's what I was looking for.'

'Be there at half past seven, on the nose. We always have a good session. If you decide to come, make sure you're on time.' He closed the door before the factory men were out of earshot.

The day had worn him hollow. He craved nothing more than the warmth of home and crawling into his bed to sleep long and deep. Rosie was right. Standing up for two dead children wasn't his fight. Nothing he could do would make a scrap of difference.

Then Simon remembered the helplessness and impotence on Billy Hardy's face, and what he'd said to Jeb Easby. The risk the man had taken in issuing his invitation. Simon's anger began to burn again. It was the spark he needed to send him out of the house and into the sharpness of the night the next evening.

Upstairs in the Pack Horse, Simon wasn't sure what to expect from the glee club. At first he wondered if Easby intended to use it as cover to tell him about the overseers. As more men filed in, Simon changed his mind. He recognized a few of the faces. Radicals, like Alice Mann's husband, James, the bookseller, talking to some others near the front of the room. He'd been on trial for sedition three years before. Several of the others had seen the inside of cells for their politics, too.

Simon stared around, assessing them. He didn't even notice Easby until the man settled next to him on the bench, holding a full tankard and grinning.

'Well?'

'You're not here for the songs.'

'Oh, we are, brother. We sing of equality and combination. And we do know a few hearty tunes.' He grinned and nodded towards the fireplace. A strong blaze was burning to warm them all. Up above, pages from the *Mercury* and the *Intelligencer* and some of the smaller newspapers were pasted to the wall, there for everyone to read. A small, slight man stood, arms outstretched. He had grey hair that sprang out from his head, a darting, elfin look to his face. A long, old-fashioned coat reached to his knees, a pure white stock was wound around his neck, and he wore a pair of polished high riding boots. He could easily have been a squire existing on a small income.

'Gentlemen,' he announced, 'we'll start the singing with *Barbara Allen*.'

An old piece, one everyone knew. Their voices rang out, full and righteous, the man conducting them through the first verse. After the refrain, half the voices trailed away and turned to each other in low conversation. By the time the second verse was done, they'd all trickled from the tune and the soft hubbub of talking filled the room.

'This is where we make our plans,' Easby said. 'I've taken a chance, bringing you here. Some folk asked around about you today. They say you can be trusted.'

'I can,' Simon said firmly.

'You'd better not tell a soul,' Easby said, and there was no lightness in his voice. 'We have a penalty for those who do. We're men who want combinations in the mills and the manufactories. Something to fight for us and give us a little power against the owners.'

'You need it.'

The man chuckled. 'They'll battle us for every inch. Them with money are hardly likely to roll over and let it happen. That's why the overseers are important to them. They're meant to terrify as much as keep things moving.'

'I told you last night what I want.'

Easby looked around the room. 'So long as you understand what *we* want, Mr Westow. *Real* changes. Do you imagine that revenge against a pair of bullies will help us?'

'Those bullies killed two children. One of them was your son.'

'You think you need to remind me?' His voice fell like iron. 'The people in this room were the ones who clubbed together and paid for our Jacob's funeral. Half of them know it could have happened to their families. Do you have children, Mr Westow?'

'Two boys.'

'We're trying to protect them, and all the others like them. But I'll warn you, think on. If you decide to do something to Seaton's overseers, you'll be setting yourself against every single one of the mill owners. Are you sure you want that many powerful enemies?'

'I'm not about to stand up and leave, if that's what you mean,' Simon said.

'You could hinder our cause.'

'How? You said it yourself: the owners aren't going to listen to you. They're more likely to set the magistrates on you and see you all transported. I'd like you to succeed. But if you truly believed you had a fair chance, you wouldn't need to disguise your meetings this way.'

'Fair chance?' Easby grimaced. 'There's no such thing for a working man in this country. Haven't you realized that yet?'

Before Simon could answer, the small man sprang up from his seat and announced another song. '*Seven Yellow Gypsies*.'

More singing that dissolved into talk. Some of the folk kept their distance from him, suspicious of a stranger's face. Others were glad of some conversation.

Six songs, seven, before the evening ended with the elfin man picking up his fiddle and playing a tune he called the *Kirkgate Hornpipe*. Simon left with Jeb Easby. They walked together towards Ebenezer Street. Just before they parted on Vicar Lane, the man leaned towards him and softly spoke a pair of names.

'You wanted to know. It's your battle now.'

Jane stood in the yard behind the Pack Horse, out of sight in a small alcove. She worried about Simon. What he was doing troubled her. Word would soon pass that he was asking questions about the mill and its overseers. That was a dangerous business, and Seaton had the money to hire men who'd kill.

Simon hadn't recovered from his illness yet; she could see it in his eyes. He was a little stronger each day, but he was still too thin, he tired too easily, he wasn't as sharp or as quick as he'd been before. It was safer if she followed him. To be there if something happened. If it didn't, there was no need for him ever to know.

She'd left Mrs Shields dozing by the fire and sharpened her knife on the small whetstone before pulling on her cloak, raising her shawl over her hair, and drifting into the night. Out here she was invisible.

Jane followed Simon from his home to the inn and saw him trail upstairs behind a group of men. A glee club, he'd said, but they hadn't done much raising of their voices in song.

Now she waited. She had no sense of anyone lurking. No danger.

She hadn't felt her father anywhere close again. Perhaps he'd decided to keep his distance; even better, maybe he'd left. No, she knew that was nothing more than hope. He'd appear when he was good and ready. This time she had to be prepared. No shock, no hesitation.

Another song, the ragged voices all coming together for a verse. After that, they began to drop out, until only two or three remained to shout out the tune. She'd noticed the men arriving, seen their silhouettes through the window upstairs; there had to be twenty of them up there.

Even in the cold night, the back door of the Pack Horse was propped open to let in air. She'd seen the serving girls hurrying up and down the steps with trays of drink; no danger of singing leaving their throats dry. Finally, she heard a fiddle play and the scrape of chairs, the shift of tone in the conversation and the sound of shoes coming down the stairs.

Jane slipped through the yard to Briggate, waiting near the crumbling Moot Hall. She was one more anonymous shape in the darkness. Simon emerged, illuminated for a second by an oil lamp over the passage. He walked with another man, their heads close together in earnest conversation as they passed through to Vicar Lane. A few more words, then they parted.

She followed Simon as he cut down Call Lane and into Queen's Court on his way home. A few dull lights hung above the door-ways, tiny glimmers cutting through the night.

Without even realizing it, he was aware of someone there. Soft footsteps behind him, keeping a rhythm that matched his own. Carefully, Simon eased his knife from its sheath on his belt, then slipped another out of its hiding place up his sleeve. He kept moving, never slowing his pace, until the passageway out to Briggate was in sight. Then he stopped and turned.

One man, eyes hidden by the wide brim of his hat. From the easy way he moved, he had to be young. Still lithe and graceful. A blade in his hand.

Simon's mouth was dry. He'd been well schooled in knife-fighting, taught by a master, but months had passed since he'd needed those skills. Before he was ill. Fear climbed up his spine. His body was tense. Every sense sharp, on edge. All he had on his side was experience. A bead of sweat trickled down his forehead. He started to raise a hand to wipe it away.

The young man moved with confidence. A feint to the right, then a fast turn to the left. He was absolutely sure of himself. Simon knew this game; no need for him to do anything at all. The man was sounding out his opponent, seeing how he'd react. Let him move and dance all he liked. The test would come when the young man decided to attack. Would Simon be fast enough to stop him?

It came quickly. A swift lunge, starting low and rising, the type of blow that could gut an opponent if it landed. But he wasn't quite as clever as he thought. His eyes gave it away just in time for Simon to move aside and slice the man's sleeve open.

He felt resistance against the blade as it cut into flesh. The man turned and came again. He was trying to force Simon back towards the wall.

It was a good idea, the sensible move; it would give him room to attack. Someone had taught him the right lessons.

Then the man opened his mouth and howled with pain. He dropped his knife, metal clattering on the flagstones. He turned, bent over double as he started to run, hands clutching his side.

At the edge of his vision, Simon saw Jane lift her blade. It would only take one more blow to finish the attacker.

'Let him go.'

She stepped back into the shadows. Another moment and the man had vanished.

Simon leaned back against the wall, closing his eyes and breathing hard. He was alive, he was unharmed. Not complete luck. But certainly nothing he'd done. Jane had probably saved his life. That was the hard truth. His heart was beating so fast that he felt as if his ribs might burst. His hands shook as he tried to return the knives to their sheaths.

A few more seconds and the man would have beaten him.

'Why did you stop me?' she asked.

Simon forced himself to stand upright. He swallowed hard and placed one foot in front of the other until he reached the opening on to Briggate. There was the assurance of noise out here, the sound of horses' hooves and the turning of coach wheels. Voices raised in laughter and arguments. All the ordinary things happening. Such a short distance between death and life.

'You'd already hurt him. No sense in murder.'

'He'd have killed you.'

'I know.' The realization that he might no longer be good enough for all this filled his head. 'I know,' he repeated quietly. 'What made you follow me?'

'The things you're doing, and you're not well yet.'

Sometimes she knew more than she ever said. 'Thank you.'

She stayed with him until he reached his door.

'I'm grateful,' he told her. 'Honestly.'

Jane gave a small nod. She was never likely to show anything more than that.

His hands had stopped their trembling as he turned the key in the lock. 'Tomorrow we'll find out who he is. I want to know who paid him.'

EIGHT

The man with the knife came again. Simon was too slow, too clumsy to defend himself. The blade felt too heavy in his hand. Every blow he tried to make missed its mark. It happened time after time. Then Simon would start awake, sitting up in bed but finding no comfort in the darkness. The dream wouldn't leave him be.

He was still exhausted when the first strands of light appeared through the shutters. But what did sleep bring? Only defeat and dread. He rose, dressed and quietly let himself out of the house, trying to shrug off the feeling that haunted him. Without Jane, he'd have been dead. He needed to admit it, to accept it.

Simon had work to do: most important was finding the wounded assassin and his paymaster. Then he needed to identify the overseers from Seaton's mill and decide what to do about them.

Another harsh morning. Frost crackled and patterned the windows of the houses as he walked along Swinegate. The mud on the streets had frozen into hard, solid ruts. Brittle ice covered the puddles. People walked with short, shuffling steps; better that than falling on their arses. Maybe Barnabas's talk of snow had a hint of truth to it.

Even the coaches at the inns went slowly and with care. The drivers knew full well that good, swift horses were valuable and expensive to replace.

The coffee cart was doing brisk business; men were eager for something warm in their bellies. The air was alive, crackling with fresh gossip. A body had been discovered during the night. This one on Leeds Bridge, in the middle of the road, found by a carter arriving in the dark moments before dawn.

Simon listened, curious but paying little mind until someone said: 'I heard he was called Collins.'

He turned, suddenly very interested. 'What was that?'

The man shrugged. 'Collins. That's just the talk. I don't know, I didn't see him.'

The gaol stood near the top of Kirkgate. It was a decrepit stone building that leaned to one side, reeking of mould and age. The wood of the door was beginning to rot and the mortar between the blocks crumbled under the touch.

Simon didn't expect to find Constable Porter here; he rarely appeared more than once a week. It was the inspector of the night watch who sat behind the desk, smoking a pipe as he wrote.

'There was a body on the bridge.'

Slowly, the man turned his gaze on Simon. 'What about it, Westow?'

'Was his name Collins?'

'It was.'

'George Collins?'

'That's right.' The man smiled. 'You've saved us the effort of coming to find you. Didn't you know him?'

'No.' That made the glint vanish from the man's eyes. 'I met him for a few seconds when I collected the candlesticks he'd stolen from Franklin Arden. That was all.'

'And you didn't kill him?'

Simon frowned and shook his head. 'Why would I do that?'

'Why don't you tell me?' The man snorted. 'It looks as if he was stabbed on Pitfall last night and managed to crawl as far as the bridge. Died there, right in the middle of the road.'

Pitfall again, where they'd dragged Sebastian Ramsey's body from the river. What had Collins been doing down there?

The man's voice cut through his thoughts. 'Where were you last night?'

Dear God, the man really believed he might have done it. 'I went to the glee club at the Pack Horse, then home to my wife and children.'

'No visitors?'

'None.' He wasn't going to mention the attack at Queen's

Court. It seemed the watch had heard nothing about that. If they had, the inspector would already be asking questions.

'Maybe you went back out.' His voice became eager. 'You ran into Collins and the two of you argued. You killed him.'

Simon grinned. 'You should make your living as a patterer. It's a good tale; a pity it never happened.'

'It's no secret that you're useful with a knife.'

Not as much as he'd once been, Simon thought. Nowhere near as much.

'So are many other people. Unless you have anything else, I'll go. The constable knows where to find me.'

'I'm sure he'll want to talk to you, Westow.'

'Maybe he should have a word with Franklin Arden and his father, too. They had no reason to like Mr Collins.' He tipped his hat and left the gaol.

Last night's attack. Now Collins's death. Something was happening. But he had no idea what it might be.

'It must have been Thomas Arden,' Rosie said. 'He was never likely to let Collins escape without punishment. That would be bad for his reputation.'

'Very likely,' Simon agreed. They were sitting at the kitchen table. At the other end, Richard and Amos were hunched over their work as they prepared for their tutor.

'Who else is it likely to be?'

'The son,' Jane said. 'Franklin.'

'It's not our business, thank God,' Simon said. 'Collins is dead. It's up to the constable now. I doubt he'll come up with much, especially if Arden is responsible. He hasn't found anything about that man Ramsey they pulled out of the river.' He looked from his wife to Jane. 'The thing I want to know is who attacked me and who paid him.'

With a nod, Jane rose and pulled the cloak around her shoulders. A touch to her side to assure herself the knife still nestled in her pocket. Before she came out she'd honed the edge again. A blade could never be too sharp.

She knew the places to go, but they'd yield little information before evening. Darkness was when the people who inhabited

the other Leeds appeared. The thieves and the vicious, the pros-
titutes and hopeless. Daylight only brought the stark sweep of a
frigid wind, the stench from the factory chimneys and unanswered
questions.

She walked, waiting for the prickling sensation of someone
following her. The chance to finally confront her father. But all
she felt was emptiness.

Once night arrived, she made the round of the dram shops.
Places you could hire a killer for a bottle of brandy and a shilling or two. She'd been in them often enough, always safe. The
men there sniffed the danger in her and kept their distance; they
realized she was more ruthless than any of them.

Jane stood just inside the door, trying to study their expressions. For one small moment, every face she saw belonged to
her father. She closed her eyes and breathed. Once, twice. Her
fingers rubbed the ridge of scars on the inside of her forearm.

Jane looked again and he was gone. In his place just curiosity
and resentment and strained expressions. Boredom. Lust. Two
people she knew. The first didn't want to talk. He sat alone
in the corner, staring down at the almost empty glass of rum. He
didn't even seem to hear as she spoke.

The second spat into the sawdust covering the boards.

'Whatever you want, it's going to cost you threepence.'

'Who would I see about a good knife man?' she asked.

He smirked. 'I thought you were handy with one yourself.'

Jane didn't say a word, simply placed three pennies one by
one on the table and stared at him until he looked away.

'Talk to John Crawford,' the man told her finally. 'You know
the Low Hurt?'

'Yes.'

'You can find him there.'

The Low Hurt. It was the name people gave to a beer shop that
had opened a couple of years before, on the far side of Timble
Bridge, across Sheepscar Beck. For many years it had been a
house. Now the lights in its windows glittered late into the night
as people came and went.

Inside was a welter of noise, bright and loud enough to make
her wince. Jane kept her hand on the knife hilt as she scanned
the crowd.

John Crawford sat alone at the end of a bench, fingers curled around his glass as if he was trying to protect it. Jane moved between the tables. Hands reached for her and she pushed them away, squeezing past a group to face him. She stood silent until Crawford realized she was there.

He cocked his head. 'What do you want?'

His words came out slurred, as sloppy as the rest of him. His stock was askew, grubby and stained with food. Grease shone on his coat.

'The name of a good knife man.' She rattled a pair of coins down on the table. His hand snaked out and cupped them.

'Why?' His eyes clouded with suspicion. 'You work with Simon Westow, don't you? I've seen you around.'

'Why would that matter?'

'What does he need with a knife man?'

'He doesn't,' she said and waited until she had his attention. 'I do.'

'What do you want him for?'

'That's my business. If you're not interested—' She began to turn away.

'I didn't say that, did I?'

'You haven't said much. All you've done so far is ask questions,' Jane told him.

'I might know one or two fellows who can do the sort of work you want. It used to be three, but the best one got himself hurt.'

'Why?' She pounced on his words. 'What happened to him?'

'Don't know.' He shrugged. 'Got a message that something had happened, that's all.'

That was the man she wanted. It had to be. 'When?'

'Not saying. I thought you wanted someone who could do the job.'

A shilling didn't loosen his tongue. Even a second didn't help.

'Why don't you want to tell me?'

'He's not the type you cross.'

She added another to the pile of coins.

'You can tell me his name now and keep the money, or I'll be waiting for you when you go home.' She slipped the knife from her pocket, letting him see the blade. 'You know I work with Simon. That means you know who I am, and what I can do.' Jane allowed enough time for the remark to sink home. 'Your choice. What's it going to be?'

He pursed his lips and took a deep breath. She could read the answer in his eyes, full of anger, impotence and fear. A thin sheen of sweat covered his forehead.

'I'll give you his name. But promise you won't say it came from me.'

'Agreed.'

'Everyone calls him Riley. He's only been in Leeds for a few months.'

'Where do I find him?'

The man shook his head. 'You don't. If I want him, I have to leave a message at the Duke William.'

'For Riley?'

'For someone called Pepper. When he receives it, he'll come and find out about the job. If the money's good enough, he'll pass on the details.'

'Who hurt this Riley? How did it happen if he's so good?' Jane knew the answer. She wanted to learn how far the word had spread.

'I don't know,' Crawford answered. 'Honest, I'm not even sure if he was working.'

She believed him; the stink of fear was too strong for the man to be lying.

'What's this Pepper like?'

He blinked. 'Very ordinary. Look away and you've forgotten he was ever there. Brown hair. Not thin or fat. He's quiet, too. You don't even notice him until he opens his mouth.'

A final penny and she left. Riley, Pepper; she'd never heard of either of them. Maybe Simon would know the names.

He sat and weighed the prospect for a long time before he strode over to Thomas Arden's house in Park Square. Pale clouds that stood high in the sky, hardly a breath of wind for once, and a chill that filled his lungs every time he breathed.

The man was at home, sitting behind the desk in his study. A fire flamed in the hearth; the room felt warm and inviting.

As soon as Arden saw Simon he began to chuckle. 'I had a bet with myself.'

'About me?' He settled into a chair with a cushioned back and carved wooden arms.

'A shilling that you'd be down here as soon as you heard Collins was dead, ready to accuse me of murder.'

'Why? Did you kill him?'

Arden's face was bland. 'No, I did not.'

'Did you arrange for it to happen? Did you ask or pay anyone to do it?'

The chuckle became outright laughter. 'You ought to have been a lawyer, Westow. So careful and precise with your words.'

Arden hadn't answered the question. 'Did you?'

'No, I didn't. The whole thing came as a surprise to me this morning.'

'What about your—?'

Arden slammed his palm down on the desk. 'Franklin isn't that stupid.'

'Have you asked him?'

'No need. I'd already ordered him to drop it all. He made his mistake. I paid to put it right. He knows not to let it happen again, and to leave Collins be.'

Simon stood. He'd learned all that was possible here. He wasn't going to mention the attack on him. Even if Arden was responsible, he'd never admit it.

'Maybe you should ask your son directly and make sure he gives you an honest answer.'

'It's not your business, Westow. You'd do well to leave it alone.' Menace flowed under the words.

'There is one more thing I'd love to know: why did you tell people I'd recovered the candlesticks?'

'Why not?' He shrugged. 'It lets people know you do your job well, Westow. And it's a reminder that if people steal property from me and mine, I'll get it back. Anything else?'

Glib words, but the truth was more complex; Simon felt certain of that. Arden was too wily to reveal the real reason. Yet he never said that his son was innocent of Collins's murder; he'd skirted around that, too. Maybe it wasn't important: in Leeds, no Arden would ever be convicted of anything. They'd never even end up in the dock.

NINE

Simon tried the coaching inns, asking for a guest named Ramsey. No luck. From there he went to the hotels. Finally, at the Great Northern, he found his man.

'Mr Westow.' Charles Ramsey was astonished to see him. Not even a handful of days since they'd met but the man had aged. The lines cut deeper into his face, his mouth turned down at the corners and his shoulders slumped under his sorrow. 'I hadn't expected to see you again.'

'I wondered how you were coming along with your investigation.'

'Nowhere, sir.' He sighed. 'Nowhere at all.'

'Perhaps you'd like some assistance,' Simon said.

'But you . . .' Ramsey was bewildered.

'I might have been hasty.' He decided not to mention what had happened to a man called Sykes in York. A letter was already on the way to the lawyer there.

'Then yes.' He smiled with relief. 'I told you, I can pay.'

'I need you to write down some things for me: the name of your brother's employer, where he lived, any of his friends you know about.'

'Gladly. If you can wait five minutes, I'll do it now.' He cocked his head. 'Might I ask what changed your mind, sir?'

'Life.' It seemed as honest an answer as any.

Two pages, penned in a firm hand. The briefest summary of a man.

'I'd been gone a long time,' Ramsey explained. 'I told you that. I can't say I knew Sebastian well. I only had this last month with him, after I came back.' A faint, wistful smile. 'I believe I'd almost persuaded him to come with me to Boston. Then . . .'

'Who's looking after your business while you're away?'

'I have a partner. We founded the firm together.'

'I can't promise I'll find your brother's killer,' Simon said. 'Please understand that.'

'Of course not, sir.' He gave a sad smile. 'But I'm sure you'll do your best.'

Simon sat in the kitchen with the warmth of the range on his back. Rosie had gone off to the market and the boys were in the parlour, listening to their tutor.

He knew a little about Sebastian Ramsey now. Just the faint outline of him. He rented rooms on Skinner Lane, a short way out of town along the Sheepscar Road. According to his brother, Ramsey was a light drinker. Not a gambler or one for the whores. A modest man. Not someone who invited violence.

But over and over, Simon's eyes strayed back to the line about Ramsey's job: for the last twelve years he'd been a clerk at Seaton's mill.

It wasn't too long since Skinner Lane had been deep in the country-side. Even now there were fields close by, and in the distance Sheepscar Bridge crossed the beck and the turnpike passed the barracks. But industry drew closer each year. He could smell the stink from the dye works a quarter of a mile away and hear the rasping grind of the rapeseed mill. No peace, no silence anywhere in Leeds these days.

Men worked in the bitter cold to erect streets of new houses. Places they'd never be able to afford for themselves. No matter; it was a job, a wage, a living, and the town was in desperate need of housing for all the people who kept arriving.

The building where Ramsey had lived looked grand enough, he thought, presenting an ornate frontage with large bay windows facing the road. But it had never been intended for one family, designed as sets of rooms to be let. Still, he must have earned a reasonable wage to afford somewhere like this.

Inside, he found only the furniture that came with the place. Charles Ramsey had already visited and claimed everything that had belonged to his brother. Wandering from room to room, Simon could catch no sense of who Sebastian had been. He checked the floorboards and the walls. Nothing loose to pry up, no hollow places a man could use to hide things.

He strode back towards town, breath blooming in a cloud to merge with the smoke hanging low in the distance. When he had the opportunity, he'd visit the dead man's friends. First, though, he needed to decide what to do about the employer.

George Mudie was sitting at his desk, chewing on a pie, a glass of brandy close to his hand. Crumbs covered his apron and chin.

'Do you recall the man they pulled from the river with his throat slashed and his hand cut off?' Simon asked.

'You have a delightful way of phrasing things when a man's trying to eat, Simon.' He placed the food on his desk and rubbed flakes of pastry from his hands before taking a sip of the drink. 'Of course I remember him.'

'Did you ever hear anything more about it? Anyone who might have done it? A reason?'

'No suspects, that's for damned certain. Someone even suggested that he might have been the wrong person. I'm told the constable's given it up as a bad job.' He stared at Simon. 'Why are you suddenly so interested, anyway?'

'His brother's paying me to look into it.'

'Didn't you already turn him down once?'

'Things change.'

Mudie swallowed more of the brandy and stayed silent and thoughtful for a long time. Finally, he said: 'For whatever it's worth, I don't think anyone has a clue. The brother you're working for was blundering around, but obviously he didn't discover much.'

'No, he didn't. Who came up with the idea that Ramsey was the wrong man?' Simon asked.

Mudie shrugged. 'I've no idea. I can't even remember who mentioned it to me. It seems that none of the usual thieves knew him.'

'If a name should come to you . . .' He smiled. 'I'll leave you to your food.'

Mudie raised his glass in a mocking toast. 'Thank you for ruining my appetite.'

'Riley.' Simon rolled it around his tongue. 'No, I've never heard of him. You've done well to find out so quickly.'

'If he's only been in Leeds for a short while, it's no surprise,' Rosie said. 'You were ill for part of that time.'

And he was still far from his best. At the very least, though, he should have come across the name.

'I know now.' Simon pursed his lips. 'I think I might have come across Pepper once or twice. I can't remember where, though.'

'We still don't know who killed Collins,' Jane said.

'We won't worry about it. It's only our business if the constable wants to ask me more questions,' Simon told her. 'There's nothing in that one for us.'

Jane slipped out into the night. She'd passed on what she'd learned, there was nothing more she could do there. Long past ten and she was ready to be home, to check on Mrs Shields and rest.

The cold came as a slap against her skin. She kept her head down as she walked, the cloak pulled tight around her. Her senses were alert and the knife ready in her hand.

Still no feeling of anyone behind her. Nothing at all today. But her father was still in Leeds. She knew he was here. She'd seen his face, just an arm's length away. It hadn't been her imagination.

People were out, drinking and cursing and singing and fighting. Knots of young men on the street, looking as if they barely felt the chill.

She ducked away from the Head Row, into Green Dragon Yard. Jane held her breath, careful. This would be a good place for him to wait for her. But there was only emptiness. Once she'd darted through the gap in the wall to Mrs Shields's house, she felt safe.

The old woman was dozing, cap on her head, strings neatly tied in a bow under her chin. Her breathing was easy, no wheezing or rasping. Jane felt her forehead and cheeks. No fever.

Sitting by the banked fire, she smiled at herself. She'd become a nursemaid, as domesticated as any wife. Yet she didn't mind. She was happy to care for Catherine Shields. Jane pulled the blanket up around her shoulders. Still smiling, she closed her eyes.

The Duke William stood just south of the river, a rough brick building on Bowman Lane, hidden away behind the wharves and the timber yards. Its custom came from the labourers and stevedores on the Aire, raw men with strong thirsts and quick tempers.

Dan Mears used blows instead of questions to keep order in his beerhouse. He had a heavy cudgel hanging from his leather apron, and he was happy to wield it the moment trouble began. Mears was a dour soul with a shaved, oiled skull that glistened under the fluttering light of a candle. A heavy, dark moustache extended from his top lip down each side of his mouth, all the way to his jaw.

Simon had come here a few times for information. This was a good time, morning, quiet, hardly a soul in the place. Mears granted him a curt, watchful nod as a greeting then stood as Simon took pennies from his trouser pocket and piled them, one on top of the other, to make a small tower on the bar. He wanted this done quickly so he could go home and give in to the weariness that reached all the way into his marrow.

'Riley,' Simon said. 'Pepper.'

'What about them?'

'Where can I find them?'

Mears shook his head. 'I don't know.'

'No?' Another shiny coin.

'Even if I knew, I wouldn't say.'

'Why not?'

'People don't sell secrets.'

Simon smiled. The man was very, very wrong if he truly believed that; it happened every single day of the year. Honour was nothing more than a word.

'What does Riley look like?'

'Never seen him.' Mears shrugged. 'I just hold the messages. Pepper's the one who comes in and checks.'

That was something, a start. 'What do you know about him?'

'Nothing.'

'How often is Pepper here?'

Another shrug. 'Two or three times a week. Every day if he's expecting something.'

'When was he in last?'

Mears rubbed his chin, considering. 'Tuesday.'

It was Thursday now. 'When he comes back, tell him I want a word.'

'I'll give him the message. What he does with it is up to him.'

Simon nodded at the money. 'That's for him, whether he comes to see me or not. There could be more.'

Temptation might work, he thought as he walked back towards Leeds Bridge. Or Mears could pocket it all and Pepper would never know. He had to take the chance.

He hadn't intended it, but Simon took the winding way home. He stood in the darkness and watched from the deep shadows when the doors opened at Seaton's mill and the workers flooded out, pale-faced, stunned after their shift. The overseers would emerge later. That was what Jeb Easby had told him. He was here now; he might as well wait.

Jane stood by the window, scraping ice from the glass with her thumbnail as she tried to stare into the yard. Frost rimed the plants. Winter was beginning early this year.

Her father had been in her dreams again. All through the night he'd tormented her, snapping and cutting at her sleep.

She needed to know why he'd come back to Leeds after all these years. What did he want with her? The only way to find out was to confront him. Until she did that, the face would taunt her each time she closed her eyes.

She raised her shawl over her head and pulled it around her throat. It was good wool, thick and heavy enough to keep out the cold and the wind. Then the old green cloak, buttoning it at the neck. A glance in the mirror, turning the gold ring on her finger for luck and safety before sliding her hands into leather gloves. She was ready.

'I didn't know you were working today, child,' Mrs Shields said.

'Just for a few hours.' She smiled at the old woman and felt for the knife in the pocket of her dress. Last night, woken with fear by a nightmare, she'd spent half an hour sharpening the blade, grinding it time after time against the whetstone. It gave her comfort and strength. 'Do you need anything?'

'No, no. We have plenty.'

The air was raw, the wind blowing enough to make her eyes sting and water. For the briefest second, as she stood by the gap in the wall, Jane hesitated and glanced back at the cottage. It would be so easy to stay there, warm and comfortable. But there was only one way she could ever feel truly safe. She plunged on, out to the Head Row.

Walking warmed her; the constant movement, searching the faces she saw on the streets. She went along Vicar Lane, Kirkgate, Commercial Street, all the way to Park Square and back again. Boar Lane and Duncan Street, a return to Kirkgate. She made the circle twice, three times. But no sense of him.

Jane bought food from Kate the pie-seller, listening as she gossiped. There were fewer wanderers today; anyone with sense would rather stay by their hearths, out of the icy cold. Idly, she ate, scarcely noticing the taste.

Then, suddenly, she felt it. It jolted her, a stab in her spine. Jane craned her neck as she looked around. Kate was still talking, but she didn't hear a word. She was trying to spot him.

Nothing she could see. But it was real. He was there, an itch that crawled over her skin. The revulsion and the fear. Everything she'd come out to face.

As she walked up Briggate, going slowly, gazing in the shop windows, Jane willed him to follow. He was there. Not close but definitely trailing behind her. She made it easy for him, staying on the main streets until he felt confident enough to draw closer.

Jane knew she was in control. She was leading him. Letting him believe he was in charge. Allowing him to think she had no idea he was there.

It was dangerous. Her father had lived here. At one time, he must have known Leeds well. She needed to stay alert, never give him the chance of an advantage. To weave her web very delicately.

It took an hour. Drawing him in. He was in no hurry to come close. She tightened her grip on the knife handle. He'd do well to be cautious. He knew exactly what he'd done to her, ending her childhood and ripping away her life. Throwing her out to die.

Jane teased him to her, the way she'd seen men on the river-bank slowly work to reel in the fish they caught. Little by little, no rush. Finally, she led him to the perfect spot, confident now that he'd follow: a ginnel that turned just before it reached a wall. It looked like a way through but went nowhere. Another wall rose. No escape. And there was an alcove where she could hide.

Jane slowed until she knew he was close enough to see her vanish through the narrow opening. She hurried, ducking away, the blade raised and ready. Her heart was beating so loud, so fast, that she was certain he must be able to hear it.

She held her breath and pushed herself back. He passed slowly, never even glancing in her direction. At the corner he turned. One more moment and he'd see the trap.

Jane stepped out to face him. She was terrified, but the time had come to put her ghosts to rest.

Bewilderment and anger clouded his expression. Then he saw her and his expression cleared.

'Jane.' It was little more than a whisper, but it sounded louder than a shout.

He took a step towards her. She raised the knife, staring at him. This was the face she'd hated for so many years. It was older now, all the excess worn away until all that remained was skin taut over the bones. His hair was wild, turning white on the temples. Dark stubble coloured his cheeks. He was dressed in a shiny coat that reached to his knees, well-worn and raggedly sewn at the cuffs. Trousers that bagged around his thighs, scuffed boots.

He held up his hands. Dirty, empty, no weapon.

'What do you want?' she asked. She heard herself, sounding firm and cold. Not even the hint of a tremor in her voice.

'I came to find you. To see you.'

'You've seen me. Now you can go again.'

'I—'

She kept her voice even, forcing down the fury that roared inside her head. 'You raped me and you didn't say a word to stop my mother when she pushed me out of the door and locked it. You never looked for me. Neither of you. You didn't care if I lived or not.'

'I'm sorry.' He lowered his head.

No apology he could offer would ever be enough. 'You owe me a life.'

'I wanted to find you, to tell you something.'

She looked at him with disgust. 'What makes you believe I'd care about anything you could say?'

He drew in a breath. 'Your mother's dead. Cancer. It happened last month.'

Jane barely noticed the words. 'She's dead. I'm alive. That sounds like justice to me.'

'She knew she'd done wrong,' he told her. 'We both did. She asked me to come and tell you.'

'What else do you want?'

The woman had turned her back on her own daughter. She'd done something no mother should ever do.

Why was pain rising from the pit of her stomach? Why did she suddenly feel something had disappeared from her life?

No. She refused to let that touch her. She wasn't going to. Not after all this time. No more. Jane wasn't guilty of anything.

'What did you think? The mother's dead, the girl can support me?' She threw the words at him.

A long silence, and then he answered: 'I wasn't even sure you were still alive. After I arrived, I asked and people told me you were working with the thief-taker. Your mother repented. She wanted forgiveness. What we did was evil. We were wrong, both of us.'

'You want me to forgive you?' She couldn't believe it.

'No. Think whatever you want of me but please know that she wished she could make things right. We changed, we tried to live good lives.'

'When was that? After she knew she was dying?' Jane struggled to keep her breathing steady. All the voices in her head screamed that he was lying. 'Do you know what I want to do?' He didn't reply, eyes fixed in the ground. 'Do you?'

'No.'

Slowly, she moved the blade from side to side in front of his face.

'I want revenge. I want to kill you.'

She watched him. His eyes were frightened, hunting for a way out.

'Don't try to move,' Jane warned. 'You'd be dead before you could even shout.' She waited until she could see the defeat on his face. 'I'm going to give you something you never gave me.'

'What?' His voice was a croak.

'A choice. You leave now. Not another word. Vanish from Leeds and never return. If you don't, I'll kill you.'

Her knife was quick, slicing his jacket from shoulder to waist. Before he could react, she stalked off. If she had to look at him any longer, she'd murder him.

As she walked up Albion Street, Jane began to shake. By the time she slipped through the hole in the wall and opened the door to the house, she was clutching at her belly, hardly able to stand. The tears streamed down her cheeks. Everything was beyond her control.

'Child.' Mrs Shields stood, enveloping her in thin arms. 'Oh my, what's happened to you?'

TEN

After the workers had passed a hush fell around the mill, as if its life had vanished with their footsteps. Simon pushed his hands deeper in his pockets and shifted his weight; small movements to try and stay warm. The cold pierced his skin and he was so tired. He heard the church clock strike the half hour and still there was no sign of anyone. Perhaps the overseers used a different entrance.

He decided to let curiosity have the better of him; he'd stay a little while longer.

Five more minutes and he received his reward. Six men emerged, stretching, laughing, lighting their pipes. Even in their heavy clothes, he could see they were all big and thickly muscled. Hard men employed to keep order through intimidation.

Easby had described the pair who hurt his son and Peter Hardy. He picked them out: Warner and Dawson.

Warner turned, heading out north, beyond the mill garth, off towards the new streets past Lady Lane. Dawson put on a billy-cock hat and began to walk in the opposite direction.

In spite of his exhaustion, Simon knew he was going to follow one of them. He'd probably known it all along. The question was which.

Dawson.

Simon remained well back on the quiet streets, far enough to avoid suspicion but close enough to keep the man in sight. Along the Calls, past Pitfall, over Leeds Bridge and through the back streets into Holbeck.

Dawson stopped at a small house a stone's throw from Marshall's big mill. He took a set of keys from his trouser pocket, selected one, and let himself in. A few seconds and the soft glow of an oil lamp filled the window before the curtains were drawn.

He doubted that the man would be out again tonight. Not in this cold. Maybe a trip to the small shop on the corner. No one had been waiting at home for him. He was either widowed or single, no children living with him. All useful information.

Simon circled the block, walking silently along the ginnel and counting the houses. High brick walls around the small yards. Farther along, two privies and an ashpit. The facilities for everyone in the row of houses. It was all fixed in his mind; now he could find the place once more.

Satisfied, he made his way home, feeling the tiredness rise through his body. It had been a long day, but there was more to it than that. The illness still had its grip on him and he'd tried to push himself too far. There was nothing he could do except pace himself, make sure he rested and hope he'd be fully recovered very soon.

At least he wouldn't be home too late; he could enjoy time with the boys before he put them to bed. Tomorrow he'd visit Seaton's again. Inside the building this time, to ask the head clerk about Sebastian Ramsey. Later, after the shift ended, he'd follow Warner to discover where he lived.

It was all knowledge, but what was he going to do with it? How far would he go with the overseers?

'Simon.' Rosie hissed his name and pushed him until he woke. 'There's someone at the door.'

An insistent fist hammered. It was still pitch dark, the middle of the night. The bedroom was bitterly cold, even with the window and the shutters closed. Quickly, he drew on his trousers and a shirt. Downstairs, he pulled back the bolts and turned the key in the lock.

Facing him was Constable Porter, accompanied by two burly men from the watch.

'What do you want?' Simon asked.

'You,' Porter said. He had a dark glint of pleasure in his eyes. 'Get yourself dressed, Westow, I'm taking you to the gaol.'

Simon blinked. He was still surfacing from sleep, trying to gather his thoughts and buy a little time. Anything at all.

'Why? What am I supposed to have done?'

Porter snorted. 'You know full well. A man named Warner.'

'Warner?' He spoke the name as if he'd never heard it before. Simon's mind was galloping. Warner? He'd followed Dawson, the other overseer. What had happened to Warner? What did the constable want?

'You heard me. Finish dressing or I'll drag you out barefoot.'

Rosie stood at the head of the stairs, cradling the twins against her body. There was only time for a few rushed whispers as Simon collected his jacket, boots and heavy greatcoat. She'd see that the lawyer arrived at the gaol first thing; he'd survive until then. Some coins for his pockets, a quick kiss and he was gone.

The gaol was colder than the street, as if years of winter were stored in the stones. The fire in the iron stove barely threw out any heat.

Porter sat, still wrapped in his thick wool coat and leather gloves.

'Why did you do it, Westow?'

'Do what?' he asked and glared at the constable. 'I've been at home with my family. I arrived about seven, haven't been out since.' He tried to keep the pressing note of worry out of his voice. How had anyone connected him to Seaton's mill and the overseers?

'How do you know Gabriel Warner?'

'I don't.' That was the simple truth.

'Someone murdered him in his house tonight.'

Simon shook his head. 'It wasn't me. I've never even spoken to him.'

'Do you know who he was?' Porter asked.

'An overseer at Seaton's Mill.' There was no point in denying he knew that; Porter had been given the information. Simon would dole out just enough of the truth.

The constable smiled. 'You see, you're damned by your own mouth. You do know him.'

A shrug. 'I know what he does. I told you, I never talked to him.'

'I have a witness who noticed you outside the mill tonight. After Warner left, they didn't see you again.'

That was it: he'd been spotted and recognized. He'd made a poor job of staying out of sight. At least he knew now.

Simon smiled. 'On the strength of that, you're arresting me?'

'Why were you there?'

'Personal business.'

'Business with Warner.'

'No,' he answered. 'I didn't speak to a soul. Is that everything?' He started to rise.

'Sit down, Westow. There's Warner dead now, and George Collins last night. I wondered about you for that death, too. Everyone knows you took some stolen silver from him. And when my men fished that corpse with his hand gone out of the river, you turned up quick enough. Maybe you were curious to see the results of your handiwork.'

Simon stared at the man and smiled. He knew he was on safe ground now. If Porter was trying to connect him to all those deaths, it meant he was groping. He had no evidence at all.

'You stand up and tell that to any magistrate and he'll throw you out of the courtroom. My lawyer will be here as soon as it's light. I'm sure he'll be happy to explain the finer points of the law to you. If you're lucky, he won't flay off your skin.'

'Put him in the cell.'

The room was eight feet long and six feet wide; he paced off the distance. A wooden shelf that was both seat and bed. The rusted bucket in the far corner reeked with years of filth. The door was stout oak, with heavy iron bars across the small, high window.

Time passed with grinding, aching slowness. The cold drove deeper and deeper into him until Simon believed his bones might snap. He ached to sleep, but the air was too frigid; as soon as he tried, his teeth started to chatter. The only way was to keep moving.

With the first hint of dawn, Simon began to anticipate the lawyer's arrival. Rosie would have sent Pollard an urgent note.

He'd be here. Damnation, though, he hoped the man would come before he froze to death.

Somehow, he must have managed to doze. Suddenly Simon heard the raised voices, the slam of a fist on the desk. A few seconds later the key turned in the lock and the cell door opened.

'Get out,' Porter said.

Simon pushed past him, into the main room. The fire burned warm and Pollard waited, a broad grin of victory on his face. He was a tall streak of a man, lanky legs that resembled stovepipes in their tight trousers.

One look and a frown. 'Let's get you home. Rosie can put some hot food in you.'

Simon nodded. He wasn't ready to speak just yet. That could wait until they were sitting in his kitchen and he had something in his belly, with the heat from the range drawing the cold out of his skin.

'It sounds as if the constable was trying to rattle you,' Pollard said. He pressed his lips together. 'He hasn't managed to come up with a single suspect in any of the killings, so he's jumping on the tiniest thing and hoping. That way, at least it looks as if he's doing something.' He paused. 'And you have to admit, you do have a connection with them all, Simon.'

He gave a quick shake of his head. 'Not with Warner. I only saw him for a second.'

'Yet someone noticed you by the mill and decided to mention it,' Pollard said. 'Someone who knew that Warner was killed a little later. That's worth thinking about.'

He realized all too well. It had gone round and round in his head during his hours in the cell. Was he being watched? He'd never spotted anyone, but . . .

'I saw Collins, that's common knowledge. For God's sake, Arden told everyone in Leeds. But Ramsey was already dead.'

'They have two things in common, Simon. There's you, of course. And they were all murdered. You're paying for my services, so like it or not, you get my advice, too: watch out for yourself.' He stood, tall enough to have to bow his head under the low ceiling. 'And try to stay out of trouble if you can.'

'I will,' Simon answered. But would he have the chance?

* * *

Jane slept until morning. A deep rest, no dreams that she could recall.

She'd arrived home racked with pain after seeing her father and hearing of her mother's death. Her skin burned with fever and she was ready to vomit. Mrs Shields made some tonic, watched as she drank it, then wrapped Jane in her weightless, spindly arms until it all began to fade.

She didn't know how long she sobbed. There was nothing she could do to stop it. She tried, but her body refused. Finally, drained, still shaking, she gathered her breath. In fragments, she gave Catherine the story. Small pieces that rasped like broken glass in her mind. They opened wounds she thought she'd hidden and locked away years before.

Mrs Shields didn't speak. She sat, softly stroking Jane's hair over and over until she began to close her eyes. But still it kept playing in her mind. Hearing his words, seeing his face.

She should have killed him. One blow. Watch him crumple on the ground and the life fade from his eyes.

Then the old woman was there, holding a mug. She hadn't heard Mrs Shields move, hadn't felt anything at all.

'Drink it, child,' she said with a smile. 'It will help.'

She tried to place the flavours. They seemed so familiar, yet just out of reach.

'All of it.'

Jane raised the cup and gulped the liquid down, feeling the calmness spread through her body.

'It will help you sleep,' Mrs Shields told her. Jane felt the blanket cover her, and settled into the comforting warmth.

Now daylight came through the shutters. She could hear birds chattering and singing in the yard. Slowly, she stretched, rose and dressed. Her mind was empty, no pain crowding and hurting her. A few brief moments of peace, the first she'd ever known in her life. Jane stood, hugging herself, looking in the long mirror and wondering at the woman she saw there.

A minute and it passed. Everything returned. Trickling back at first, then the flood gates opened to bring the worries and the fears cascading around her.

Without them she'd felt different, light and made of gauze, as if she might float away. The feelings, the hurt, the sorrows, they weighed her down, kept her here. She ran her fingers over the scars she'd put on her arms across the years. Each one a reminder of some failure. But she wouldn't add to them. Not for him. If she cut herself over it, he'd won, and she wouldn't offer him that satisfaction.

'Did you sleep well, child?'

Jane nodded. The pain of seeing her father had vanished. She could only recall it dimly, as if it had happened long ago. She had an appetite, wolfing down the porridge that Mrs Shields cooked and the bread thickly spread with butter.

The knock on the door took her by surprise. They weren't expecting anyone. She opened it a crack, the knife in her hand, poised and out of sight, then saw it was Simon. Anger was bubbling through his veins.

'I need you to follow me,' he said. 'I'm being watched.'

He told her about his arrest and everything the constable appeared to know.

'I don't believe someone just happened to spot me outside Seaton's mill and mentioned it. Stay behind me when I go out later. See if anyone's following me.'

'What do you want me to do if I see him?'

'Tell me; we'll take him.'

She nodded. 'Anything else?'

'Not for now,' Simon told her. 'I'm going to sleep until dinner.'

He woke to see Rosie sitting on the bed, smiling down at him. A white cap covered her hair, the apron over an old dress of plain brown muslin. He knew it well, a high Empire waist that fell all the way to the ground. Out of fashion now, but the style suited her.

'I had no idea I was so amusing to watch while I slept.'

She took his hand. 'I'm glad to have you home. I was worried when the constable took you off to gaol.'

'I told you: Porter had nothing.'

'Yes, he did.' Her voice was stark, sober. 'He had power.'

'Not enough, and he has no clue how to use it.' Simon sat up and rubbed his face. 'There are too many things going on that I don't understand.'

'Simon . . .' she began.

'First it was Ramsey pulled out of the river. Then Arden passed word that I'd found those candlesticks. Someone attacked me. After that, both Collins and Warner were murdered. The lawyer pointed it out: I'm the common factor. If I don't do anything, sooner or later something's going to stick.'

Rosie stayed silent, her strong fingers kneading his palm.

'What do you need from me?' she asked.

'For now, just look after yourself and the boys.'

Before he'd even finished the sentence, she had a knife in her hand and a glint of anticipation in her eye. What he needed wasn't enough for her.

'What else?' she asked.

'There'll be more,' he promised, and kissed her. 'I should be up and dressed. Jane will be here soon.'

Simon thought he caught a glimpse of Jane from the corner of his eye. She was so good, so invisible that he'd forgotten she was there.

Ramsey's friends were all at work. Not gentlemen of leisure. No answer for the first two names, while the landlady at the third said her tenant was at his place of business.

At the Talbot he bought a bowl of stew and a mug of beer, sitting with his back to the wall, watching the faces who came and went. One or two were familiar, but not friends, no one who might be able to tell him things he wanted to know.

He was ambling down Kirkgate, close to the parish church and Timble Bridge, when Jane emerged from the opening to a court.

'There's a man who's been behind you for a while,' she hissed. 'He's thirty yards back. Buff coat and dark hat. I'm going to take him.'

He let half a minute pass then turned back and let out a low, long whistle. She replied with a yell. He followed her voice into the dark entrance to a yard, a close passage little more than five yards long. She had a man pressed back against the wall. He was trying to keep his throat clear of the tip of her blade.

A quick search brought a single knife. No spare anywhere on his body. A man with no imagination, Simon thought. Either that or he didn't expect any trouble.

'What's your name?' A tiny prod from Jane made the man wince.
'Yates,' he said. 'Cornelius Yates.'

'And are you interested in where I go on your own account, Mr Yates, or is someone paying you to follow me?'

ELEVEN

N o reply. Simon took a firm grip on the man's jaw and turned his head until Yates had no choice but to look at him.

'I'm not asking for the pleasure of hearing my own voice. I want an answer.'

Yates cried out and tried to squirm away. Jane had sliced across his palm, then held it up for him to see.

'A man called Pepper paid me.' The words rushed out of his mouth.

Interesting. He hadn't anticipated that.

'Why?'

'I don't know.' The young man was sweating, holding the bleeding hand away from his clothes and biting his lip against the pain. 'He told me to follow you and find out what you want, that's all. Not to hurt you.'

'How do you tell him what you've discovered?'

'I write it down and leave it for him at the Duke William.'

Simon thought for a moment. He had plenty of questions, but Yates wouldn't be able to answer most of them. Still, there might be something he could use.

'You must have seen him when he hired you. Where did you meet?'

The man blinked, then replied, as if it was obvious: 'The Duke William. He sent me a message to be there at a certain time.'

'Have you done this work before?'

'A little.'

Simon kept the questions coming, one after the other, relentless. He knew this was the only chance he'd have; as soon as Yates ran off, they'd never see him again.

'What does he look like?'

'Ordinary,' the man answered after a moment. 'Brown hair, not long, not short. Medium height, not stout or thin. Brown clothes.' He shook his head. 'That's all.'

It tallied with what the landlord of the Duke William had told him. A nondescript man. Simon stepped back.

'Did you follow me yesterday?'

'Yes.' His voice trembled. 'I left a message for him last night to say where you'd been.'

'Get out of here,' Simon said. 'Tell Pepper I want to see him, not anyone else.'

They watched Yates hurry away with a grubby handkerchief wrapped around his hand.

'Pepper again,' Jane said.

'I know.' He rubbed his chin and sighed. 'I'm curious. Who the hell is he?'

More than that: Yates had told Pepper. But who had Pepper told? Who was paying him? Who wanted Simon dead?

'Do you want me to find out?'

'If you can. I think it's time.' He sighed. 'I should be safe enough for now.'

South of Leeds Bridge, things were busy by the river. Late in the afternoon, with dusk rapidly falling, but people still moved along the wharves, loading and unloading the barges that were moored. Some vessels left; more arrived. Shouts and curses rose into the air. Jane smelled the scent of fresh-cut wood from the timber yards.

But she saw very few people on Bowman Lane. Down at the far end, close to Black Bull Street, stood the Duke William.

Jane picked her way along the road. No cobbles here, just hard, rutted dirt under the soles of her boots. It was shaping up to be a bitter night, a raw wind blowing from the west. She gathered her cloak tighter and pulled her shawl close around her face.

She'd spent the afternoon asking questions about Pepper in town. A few were familiar with his name, but the only way they knew to find him was through the Duke William. He'd managed to isolate himself, to become a mystery. But *someone* had to know him, where he lived, what he did. All she needed was to find the right person.

No one had followed her. She'd had no more sense of her father; he seemed to have vanished. The pain and rage that coursed through her when she had him helpless had taken her by surprise. But once it ebbed, she felt sharper. Clearer. He was a weak little man. He could never hurt her again. She'd banished him from her dreams.

It was simple to remain hidden out here, with so many places where she could watch the door of the Duke William without being seen. Not many came and went; the landlord must be spending more on coal to heat the place than he made on beer.

Jane stayed for four hours, hearing the lonely toll of the bell on the Parish Church as it marked the time. Close to eight she eased away. Her legs were stiff, her body ached with cold. No one who resembled Pepper had gone in or out. She needed a better way to find him.

Seaton's mill was large, the noise loud enough to deafen. Machines roared and screamed, so many of them, row after row, all the sound echoing off the high ceiling. He coughed after each breath as the fibres in the air caught in his throat.

'This way.' The man guiding him had to shout to make himself heard.

Men and women worked the looms, heads down, eyes focused on the machines. A few glanced at each other, seeming to speak. Simon watched: how could they hear anything in all this noise? Then he realized – they were lip-reading. Children darted under the looms and back out again, changing the bobbins or mending a broken thread. Dangerous work. Deadly. The overseers strode around, shouting, threatening, using the sticks they carried to make sure production stayed high.

'Through here.'

The office was quieter, separated from the factory by a wall with glass windows. But it was still far from silent. Nowhere in this place could ever be quiet while the shift was running.

Simon counted ten men bent over ledgers and invoices. One desk empty. Was that where Sebastian Ramsey had worked? he wondered.

The head clerk's desk faced them, like at teacher with his class. At first he was reluctant to move away and talk.

'I don't know what they'll get up to if I'm not here,' he said with a doubtful look.

Ramsey had been a conscientious employee, the man explained. Always on time, worked well without prompting. He'd rarely been ill over the years he'd been employed in the office. Everything straightforward and ordinary. But Simon felt that the man wouldn't have mentioned it if things had been different. He wanted his world to be ordered and simple. No difficulties on his road.

'One last thing,' Simon said. 'Do you often see Mr Seaton here?'

'Mr Seaton?' The head clerk frowned as if the name astonished him. 'No, no. He's never been in my office. Never at all.'

The darkness was rising when Simon came out through the large door. He was tired; the morning hadn't brought enough sleep to make up for the broken night. But there were still one or two things to do today.

The man had just placed the key in the lock when Simon gripped his wrist. Dawson turned, eyes wide, terror on his face.

'I want to talk to you,' Simon said. 'About Peter Hardy and Jacob Easby. You remember them, don't you?'

'I don't know what you're talking about.' He tried to pull away, head turning, looking around for anyone who might help.

'I'm not going to hurt you.' He kept tight hold of Dawson's arm, fingers pressing hard enough on the man's flesh to make him wince.

'You're the one who murdered Harry Warner.' The man's voice was raw and fragile.

'No. I never spoke to him. I didn't go anywhere near him.'
'Then—'

'I don't know. But it wasn't me.' He nodded towards the door where the key still hung. 'Why don't we go inside and talk about two dead children?'

Dawson was shaking. He probably still believed Simon had killed the other overseer and now he was going to die. Good.

Let him imagine that and have the fear of God running through his veins. He could be on the receiving end for once.

'Sit down.' Simon lit the oil lamp, trimming the wick until it gave a warm, wide light. A single room with a fireplace, table, two old wooden chairs. A cupboard for food and crockery. Stone sink. A stairway leading up to a bedroom. For a man on an overseer's wage, he lived a very spare, modest life.

'You know who I am?'

Dawson nodded, terrified.

Simon moved behind him and began to speak: 'When I was a boy, I was in the workhouse and they sent me to work in a mill . . .'

He made the man listen to it all. The pain, the humiliation, the things he saw. When he finished, the room seemed to be filled with sorrow.

Eventually Dawson asked, 'What do you want me to say?'

'I want to know why you beat those children and all the others.'

'You know why.'

'Tell me anyway,' Simon said. 'Make me understand.'

He coughed, stammered. 'So they learn and remember to do it properly the next time.'

'No.' Simon shook his head. 'There's more to it than that, isn't there?' He leaned close and whispered in the man's ear. 'You enjoy it, don't you?'

He kept pushing the man. He wanted Dawson to admit the pleasure he took in his work.

'Yes, I like to see them scared,' he said finally. 'I like their pain.'

Dawson was a bully. A man who loved to show his strength by exercising power over children. No note of regret or guilt in his voice. To him, everything he'd done was natural.

'If I don't do it, someone else will,' he said. He shrugged, folded his arms and sat back.

'Then it's going to be someone else, Mr Dawson,' Simon told him, 'because you won't be doing it again. You need to understand something: that part of your life has ended. Don't think you can fool me. If you ever beat another child, I'll hear about it. Believe me, I will, and I'll call on you again. Next time, though, we won't be talking like a pair of fine gentlemen. Do I make myself clear?'

The man turned pale. 'I'll lose my job.'

Simon slammed his hand down on the table. The oil lamp jumped, and shadows danced across the room.

'The Easbys and the Hardys each lost a son. That's a damned sight more than a job. You can find work. Remember, though, wherever you go, if you hurt anyone at all, I'll know, and you can expect another visit. Trust me on that. Trust me with your life.'

'Did you kill Harry Warner?' Dawson asked again. His hands were trembling, beyond control.

'I told you before: no. I didn't lie about that. And I won't kill you, either. But I'll give you this promise: unless you change, I'll make you believe you've gone to hell.'

Simon left. His anger was molten. He wanted Dawson so terrified that he'd spend a lifetime glancing over his shoulder. He wanted the man to change. Perhaps he would, at least for a while. Still, Dawson had been right about one thing; if he didn't do the job Seaton wanted, someone else would. There'd never be a shortage of candidates.

Simon had done what was in his power. It didn't come close to justice for two dead children. Still, if he made Dawson pause before he took the rod to another child's back, that was one tiny victory.

As he walked, though, questions kept niggling and gnawing at the corners of his mind. Why had Warner been killed? His death figured into everything else, that seemed obvious. The same with Sebastian Ramsey. But however he moved the pieces, he couldn't see how they fitted together.

He ached to be home, feeling the heat from the range, lying under the blankets in bed with the warmth from Rosie by his side. He was drained, he needed to sleep. But there was still one final task he hadn't been able to do during the day: talk to Sebastian Ramsey's friends.

Three names, all of them at home. But with the night so cold, who would care to go out? They were young men, courteous and thoughtful, all of them shocked that Ramsey had been killed, and even more horrified by the maiming. If Sebastian Ramsey had a hidden life, none of them had ever caught wind of it. He'd been normal, sober and content with his lot. Not sure if he wanted to take up his brother's offer of a move to the United States.

'I appreciate your honesty, sir,' Charles Ramsey said as they walked along Boar Lane the next morning. A piercing wind that sliced at the flesh had blown away the smoke which usually covered Leeds, leaving the sky a clean, glittering blue. But something in the air made Simon wonder if Barnabas Wade's prediction of snow might not be just over the horizon.

'At least you know what I've found. I wish there was more.'

'So do I.' Ramsey pursed his lips. 'I'd like you to keep looking, Mr Westow.'

'I can,' Simon agreed with hesitation. 'But I don't think I'll learn much. Maybe it's best to let it simmer for a few days then come back to it.'

Ramsey seemed surprised, then nodded. 'It's your business. I'm told you're good at it.'

'There is one thing. Your brother's friends said he wasn't sure about moving to America, but you thought you had him convinced. Were you right or were they?'

Sebastian Ramsey was young. He had no sweetheart, a fair wage but no great prospects in his work. Meanwhile, his brother had done well for himself, offering a new life with endless possibilities. It looked like a straightforward decision, but he hadn't been so sure.

Charles Ramsey gave a tight, sad smile. 'Sebastian wasn't an adventurous fellow. He liked steadiness in his life. I can't speak for what lay in his heart. I like to think I was close to talking him round, but . . .'

There were people like that. They found it safer to live in a rut.

'I won't give up, I promise you that.'

'Thank you.'

TWELVE

Jane crossed Leeds Bridge. Ahead of her, the Huddersfield road stretched out broad and wide. She saw a coach rattling away into the distance. Closer, an overloaded cart made its ponderous way to town. Houses stretched ahead as far as she could see. Leeds was growing quickly, sprawling on both sides of the river.

Breath clouding in the air, she slipped off into a cluster of streets. No girl walking in a shawl or cloak would attract any attention. Anonymous and forgotten in an instant. The place she wanted stood on the corner. A grocer's shop with the paint bright and fresh, the lettering picked out in white over the door. She glanced up at the words but they meant nothing. Jane had never learned to read, never felt the need.

The shop smelled clean, a mix of beeswax polish and lavender. The floor was neatly swept, with sacks of flour and beans stacked against the wall. The counter glistened. The old woman watching her wore a long, starched apron that reached to her ankles, a brilliant white cap covering her hair.

'Morning.' There was a hint of suspicion in the smile that didn't reach her eyes. 'What can I do for you, pet?'

'Are you Miss Spinks?'

The woman hesitated for a moment, cautiously eyeing Jane up and down. 'I am, yes. Why? Do I know you?'

'Mrs Shields said I should come and see you.'

Suddenly she was welcoming and open. 'Catherine? I haven't seen her in a long time. How is she?'

'Her chest was bad, but she's recovering,' Jane said. 'She's eager to be doing more again.'

Mrs Spinks beamed. 'That sounds like her all right, never one for sitting idle. But you tell her that if she goes out when it's parky like this, it won't do her any good. You must be that lass who lives with her, the one who works with the thief-taker.'

'I am.' Jane wasn't going to say more. The woman had already heard too much about her. 'She said you know everyone round here.'

'Well, I suppose I ought to after all these years. Who are you trying to find?'

'A man called Pepper. He uses that name, anyway.'

She gave a wry smile. 'Oh, I know him right enough. Half the time you'd never know he was there, mind. He's the type that you can blink and you'd stop noticing him.'

Jane felt her hopes rise. The night before, when she was trying to puzzle out a way to trace Pepper, Catherine Shields had told her about the friend who kept a shop in Holbeck.

'Shopkeepers always know the people in their area,' she'd said. 'Didn't you say the beerhouse is in Holbeck?'

'More like Hunslet,' Jane had replied.

'Still, it wouldn't hurt to go over and ask. Tell her I sent you.'

'I will,' Jane said. All she had to lose by it was the time spent walking. And now it looked as if it might pay off.

'Always liked to be called *Mister* Pepper. He used to have a place right around the corner,' Miss Spinks continued. 'Then he moved. Let me think, it'll come in a minute.' She frowned, tapping a fingernail against her teeth, then beamed. 'That's right, I remember. Someone told me he'd gone over to Hunslet, somewhere on Grey Walk.'

Jane felt a surge of gratitude. She was close now. She'd find him.

'Do you know where exactly?'

Miss Spinks shook her head. 'I never asked. Go and talk to Ged Marsden. He owns the butcher's shop on Hunslet Lane, right where it turns. Likely he'll have the address.'

'Thank you.'

'No need, pet, I haven't done anything.' The woman sighed. 'But I want you to tell Catherine I'll come up and see her one of these days.' She glanced out of the windows and gathered a shawl about her shoulders. 'Once the days get longer again, and a bit warmer. Give her my blessings.'

'I will,' Jane said. 'I promise.'

Marsden the butcher was easy to find, with his shop on the main road, carcasses hanging on display inside the window. Even in the cold, flies buzzed and gathered around the meat. He had a broad, fleshy face, with pale, curly hair that was retreating along his skull, and a nose that stood out red and blotchy from years of drinking.

He listened as Jane explained why Miss Spinks had suggested she visit him.

'She's right, he has a house on Grey Walk. Comes in and buys his meat once a week. Demands his bill, just like a gentleman, but he always pays prompt, soon as he gets it.'

'Which house is his?' she asked. She felt her eagerness like an itch. She was eager for the information, to be able to hurry back to Simon and tell him.

'It has a blue door, you can't miss it. On your left as you walk off towards Leeds.' He said it as though the town was somewhere distant, not just a few minutes away. But perhaps that was how he saw things. This neighbourhood was his life. He probably lived above the shop, his customers coming from the streets close by. Almost everything he needed was within an easy stroll. The air was cleaner here, not even a handful of manufactories. But more houses were being built; she'd passed some on her way here. Life was changing right in front of his eyes.

'Thank you.'

'He must have someone staying,' Marsden added. 'Just yesterday he came in wanting some oxtail to make soup.'

Worth knowing, she decided as she marched along Grey Walk. She didn't turn her head. Never checked to see if anyone was watching. Just carried on, catching the deep blue of the door as she passed, touching the gold ring through her glove without thinking. The house was part of a terrace, better, more solid than so many of the cheap houses being thrown up elsewhere in Leeds.

And someone staying . . . what safer place for Riley the knifeman to recover? They needed to pay a visit and find out.

Simon began to smile as she told him. By the time she'd finished, he wore a broad grin.

'That's remarkable,' he told her. 'I can't believe you managed it so quickly. I had no idea how we'd find him.' He checked his knives. 'No time like now to meet them. Are you ready?'

He worked things through in his mind as they strode off into Hunslet. If Pepper shopped for his own meat and paid his own bills, he didn't have any servants. That made sense. The man was cautious; his arrangement with the landlord of the Duke William proved that. He certainly wouldn't expect anyone to trace him. That showed just how good Jane had become at this business.

No servant, he thought again. That meant Pepper would answer a knock on the door himself. Time to give him a surprise.

Simon brought his fist down hard on the wood, feeling it reverberate through the house. He had one knife concealed in his hand, the second loose and ready in its sheath on his forearm.

The street was quiet. Noon and still freezing. His breath steamed in the air. He kept an eye on the handle as it started to turn.

The door was drawn back two inches, just enough for a man to peer out. Simon was ready, hitting it with all his weight, sending the man inside sprawling. By the time he could begin to recover, Simon had already kicked the door closed and was standing over him, both knives drawn, as Jane hurried to search the rooms.

'You're a very elusive man, Mr Pepper. It's been the devil's own job to track you.'

He was as bland and forgettable as everyone said. A perfectly ordinary face, light brown hair and an average build. No marks to make him stand out. Clothes in dun and fawn. Someone to pass on the street and never even notice.

Quickly, Simon checked him for a weapon. Nothing more than a dull knife, but why would he need anything at home?

'There's a man in the bed,' Jane shouted. 'He's bandaged, not well enough to move.'

'Let's go upstairs and have a talk,' Simon told Pepper. The man was lighter than he'd expected, hardly any substance to him as Simon dragged him to his feet. 'Go on.'

He kept a careful distance; he'd seen all the tricks before. But Pepper was docile, saying nothing, his eyes blank and his face empty.

A small fire burned in the grate, a bucket of coal on the hearth. The man in the bed looked to be in pain. A small bottle of some medicine sat on a table, next to a glass.

'Pepper and Riley.' Simon smiled. 'Quite a find to see the pair of you together. I'm sure Mr Riley remembers me. After all, he tried to kill me the other night.' He turned to Pepper. 'And you must know me, too. After all, you employed him to do it.'

No answer from either of them. Jane stood by the closed door. Alert, eyes hooded, blade poised.

'Who paid you to have me attacked?'

Pepper gave a small shake of his head. Before he'd finished, Simon had grabbed his stock and pulled him up on the tips of his toes.

'That's not an answer.' He moved his knife so the tip touched Pepper's belly. The man's eyes bulged, but his mouth remained closed. From the corner of his eye, Simon saw Riley struggling in the bed. He was no threat at all. Not today. The man to break was right in front of him.

A touch more pressure from the knife, a small jab to pierce the skin so Pepper felt the warm trickle of blood seeping into his groin. Enough to convince him that Simon was serious. He kept his eyes locked on Pepper's face, judging the panic, the thoughts as the man weighed his chances of staying alive. Another small tug, lifting him even higher.

'Well?'

'Arden.'

The answer came from behind him. Simon didn't turn; he watched Pepper's response. Hopelessness. It was true.

'Father or son?'

He shook Pepper. The man was light, but the muscles in Simon's arm were cramping, growing weary.

'Which one?' he repeated, digging the knife point deep enough to make the man squirm again.

'Father,' Pepper said. A rough, desperate whisper.

'If I discover you're lying, Jane will come and find you.' He nodded towards her. 'I think she'd enjoy killing you. And it would all be for the want of a single word. Now, think carefully, Mr Pepper: are you positive it was Thomas Arden?'

'Yes.' He gasped, hardly able to breathe. Simon let go and the man collapsed, dropped like rubbish to the floor.

'I'd suggest you don't tell him you passed me that information,' Simon said. 'Not if you want to stay alive.'

*　　*　　*

'Now I know who's behind it,' Simon said as they walked back to town. His face was set rock hard, voice grim. Maybe a part of him had expected to hear the name, but it still had arrived as a shock. When the word crossed Riley's lips, though, he knew it was true. Deep in the pocket of his greatcoat, his fingers caressed the hilt of his knife.

'Why?' Jane asked. 'Why would he do that? We found the candlesticks for him. He was praising you all around Leeds.'

'I don't know,' Simon answered. This wasn't one of Arden's games. This was life and death. Arden must have been behind the overseer's death and passing Simon's name to the constable. He glanced at her and shook his head. 'I really don't understand.'

'What are we going to do about it?'

We, he thought with gratitude. She was with him. Arden would certainly see her that way. Simon's assistant, his ally. What *could* they do about it? He didn't understand why Thomas Arden would pay someone to kill him. He did know that the man was untouchable. He had money and power, he had influence and important friends who owed him favours. Simon couldn't use the law to touch him.

Maybe Arden really had been responsible for the death of George Collins, never mind his denials. He was certainly ruthless enough.

'Don't forget that Arden has a bodyguard,' Jane's voice cut into his thoughts. 'We'll need to watch out for him.'

Will Perkins was his name. He'd stayed well out of sight on the times Simon had seen his boss. Not visible, perhaps, but likely always close. Just in case. That was his job.

Simon had seen Perkins in a brawl once. With four blows, he'd dismantled his opponent and left him knocked out on the ground. Bigger than his master and more casually brutal, Perkins had served in the Thirty-Third Foot, rising to sergeant before he'd had his rank stripped away and been cashiered out for theft.

He exuded violence, carrying his old army bayonet in a sheath that hung from his belt. But there was more to him than that. He'd led men; he could think, too. And he'd be standing in the way if Simon had to confront Arden. Perkins wasn't a subtle man; maybe that was why Arden had hired someone else to try and kill. Maybe.

'I need to think about this,' he said, and she nodded. 'Come to the house in the morning. We'll talk about it then.'

THIRTEEN

'**W**as Miss Spinks able to help, child?'

Jane hung up the cloak, knelt and prodded the fire with a poker to send the blaze roaring. They were luckier than so many in Leeds; they had ample money to afford coal and food. In this house they'd never go cold or hungry.

'Yes, she was. Thank you.' She smiled. 'She sends you her blessings. I found the man I wanted because of her.'

'How did she look? It's been an age since I was over there.' Her voice held a soft, wistful note.

'Maybe we can go in the spring,' Jane said. It was idle, hopeful chatter; Mrs Shields would never again be strong enough to walk to Holbeck and back again. They both knew it, but the pretence, thinking about it and making vague plans for when the weather grew warmer gave a sense of the future.

She'd been honest with the shopkeeper; the old woman really was recovering. Her cough had almost vanished, she had colour back in her cheeks. But the damp spell had exacted its toll on her body. Or perhaps she was simply growing old; Jane had never asked Mrs Shields her age. Still, her mind was sharp, not like many Jane had seen, and her memory was crisp.

The rest of the day passed slowly. Jane lit the lamps and cooked supper for them. Catherine Shields told stories of the Leeds she remembered when she was younger. Before any of the factories were built. She'd watched the first of them rise, course after course of brick at Bean Ing Mill that climbed higher than anyone in the town had ever seen.

In those days, she and her husband had lived in Park Square, in the days when it was still brand new and the most elegant address in Leeds.

'It was to the west of town, you see, before any of these manufactories, so the air blew in fresh from the hills, and we were away from all the dirt. The houses were all so beautiful and neat.' She smiled, floating into her memories. 'My husband did well as a lawyer. Then he died and I found out we didn't have as much as he'd always made me believe.' She shook her head, slipping back out of the reverie. 'So many people you think you can trust fail you in the end.' She reached out and took hold of Jane's hand with her thin fingers. 'But you've had that, too.'

'Yes.' She didn't want to think of her parents. Not now.

'I had to sell the house and dismiss the servants. I had a lovely maid. Georgiana . . . a pretty thing, always so kind. I cried when I had to say goodbye to her.'

'Did you ever see her again?'

Mrs Shields shook her head. 'I found her a position with a family in Bradford. Then I discovered this little cottage. It was tucked away, just the right size for me. It felt perfect. I had to learn to do things for myself. I realized how much I'd been coddled. I'd grown up with nursemaids and governesses, all the things a young lady should have. After that I had a husband. Do you know what I realized in the end?'

'What?' Jane asked.

'I was happier on my own. Until you came along.'

'Me?' she asked in disbelief. She loved the woman, but sometimes she felt as if Catherine Shields had taken her in out of charity.

'You,' Mrs Shields repeated. 'You're my gift. The grandchild I never had. I like a small life. It's kept me alert. And I know I'm lucky to have enough for my needs. With you here, I feel safe, too.'

'You know I'll take care of you.'

'I do, child, I do.' She placed her hands on the chair arm and pushed herself up, waving away Jane's help. A peck on the cheek from dry lips and the woman hobbled into the bedroom.

Jane banked the fire for the night. She wasn't tired yet, but there was no sense in staying up and wasting coal. The blankets would warm after a few minutes.

She wasn't going to allow Thomas Arden to ruin her sleep. She'd do whatever Simon needed, but he had to be the one to discover the answers to his problem.

The snow arrived overnight. Silent and soft, it continued past dawn, from clouds plumped and full. Enough had fallen to leave a light covering over the pavements and the cobbles. Within an hour it was trodden into slush and erased by cartwheels. But it showed no sign of stopping. The coaches kept to a sedate pace, the drivers careful with their beasts instead of roaring through town at a gallop.

People walked carefully, keeping their heads bowed, eyes on the ground ahead of them. Everything was wet and slick underfoot. The women with money walked on pattens, shoes and dresses raised from the wet, and kept their hair dry with hats. The poorer ones clutched their shawls tight and got their feet soaked. People tumbled and others helped them up again. Today would bring plenty of sprains and broken bones, Simon thought as he moved through the crowds.

Sunday, and the factories and offices were closed, but Simon picked up snippets of news as he went around. There were places in the countryside, towards Skipton and up around Ripon, where the roads were almost impassable. Not too far away. If the snow continued, another day would probably bring a halt to all travel; people would be trapped in Leeds until a thaw came.

At the Bull and Mouth, Barnabas Wade was already trying to sell stocks to the unwitting; an early start to take advantage of the weather.

'The year might turn out well, after all,' he said triumphantly. 'Give me a few days to wear them down and they'll be happy to sign over their fortunes.'

'It looks as if you might have your wish,' Simon said. 'Have you heard anything about Thomas Arden coming after me?'

'You?' He squinted and stared, as if the question had dragged him from richer thoughts. 'No, nothing; why? Someone told me what happened to that overseer. The constable took you in for that.' He stopped himself 'You didn't—?'

'Do you really think I'd be standing here if I'd killed him?' It wasn't an answer, it meant nothing, but it would be enough to satisfy Wade. 'I just wondered if anything had been floating on the wind.'

'Not that I heard.'

'Did you find out more about Arden or Seaton yet?'

'I'm sorry, Simon, I've been busy.' He raised his head and began to smile as a coach rattled into the yard. 'More trade.'

Simon was surprised to see George Mudie at work, typesetting a broadside ballad about a man who vainly tried to save his young love when her house was cut off by a blizzard.

'It's enough to turn your stomach,' he said. 'But it'll sell, and that's what matters. Pay a few of my bills.' He shrugged. 'Did you ever find your man Pepper?'

'Yes,' Simon replied. 'He told me who wanted me dead.'

That was enough to make Mudie stop. 'Go on, are you going to say?'

'Thomas Arden.'

Mudie frowned as he tried to find some sense in the idea. 'Why would he do that?'

Simon shook his head in frustration. 'I was hoping you might be able to tell me.'

'I can't. But watch yourself, Simon. You know what he's like.'

He did. That was the problem.

Jane placed three pennies in the man's tin cup. The snow fell around him, settling and sticking to the ground. He sat on a ruined old blanket, legs stretched out, daring the churchgoers to go around or step over them. Most did, not even glancing down to see that one of the limbs was made of roughly carved wood below the knee.

Charles Dodson looked up at her and nodded his gratitude.

'You always have a kind heart when you go by. God bless you for it, miss.'

She often gave him money. She spared a little for many of the beggars around town. Why not? She knew their lives. She had enough, they had nothing. But this time she wasn't going past; she'd come here to see him.

He wore the faded, tattered remains of his army jacket. For years he'd been a soldier in the Thirty-Third until he lost his leg to an unlucky French shot at Quatre Bas, right before Waterloo.

In the army since he was young, he had no trade that he could work and there was no pension for a soldier. No choice beyond a mug, a place on the street and the prayer of charity.

'Did you ever serve under a man called Will Perkins?' she asked. 'Wasn't he a sergeant in your regiment?'

Dodson ran his tongue around his mouth for a few seconds, then looked away from her.

'No,' he answered. 'I don't think I ever knew him.'

It was a lie, not even a good one. She dropped another two coins to jingle in his mug.

'I just want to know what he was like,' Jane said. 'I'll never tell him you said a word, I promise.'

The fear flashed in Dodson's eyes, but the money was making him start to waver. She added another coin. Maybe it was wrong to use him, but she needed the information, the edge. If Arden's bodyguard came for them, her life and Simon's might depend on it.

'You swear?'

'Yes.' She squatted next to him.

'Perkins was a bastard. It wasn't just me who thought it, we all did. He stole from us all, that's why they drove him out. He loved to have us flogged, to see us bleed. The smallest thing meant a flogging. When we were out in India he'd place wagers with the other sergeants over which men would end up dying from the whip.'

'Did he fight or run?'

'Oh, he fought, all right,' Dodson replied without any hesitation. 'He revelled in it. He liked the blood, he loved to kill. He'd be there with the rest of us, right up at the front. I'll give him his due for that. Got himself a medal or two for it. The way I heard things, that's what earned him his stripes in the first place.'

'Why did you follow him?'

He considered the question for a long time before he opened his mouth.

'What else were we going to do? We all knew the penalty if we killed him and it came out. Worse still if we tried and failed. We'd seen what he was like. Perkins never took prisoners, you see, even if they surrendered. He was born without mercy, that one. He liked to gut them, then leave them to die and smile at their screams. If we tried to put them out of their misery, it was a court-martial for insubordination.' He let the memories ripple away into history. 'He got his due in the end. Stripes on his own back before the army sent him packing. He's Thomas Arden's man now. Why do you want to know?'

'Business,' she said. It was probably safer if she didn't say more than that.

'I'll give you a tip, then: if you have to face him, he fights as dirty as they come, and he's forgotten more tricks than you'll ever learn. But his right knee is weak. Hurt that and you might be able to take him.'

Dodson smiled at the thought as Jane let another coin rattle in the cup. She rose in a quick, easy movement.

'You've helped. Thank you.'

'He has a cunning mind, too. Be careful around him.'

'I will,' she promised.

The snow kept falling.

FOURTEEN

Simon watched Rosie's face as Jane explained what she'd learned about Perkins. He could see the fire in her eyes, the tense, tight way she held her body.

'Hard to say which one's more dangerous, master or man,' she said once Jane had finished. Rosie turned to her husband. 'We need to know why Arden wants you dead.'

'There's no reason that I can see,' he told her. The question had dogged him all through the night, dragging him awake time after time. He was weary, aches in his back and his knees like an old man. His mind felt dull with the weight of it all pressing down on him. Not recovered yet. The echo of the words rang softly in his ears.

At least the snow had ended. Thankfully it was only a couple of inches, not enough to bring Leeds to a standstill. Simon had been up early, walking to the coffee cart to catch the gossip. For a little while at least, the world had been white, all the sounds muted to softness. He'd stood, listening to the talk as he drank. But nobody was saying anything useful.

Rosie shook her head. 'There has to be *something*. He was happy enough with the work you did for him.'

A loud, heavy knocking. Simon rose, passing the parlour where the tutor was teaching Amos and Richard. He kept the knife behind his back as he answered the door.

'Who was it?' Rosie asked when he returned. 'You were gone long enough.'

He held up a sheet of paper. 'I wrote to Robert Archer, that lawyer in York. I thought he could find out a bit about Arden's time there. The reply came with the mail coach.'

'What does he have to say?'

'More or less what I'd already heard. Plenty of rumours, but nothing that ever came close to court. If there was any danger of that, witnesses decided to leave York or suddenly couldn't remember what they'd seen. He let it be known that he might have committed a murder or two, although no bodies were ever found.' He shrugged.

'Does he say anything about Arden starting out as a highwayman?'

He scanned the page again. 'It's true enough, he claims, although Arden was never arrested for it. He always had another man with him. They moved into crimes that offered better returns and made enough money for them to go on to legitimate things.'

'Who was it?' Rosie asked. 'Does he give this other man a name?'

'Oh yes,' Simon replied. 'He does. Turns out they both moved to Leeds at about the same time.'

'Who?' she asked again. But it was Jane who answered.

'Seaton,' she said.

'How did you know?' Simon looked at her face. 'I'd never heard of any contact between them.'

'It's the only thing that makes sense. You'd been asking around about the children who died at Seaton's factory. After you said he'd worked with someone else and moved here, it fell into place.' She shrugged and looked down.

'Seaton passed word to Arden, and he arranged to take care of the problem.' Rosie clenched her jaw. 'What are we going to do now?'

Simon placed his elbows on the table and cupped his chin.

'I—'

'Please don't say bring Arden down, Simon,' Rosie warned. 'You know we don't have a hope of that. Try it and he'll take his revenge on us. All of us.'

The whole family, she meant. With their sons as targets.

'I'm not going to say anything yet,' he told her. 'There's still too much I don't understand. Did Seaton murder one of his own overseers through Arden? Why would he do that? Did Arden kill George Collins? That makes no sense. If he was trying to make me appear guilty, he'd have pressed harder. A word or two from him and I could have been on my way to the assizes now. In the end, the only thing that happened was the constable questioned me once.'

'Maybe Arden and Seaton weren't behind the overseer's death,' Jane said. They both turned to look at her.

'What do you mean?' Rosie asked.

'It could be that someone else wants revenge for the children.'

'Who?' Simon said.

'The parents, perhaps. A relative.'

He sat back in his chair and rubbed his chin. Of course. He'd been too quick to let himself think he was the only one who might take some action, some retribution for the children. Stupid. There would be others who'd feel the loss very keenly.

'I'll go and talk to them later.'

He glanced out of the window. The snow was starting again. Large flakes that barely seemed to drift down through the air. He hoped it wouldn't keep falling and leave Leeds isolated. At least Barnabas Wade should be happy with a captive audience of stranded travellers. Maybe he'd even manage to sell a few more of his worthless shares.

'We still have the problem of Thomas Arden,' Rosie said.

'It's not just him.' Simon tapped the letter with his fingertips. 'Now we have to think about Seaton, too. We're not going to find any answers sitting here.' He rose from his chair, and without a word, Jane followed.

'I need us to work together, not separately,' he told her as they marched down Swinegate. 'Riley would have killed me if you hadn't been there. Perkins could very likely destroy me without breaking a sweat. We both know I'm not back to who I was yet.'

He saw her nod. It was a hard admission to make, to speak the words. But she'd realized it well before he had; that was why she'd followed him to the glee club.

Fresh snow was already filling the prints that feet and cart wheels had made that morning. By the time they reached Briggate he had a coating of it on the cape of his greatcoat and it had settled on the shoulders of Jane's cloak.

'Arden already has a new overseer,' he said. 'I heard it earlier at the coffee cart.'

'Who?'

'I don't know his name. If Dawson listened to our talk, he'll need another one, too.'

'What good does it do?' Jane said. 'They're easy enough to replace.'

'If we scare a few away, then others might have second thoughts.'

'No, they won't.'

Deep inside, Simon knew she was right. It was nothing more than wishful thinking. There was never going to be a shortage of men who'd be happy to bully and be paid for it. More than that, it wouldn't bring any real justice for Peter Hardy and Jacob Easby.

'It won't stop Seaton,' she said.

'Probably not,' he agreed. But at least it felt as if he was doing *something*. At the moment he had nothing better to offer.

They walked quietly through town. Simon stopped here and there, talking, asking questions and passing coins for information to men he knew. She stayed outside, watching faces, making sure no one was following them. Very few people on the streets, and they all seemed to hurry along, anxious to be back in the warmth.

There was a strange sense of peace about the morning. No whip cracks or shouts from the coach drivers. She glanced through the windows of the inns. Men and women sat at tables. Some ate, others talked, a few stared glumly into the fire.

Jane tried to imagine a life on the move. She'd been to York once, riding in a carriage. So high off the ground that she was terrified she'd fall. If she had to go somewhere, she'd use her own two feet.

In the past she often used to imagine leaving Leeds. Picking a new name, a new town where nobody knew her or her history. With the money she'd earned working for Simon, she could afford to do it. In the end she'd stayed, and now all those thoughts had vanished. She had a home with Mrs Shields. A real home. She wouldn't allow the appearance of her father to change that. He would be the one to go. Perhaps he already had; she'd certainly had no sense of him close by since their meeting in the ginnel.

Dusk came early. The falling snow had turned dirty, blackened by all the soot from the factory chimneys. It lay thick and crusted on the ground and gave a strange light to the streets.

'I want to go to Seaton's factory and take a look at this new overseer,' he said. 'No one's been watching us, have they?'

Jane shook her head and stared for a moment but said nothing. She didn't understand the point of it. Even if Simon tried to explain himself, she knew she still wouldn't be able to see the sense in going there. He was tempting trouble, and that was always quick to arrive; it needed precious little encouragement. She found a dark space from where she could watch him, and stood with one hand in her pocket resting on the hilt of her knife.

The workers left, a stream of people eager to flow away from the mill and out into the night. A few minutes and the streets around the building seemed empty. Almost six inches of snow covering the ground now. Jane didn't watch the doors; she kept her eyes on Simon.

She only glanced over when the small knot of men came out. Then she gripped the knife hilt more tightly and drew in a breath. Simon started to follow one of them when he left the others. Jane stayed behind him. Over Lady Bridge, then Quarry Hill. On to High Street. Simon stood at the corner for a minute, hidden but keeping his eye on the man.

Finally he turned away, moving fast; she caught up to him by the wall of St Peter's burial ground.

'Nobody was behind you. No one lurking down by the mill, either.'

'The one I went after . . .' Simon's voice was bitter. 'There are some faces you can't ever forget.'

'You know him?' she asked in disbelief. 'How? How could you?'

'He started as an overseer at the mill where I worked when I was thirteen. A few months before I walked out. His name's Truscott.'

'Joseph Truscott,' Jane said. 'Joe, that's what he likes to be called.'

Simon stopped. He placed his hands on her shoulders, eyes searching her face.

'How do you know him?'

'He's my father.' He had nothing to say. 'He came back to Leeds. He said he wanted to let me know my mother had died. I told him to leave or I'd kill him.'

'He didn't listen.'

'No.' A single, sharp word, but enough. 'Which house is it?'

'Halfway down on the right. A dirty black door, next to the one where the paint's peeling.'

'I'll take care of it,' she said. Her job. She wasn't going to let Simon take this away from her.

He nodded. 'Don't kill him.'

Seconds passed as she remained silent.

'He'll be alive,' she promised. 'He'll just wish he wasn't.'

Simon knew what Jane's father had done to her. She'd never told him; it was Mrs Shields who explained it as they sat quietly in front of her cottage one sunny, dusty day during the summer. Summer . . . that seemed like a different life, back when every-thing bad lived in another country.

He knew he could never imagine what had happened to her. But however much he hated Joseph Truscott, Jane deserved the chance to finish things with him for herself.

He realized he hadn't noticed if Dawson had been among the group of men. As soon as he'd spotted Truscott, the rest of them had gone from his mind.

'Did you see Dawson with the others?' He described the man.

'Yes.' She narrowed her eyes as she thought, then nodded 'Yes, he was there.'

He hadn't heeded Simon's warning. In the morning he'd have a few more words with Dawson. For now, all he wanted was to be at home. The day had drained him.

'You can't do anything about Arden until you know what he's planning,' Rosie said. Amos and Richard were crouched on the floor, absorbed in a game of marbles with coloured balls made of alabaster. 'He's never been one to think small. It'll be some scheme to line his pockets. You can guarantee that.'

Jane watched her father's face contort and did nothing to stop his agony. She woke in the darkness, for a moment not quite sure what was real and what had happened as she slept, caught in dreams of violence and the satisfaction of inflicting pain.

It slipped away like mist. But she'd make certain it happened. Her father had a debt to pay. She listened to the room, all the tiny noises and creaks of a house that sounded like comfort and calm. After a few minutes she drifted off again, untroubled by anything more.

Early morning, with yesterday's snow still solid on the ground and a heavy frost crackling on the windows, Simon waited in Holbeck as Dawson came out of his house. The man took his time, staring up and down the street, wearing a hunted look, before he locked the door and began to walk.

He kept glancing over his shoulder, worried that someone might follow. Sensible enough. But Simon cut through the streets, waiting around a corner as Dawson appeared.

'On your way to work?'

The man stood still, panic spreading across his face. He didn't know where to turn, frozen in place and terrified.

'You were going to leave your job, Mr Dawson.' Simon's voice was calm and even. 'Or perhaps I wasn't clear when we talked.'

The man seemed to have difficulty swallowing.

'I need the money,' he said. 'There aren't many jobs for overseers.'

'You're no longer an overseer,' Simon said. 'We agreed that, didn't we? You're not going to hurt any more children. You won't be going back to Seaton's mill.'

'But if I just leave I won't get a reference,' Dawson told him.

'And if you don't, I'll make you regret it until you die. That's an interesting dilemma for you, isn't it?'

'I won't touch them. I promise you.'

He was pleading. Begging. Yet there were still two dead children, and he'd had a hand in that. How many more that Simon had never heard about?

'Enough. You have to decide.'

Dawson stood his ground longer than Simon expected. But the trace of defiance quickly disappeared. He nodded, moved his gaze to the ground, turned around and walked away. His shoulders were slumped. Defeated. Humiliated.

FIFTEEN

S he was waiting as he left for work in the morning, listening for the crunch of his boots through the packed snow. He was humming a tune to himself, thickly wrapped against the weather, surprised to look up to spot her in front of him.

For a moment he said nothing, his eyes full of fury. Then he brought his hands from his coat, opening them. Empty.

'You see?' he said. 'I'm no threat. All I'm trying to do is earn enough to live.'

'I told you to leave Leeds,' Jane said.

'I know you did. But I need money to be able to go. I saw someone I knew from before and he said a job had come up.' He smiled, but his gaze moved around. 'It's not for long. Honestly, Jane. Just until I—'

She didn't give him the chance to finish. She couldn't bear to hear him speak her name. Her knife flashed. As he started to howl and cover the hand where she'd severed his little finger, she brought the blade down again, slicing through the flesh of his cheek. Jane stood until the first drops of blood appeared.

'I warned you once. Go while you still can,' she told him, then turned and strode off.

She'd kept her promise to Simon; she hadn't killed him. But she'd desperately wanted to see him dead.

Two overseers not at work today, Simon thought when Jane told him what she'd done. Seaton would have to retaliate for that.

'We need to stay ready,' he said. 'They'll be coming.'

The glee club was busy, men filling the benches upstairs at the Pack Horse. As they started on the first song, a full-throated version of *The Game Of All Fours*, Simon leaned toward Jeb Easby. His voice was hardly above a whisper.

'Do you have any idea who killed Warner the overseer? Not yourself or Mr Hardy, was it?'

The man shook his head. 'Us? Of course not. We're not that stupid. Why? Do you know anything? A pair of them didn't come in today. Was that . . .?'

Simon nodded. That was enough, no explanation needed.

Easby remained silent for a long time while the singing died away to a pair of strained voices.

'Be careful,' he said finally.

'I will.' A nod, then Simon stood and left, the ragged melody of the chorus following him down the stairs.

Jane followed Simon back to the house on Swinegate. Twenty yards behind, flitting from shadow to shadow with the knife in her hand. There was no danger waiting. She watched until the door closed behind him and she heard the bolts being shot home before she began to walk.

She turned off Boar Lane on to Albion Street and knew someone was there. She had the sense of him before she could see anything. Tightening her grip on the hilt of the blade, she peered into the darkness.

Suddenly he was in front of her, no more than three yards away. As if he'd appeared from nowhere. Looming like a giant. Tall, broad as a house. If she allowed him to come close enough, he'd be able to crush the life from her.

The bayonet that usually hung from his belt was in his right hand.

Perkins. Arden's bodyguard, grinning at the sight of her.

'You and your boss, you've been poking in places where you don't belong. Causing trouble for Mr Arden's friend.'

Jane didn't reply. She was watching him, her mind racing over the advice Dodson the crippled soldier had given her. A dirty fighter, brutal, with years of experience. If he won, he'd leave her for dead without a qualm.

A weak right knee. That was what Dodson had said. Not much, but it was something.

Perkins moved towards her. Only a single pace, but it was enough. He was going to use his size and weight against her. He had to be in his fifties now, grey hair cropped close against his skull; old for work like this. But he still had power. What he'd lost in speed he made up for in trickery.

Jane could see it in his eyes; he believed she was an easy target. A girl who'd have no fight in her. He took another pace forward. She tried to feint to her right, but he was already moving to stop it. Old, but not so slow. And not slipping on the packed, frozen snow.

He wanted to keep her moving backwards until she was pinned against the wall. Once that happened, he could take his time. Finish her as quickly or slowly as he wanted.

She was watching. His eyes, his hands. His feet. They'd give the clues. Even knowing she might die here, she felt calm. She touched the gold ring. A single step back, to see what he'd do. His eyes glinted, as if he already sensed victory.

Good, she thought, let him. Maybe he'd let down his guard a little.

Perkins swung his arm, the bayonet slicing through the air. But that wasn't the danger; it was a diversion, he'd put no power into it. He was shifting his balance, preparing to kick her. As soon as he raised his foot, she darted forward with a kick of her own.

She put all her weight behind it. She felt the hobnails on the sole of her boot crash into his right knee. Something gave in his leg. He staggered, arms out to try and keep his balance. Mouth shut tight to stifle the cry. Eyes filled with fury and surprise.

She could run. He wouldn't be able to follow. But if she did that, Jane knew he'd recover and come for her another time. When that happened, she wouldn't have the smallest chance of staying alive.

The thoughts flew through her head in a moment. No hesitation. She kicked his knee again. This time it gave way. He fell on to the pavement, scrambling backwards so he could try to defend himself.

Jane brought her foot down once more and ground the sole of her boot into his skin. She watched his face. Perkins kept his mouth closed. He wouldn't give her the satisfaction of crying out. He wasn't going to show his pain.

She'd damaged him. He wouldn't be able to walk for a little while. When he did, he'd probably be slow and limping for the rest of his life. For now, though, he still had his bayonet. If she came too close, he'd lunge for her. Even on his back, she didn't doubt he was capable of killing her.

Jane picked her moment carefully. The pain from the knee had to be enough to distract him. She brought her foot down on it yet again. Short, sharp. But it was no worse than he'd doled out to others, if Dodson had told her the truth.

For one brief second Perkins closed his eyes. That was enough. She struck, knife slashing across the back of his hand. The man couldn't help himself. His fingers opened and the bayonet tumbled into the dirty snow. Then she had it. A big, awkward weapon. Too heavy for her, like trying to heft a piece of lead.

That didn't matter. The important thing was that he didn't have it any more. She'd taken it away from him. She'd left him defeated and helpless. He'd never be able to tell anyone the truth about tonight. Perkins could never admit he'd been beaten by a woman.

'Going to kill me now?' His voice was a soft, pained rasp. He took a breath and tried to smile at her. 'You won.'

'Yes,' she told him. 'I did.'

One final look, then she turned and walked up the street.

Simon watched as Jane brought her hand from under the cloak and dropped the bayonet on the table. He looked up, trying to read her face, but she showed nothing; she never did. Rosie gave a small gasp.

'Nobody told me he was dead.' He'd been out early, rested after a good night's sleep, but there'd been little gossip to hear at the coffee cart.

'He was alive when I left him.'

'How?' He'd never heard of anyone besting Perkins. No man, no fighter, and certainly not a woman barely half his size.

'He was waiting when I was on my way home, after I followed you back here.' Her eyes looked at something Simon knew he couldn't see. 'He said we were causing trouble for Arden's friend.'

'That proves the connection between Seaton and Arden,' Rosie said, then frowned. 'How did you manage to do it?'

'Someone told me that Perkins has a weak right knee,' Jane answered.

Simon stared at the bayonet, then picked it up, weighing it in his hand. Heavy and deadly. He ran the ball of his thumb along the blade. Honed sharp enough to kill with a stroke. Or cut off a man's hand.

'How bad was he when you left him?'

'He won't be able to do more than hobble,' she answered after a second.

He stared at her. Jane constantly surprised him. At times like this, she terrified him. Sitting there, looking completely unaffected by her fight with Perkins, as if it was a matter of no account. Not a scratch on her that he could see. No lingering fear behind her eyes of what might happen now. Good enough to beat a fighter that Simon feared, and clever enough to leave the man alive. Perkins would want his revenge, he'd crave it. But he'd let it lie. To do anything else would be to admit he'd lost to a girl. And he wasn't in a fit state to do anything if what Jane said was true.

'What are we going to do now?' Rosie asked.

Two overseers who hadn't shown up at the mill the day before. Word would spread about that. Seaton would recruit others quickly enough, but the damage was done. And Arden was without the bodyguard he'd trusted for so long.

The pair of them would be starting to worry.

The next move was theirs. Nothing to do but wait and see what they did.

No, perhaps there was something he could do. Perkins was helpless. This could be a good time to ask him what he knew about Sebastian Ramsey's death, and maybe the killing in York of a man named Sykes all those years ago. The man might be persuaded to answer.

When he asked around, though, Perkins seemed to have disappeared. He'd last been seen in the Low Hurt the night before. A little after eight someone had come and talked to him. He'd listened, finished his glass and left.

'Who was it who came?' Simon asked. There was a coin for anyone who could give him an answer, but nobody remembered.

He hid the bayonet in the secret drawer under the stairs at home. Out of sight and away from Richard and Amos. Two roughhousing boys near a weapon like that? It was a recipe for a funeral and mourning. Yet he wanted to keep it close. It might have a use.

For two hours Simon moved around Leeds. No more snow had fallen during the night. What remained was packed down solid and crusted with black soot. But still no sign of Perkins, and no one had heard a word about him today.

Simon had reached a wall in the investigation into Sebastian Ramsey's death. He'd inflicted some damage on Seaton and his mill. But in the thick dusk, he walked by the building again. Simon had turned up the collar of his greatcoat and pulled down the brim of his beaver hat until his face was well hidden.

Three men stood guard, paying attention to every person who passed. Scabbards hung from their belts and they kept a hand on the hilts of their swords. When the doors opened, the workers emerged cautiously, casting glances at the men who waited and watched.

Simon drifted away with the crowd; no sense in drawing suspicion. Seaton was taking no chances. But who knew what might happen?

For four days, things remained quiet. October became November. The cold remained and the filthy snow grew dirtier as it remained on the ground. Wind rattled the last of the leaves from the branches, leaving the trees stark and bold and bare.

Simon slept later in the mornings, sat and read the newspaper in the evenings. It would be all too easy to enjoy a life like this, he thought. Little to do and time to take pleasure in it. For now, it gave him the chance to feel his strength beginning to return.

'You're definitely looking better,' Rosie told him. She stood, taking a rest from sewing and darning as she rubbed her fingers. 'There's more life in your eyes.'

'A little,' he agreed. But he was still a long way from the fighter he'd once been. The illness hadn't let go of him yet. He'd need to practise with the knife, to work on his speed and improve the way he reacted. He knew his reputation. But that only lasted until you went up against someone better.

He woke to the steady sound of dripping water. Not as cold outside, the snow beginning to melt. The pavements turned to lakes of grey slush. He ate breakfast with Richard and Amos, asking them about the work they'd done for the tutor, questions to test how much they'd remembered.

Once their lesson began, he kissed Rosie, laced up his heavy boots, buttoned up the thick caped greatcoat and left the house. Mild enough for a thaw, perhaps, but still far from summer.

He walked gingerly, watching ahead and up, pulling back before snow slipped off a roof and down to the pavement. His hand stayed in his pocket, gripping the knife. Perhaps he was safe, but it was impossible to predict what Arden and Seaton were planning.

Finally he slipped through the gap in the wall at Green Dragon Yard, through to Mrs Shields's cottage. Jane answered the door, gazing beyond him as if someone might be there before inviting him inside.

Jane studied him. Not as awkward as he'd so often been since the illness. His movements flowed, almost the way they had before. Not quite the same, not yet, but improving day by day.

While Simon and Mrs Shields talked, she sat in the corner, half-listening, looking out of the window. She had no sense of anyone else around, but it was better to be certain. What kind of revenge would Perkins want?

The last two evenings she'd gone down to the mill, finding a spot where the guards couldn't see her. She'd spotted Simon, smiling as he let himself be carried away by the flow of labourers.

Jane had kept to her place, waiting until the foremen emerged. Four of them. But not Dawson, the man Simon had warned off. Her father wasn't there either. Not one evening, nor the next. Perhaps he finally understood her threat now he was scarred and missing a finger.

Early that morning she'd gone over to High Street, standing in her heavy cloak with her shawl pulled over her hair. One or two early workers passed, not giving her a glance. She was just another girl, invisible in this town.

Jane kept her eyes on the house with the dirty black door. She waited an hour, until long after the shift had begun. But it never opened.

When she knocked, the landlady told her the man had moved on. She didn't know where; he'd never said. He'd had a bloody rag wrapped around his hand and a deep cut on his cheek, as if he'd been in a fight.

'He'd only left for work five minutes before,' the woman said. 'I took one look and said I wanted him gone. He just had the one small bag. More like a satchel.'

'Did he say if he was staying in Leeds?' Jane asked.

'Not a word.'

She left a penny with the landlady for the information. Maybe this time he'd really learned. She'd allowed him to leave alive. If he ever returned, she'd have no choice but to kill him. She'd given him warnings; she'd offered him chances. He was nothing to her.

Mrs Shields shuffled through to the kitchen. Jane watched her affectionately.

'Have you heard anything more about Perkins?' Simon asked.

'No,' Jane replied. 'I haven't asked about him. Why would I?'

'He seems to have vanished.'

She shrugged. That first night, the bodyguard had visited her in her dreams, overpowering her, that bayonet raised. She'd woken and padded around the house until she'd banished his presence. Good riddance.

'Did you want him?' She frowned.

'He must be recovering somewhere.'

'Do we have any work?' she asked.

'Not at the moment,' Simon told her and started to smile. 'This weather's probably keeping everyone at home. The criminals, too.'

A pity it wasn't true, Jane thought. Simon knew it as well as she did. Those addicted to the night would be out there, no matter the weather. The same with the poor, who had no choice. But until someone wanted stolen items to be retrieved there was little for them to do.

'You should enjoy the rest,' she said.

'I need to work with my knife. I'm too rusty. Perhaps if we practised together . . .' He looked away from her, down at the faded Turkey rug that covered the floorboards.

'All right.' She could learn from him, too.

He was sweating, completely drained as he walked home. Water from the melting snow sluiced down the road, lapping over his boots. An hour going against Jane had challenged all the skills he thought he possessed. Survival had been her teacher and she'd learned well.

They'd worked hard, one bout after another. She'd started out by defeating him easily. So quick that she made it seem simple. Slowly, though, Simon's limbs and muscles remembered how to move. His eye grew sharper.

By the time they finished, each fight was equal. He knew it wasn't as good as he could be, and nowhere near where he needed to be. But he could barely hold his arms up any longer and the knife weighed like a millstone in his hand. Simon was exhausted; Jane didn't even look tired.

Still a long way to go, he thought as he unlocked his front door. The twins were waiting, pouncing on him like a pair of eager hounds even before he'd hung up his coat and hat. Rosie appeared in the doorway to the kitchen, holding a folded sheet of paper.

'A boy brought it a little while ago.'

He took off his boots, stuffed them with old copies of the *Mercury* to help the leather dry out, and took it from her. A single glance.

'Have you read it?'

'Yes,' she answered. 'What do you think he wants?'

Simon looked at it again.

It's time we talked. Tomorrow, outside the Moot Hall at nine. Arden.

More a command than a request. But Thomas Arden was used to having people bend to his will.

'Only one way to find out, isn't there?'

SIXTEEN

The air had warmed further during the night. The streams of melting snow flowing along the road had become a spate. Some islands of ice remained, but they grew smaller by the hour.

People picked their way along the pavements, watching where their feet were treading. Simon stood outside the Moot Hall and listened as the clock in the Parish Church rang nine.

Market day and a few had braved the roads to trudge into town to set up their goods for sale on trestles ranged either side of Briggate. They cried out their wares, the carrots and onions and potatoes. Sacks of apples and pears. Dried peas and beans.

Women and servants milled around, haggling over prices, putting food in their baskets, handing over coins. He always enjoyed watching the trading and hearing the sellers.

'Life goes on when there's money to be made. Doesn't matter about the weather.'

Simon turned towards Arden's voice. He started to reach for the knife in his pocket, but the other man simply stood, amused.

'I'm not likely to start anything with all these people around. I didn't think you had me pegged for that much of a fool, Westow.'

'You wanted to talk.'

'We can do it here and let everyone overhear our business,' Arden said. 'Or we can walk.' He took a few paces and stopped. 'Are you coming?'

He had no choice but to hurry after the man.

'Why did you send the message?'

'I imagine you can guess. You're causing plenty of problems for a good friend of mine.'

'Seaton.'

Arden nodded but he didn't speak the name. 'It's not just that. Your girl crippled my bodyguard.'

'He'd have killed her.'

'Now he's useless to me. I've had to let him go.'

The man had no sympathy in his voice, Simon thought. Only disgust that Perkins had lost.

'He had it coming.'

'Between the pair of you, you're giving us too much trouble. That's bad for profits, Westow.'

'Your profits aren't my concern.'

'We thought it would be helpful if the three of us talked.'

'Three?'

Arden nodded. 'You, me and Seaton. See how we can end this. He suggested we meet at his farm.'

'Why there?' Simon felt the creep of suspicion in his mind.

'He doesn't like to come into town, and it's a busy time for him. It's the season to slaughter some of the stock. Setting meat aside for the winter.'

'No.'

'It's not a negotiation, Westow. This is what he wants.'

'Is it?' Simon asked. 'What about you?'

A shrug. 'I like the idea. You'll be safe enough, I guarantee it.'

'And what's your guarantee worth?'

'You'll go home alive and in one piece. Not a scratch on you. The three of us talk and come to an agreement, that's all.'

Simon shook his head. 'No. Or do you have *me* pegged for a fool?'

Arden frowned. 'I'm not going back and forth on it, Westow. You'll do it, or Perkins will tell the constable that your girl attacked him. I'll pay him to do it. He's going to need money. After all, he has the injuries to prove it.' A small hesitation and a dark smile. 'I'll back him up. Do you really want her in prison or transported to Van Diemen's Land? The jury will convict, I'll make bloody certain of that.'

In Leeds the courts would do whatever Arden desired.

The man waited a few seconds. 'Well?'

A nod, an admission of defeat. 'When?'

'The day after tomorrow. His house is by the milepost on the

Harrogate turnpike. Look for the one that reads Leeds, three and a half miles. Seaton owns the large house set back from the road. Be there for nine, there's plenty to do. I knew you'd see sense.'

'Did I have any choice?' Simon asked.

'Of course not. That's the secret of doing business. You make sure your opponent isn't left with any other options.' Arden tipped his hat. 'I'll wish you well and see you the day after tomorrow.'

They hadn't gone far, only to Commercial Street. Simon stood in front of the Leeds Library and watched Arden march off towards his home in Park Square.

'What did he want?' Jane asked. She'd appeared from nowhere in her cloak and shawl.

'Seaton wants to meet me and Arden the day after tomorrow.'

'Where?'

'His farm.'

'That place he has out in the country?'

'Yes.' He saw the worry flash in her eyes. 'Don't worry, I'll be fine.' Simon could never tell her the reason he'd agreed.

'I'll come.'

It wasn't going to be a place for her to be seen. 'Not all the way.'

For a moment he thought she'd argue. Finally she nodded.

'More practice with the knives this afternoon?' he asked. God knew he needed it more than ever now. And it changed the topic.

'You agreed to go out there? On your own?' Rosie's voice exploded in the kitchen. She stood with her hands on her hips.

'What choice did I have? I told you what he threatened to do.'

She breathed slowly, staring at him, face set in anger and fear.

'I'm coming with you.'

'What about the boys? They—'

'I'm coming with you.' Her tone dared him to object.

'All right,' he agreed after a moment. Arden and Seaton would underestimate her; all too often, people did. She could look very feminine, a demure lady in her silk gown, but Rosie had a core of steel. She could be as deadly as Jane. She'd killed before, a time when it was the only way to keep alive. If she had to, he knew she'd do it again, without any hesitation.

*   *   *

An hour working with the knives. As soon as he settled into his crouch, Simon forgot everything else. All that mattered was his opponent and survival. He fought a little better than the day before. The bouts were more equal, but he was still tiring too easily. Towards the end of the time his concentration began to slip. He made mistakes that left him open.

'Enough,' he said. As she slipped her knife back into its sheath in the pocket of her dress, he asked: 'More tomorrow?'

'Yes.'

Jane walked down towards town. The sparring had warmed her and left her feeling sharp. Simon needed it. He'd still lose against any fighter worth his salt, but his skills were returning. A few times he'd come close to beating her. It was good for her, too, honing her, keeping her alert.

She'd just reached the Head Row when she felt it. The familiar crawl up her spine. Someone was following her. She knew exactly who it was.

She wanted to be home, to make sure Mrs Shields was fine. But not yet, not with him on her heels. If he didn't know where she lived, she wasn't about to lead him there. Instead, she wound her way around the streets, down towards Briggate.

As she passed, Jane glanced at the reflections in shop windows. Nothing. He was still there, though; she could feel it.

She plunged through the ginnels and alleys, and then she was alone. He'd learned enough to keep clear of places like these. Ten minutes later she emerged on Basinghall Street, free and clear, hurrying home.

Morning and only a few tiny mounds of snow remained, as black as the buildings now. The roads had turned to mud, sucking at his boots as he walked. Another good night's sleep; the physical effort of practising with the knives had worn him out.

Simon had gone to the coffee cart at first light, sipping from the tin cup and listening as people talked. No more murders, very little crime to entertain them. When he walked to the print shop, Mudie was dismantling the printing press, too caught up in his work to pass the time, and it was far too early to find Barnabas Wade at the inns.

He stepped back as a coach passed, the driver urging on the horse, sending a tall spray of dirty water over people on the pavement as it lurched through a puddle.

At home, while the boys worked in the parlour with their tutor, Simon sat in the kitchen, drawing the blades of his knives over the whetstone. The same movement again and again. He performed it without thinking until all three blades had edges as sharp as razors. Ready for the next day. He placed them in their sheaths: one on his belt, a second in his boot, and the third hidden up his sleeve. Now he needed to be faster using them, to be as fit as he'd been before the illness.

He was improving; he could feel it. Every day he grew a little stronger, not tiring quite so easily. But there was still so far to go. He needed to be sharp for the meeting with Seaton and Arden. Maybe having Rosie with him was a good idea, after all.

'You're miles away,' she said.

'Thinking,' he told her with a smile. 'Do you want to come out and practise with us this afternoon? I'm sure Mrs Fenton next door would look after the boys.'

Rosie shook her head. 'You never know who's watching. Better if they imagine I'm a wife and nothing more.'

'Arden will probably know your history.'

She shrugged. 'Men believe what they want to believe. A pretty gown and a bonnet . . . but hire a chaise for tomorrow. I don't want to walk all the way there through a quagmire.'

It was easily enough arranged. The ostler was grateful for the business. He paid and set out for Woodhouse Moor to meet Jane. But his mind was looking ahead to the next morning.

Simon had never met Seaton, didn't believe he'd ever even seen him. He remained a grey figure, a shadow. Most of the men who owned mills and factories spent hour after hour at their businesses, keeping a close eye on the money. Why was Seaton so different, he wondered?

He doubted he'd find an answer. Very likely he'd never have the chance to ask the question.

'We have someone behind us.'

He'd been too lost in his thoughts to hear Jane approaching. She kept pace with his stride.

'Anyone we know?'

She shook her head. 'Whoever he is, he'd be a fool to take us both on.'

Simon grinned. 'Probably one of Arden's. We might as well treat him to a show.'

A full hour. No breaks, no rest, moving straight from one bout to the next. By the time they finished, Simon was covered in sweat, his linen damp and his heart thudding from effort. Jane was barely breathing hard; she looked as if she could have lasted much longer.

He ran a handkerchief over his hair. Wringing wet. She'd put him through his paces. But he needed to be pushed, to be made to work.

'Do you still see our spy?' Simon asked as they strolled back towards town. A grey day, thick clouds on the horizon and the first harsh notes of a chill on the breeze. The mercury would drop tonight.

She took her time before answering. 'No, he's gone. I'm sure of it.'

'Tomorrow,' he began. 'Rosie's coming with me.'

He saw Jane hesitate and frown before she nodded.

'What about me?'

'I'd like you somewhere near. Seaton—'

'I asked. I know where he lives.'

'We're taking a chaise. You can—'

'I'll walk. No one's likely to spot me that way.'

'We'll be there for nine. You'll hear me shout if I need you.' For a moment he considered telling her exactly why she couldn't be with him. No, he decided. Leave it as it is, even if she didn't understand. Better she never knew.

Up early and into his good clothes. Rested and fresh from a long, unbroken night of sleep. Colder weather had returned with the evening; there was frost inside the windows. He scraped it away. Bitter outside; all the water on the streets had turned back to ice, the mud was solid as rock.

The familiar route to the coffee cart was treacherous, slow and slippery. He'd need to be careful driving the chaise.

No gossip to begin his day, but the hot coffee warmed his insides. Was he doing the right thing going to Seaton's? What was there to discuss? Too many questions and no answers yet.

SEVENTEEN

Simon held the reins loosely, letting the horse move at its own pace. That was best when the roads were so rutted and frozen. Next to him, Rosie clutched his arm, silent, her face pale and frightened.

Finally, he reached the milepost. Exactly as Arden had described. A carved arrow pointed back towards Leeds. In the other direction: *Harrogate 12 miles*. Simon stopped, flexing his fingers and studying the land around. He didn't try to spot Jane. She'd promised she'd be here, and he trusted her word. Other eyes were certain to be watching him. No sense in giving her away.

There was only one large house in sight. A neat building of stone that had weathered to the soft colour of honey. He pulled the watch from his waistcoat pocket. Almost nine. A slow journey, but he was happy to have arrived at all with the roads this dangerous. The air hadn't grown any warmer. Going home would be hard work.

Home? First they had to last through this.

'Ready?' he asked as he turned to Rosie. Saying nothing, she nodded.

A groom was waiting to help them down and take the horse.

'Just go around the back of the house, sir, over towards the barn,' he told them. 'They're already at it.'

A path led round the building. No elaborate gardens for Seaton. This was a working farm. Chickens pecked at the ice between the cobbles of the yard for their food. Fields rolled off into the distance, bounded by hedges or drystone walls.

He followed the voices, giving Rosie a smile to reassure her.

She kept her head down, eyes on the path ahead, her body stiff and tense.

A group of men stood around talking. Half of them drew on clay pipes and blew smoke into the air. A bottle moved quietly between them. They were gathered by a bench, next to a long wooden trough and a device that looked like a pulley. A fire burned bright, giving off welcome heat that shimmered in the air. A metal cauldron of boiling water hung suspended above it.

It was easy enough to spot the ones who'd do the work; they wore heavy leather aprons over their waistcoats and shirts. No coats, sleeves rolled up, even in the raw weather. Heavy boots that buttoned up the side.

Arden he knew. It was the man at his side who interested him. He wore a high-crown hat and a long oilcloth riding coat that ended just above his ankles. Old moleskin trousers and sturdy boots. He stood slightly apart, gazing at the others, his face full of concern. He barely bothered to turn his head as he noticed Simon and Rosie. A soft word, then Arden was coming towards them.

'Mrs Westow,' he said, removing his hat. 'I hadn't expected to see you.' His eyes flashed anger at Simon.

Rosie graced him with a smile. 'I was curious to see what happens out here.'

She was dressed up, wearing a warm gown of wool dyed a deep purple; its elaborate lace collar had been crafted by the Moravians in Fulneck. Flannel petticoats underneath, everything covered by a thick cloak and decorated black hat. A lady's winter wardrobe. At least she'd left the dainty shoes at home and put on sturdy boots.

'Allow me to introduce Mr Seaton. This is his house and land.'

'Not just land. This is a farm, Thomas.' He spoke softly, pride hiding behind the words. There was no smile; Seaton had the look of a man without humour. With his pale blue eyes, a beak of a nose and a small mouth, he wasn't attractive. 'We work here,' he added with a small nod. 'As you'll see.'

Another word and one of the labourers left, returning with a pig. It trotted beside him like a dog, all the way to the bench. It was a thick, sturdy beast, nearly as heavy as a man. The labourer scratched its snout then moved away.

Another of the men came up on the animal's blind side and swung a hammer, catching it hard between the eyes.

Rosie gasped and dug her fingers into Simon's sleeve as the blow landed and the animal crumpled to the ground. The men hefted it on to the broad bench, neck protruding over the end. and placed a large bucket underneath.

'Are you sure you want to watch this?' Arden asked Rosie. 'It's not a sight a lady ought to see.'

'It's all right. I know what's going to happen.' She stared at him as she replied. 'It took me by surprise, that's all.'

Seaton gave the signal. One of the men drew a broad knife across the pig's throat. A single, loving stroke, but with enough strength to slice through the flesh and the fat. Blood poured into the bucket, warm and steaming in the bitter morning.

'She didn't scream,' Seaton said with satisfaction. 'Perfectly happy when she died. I know it's hard to believe, but it makes a difference to the way the meat tastes.' He didn't turn to face them, keeping his eyes on the pig as it bled.

Rosie's fingers kept their firm grip on Simon's arm, but she was still watching. So was he. It was gruesome, but something people had done for centuries. All the pork, the bacon and sausages they ate began with this. The man had been right; the pig had seemed calm and content before the hammer stunned it. No cry as the knife took its life.

'Enough,' Seaton said as the stream of blood eventually weakened to become a hesitant trickle. Four of the farm workers each took one of the animal's legs and lifted it into the trough. Ladle by ladle, boiling water from the cauldron was poured over the skin.

'This softens the bristles so we can remove them,' Seaton explained. Another minute and men busied themselves with scrapers, dragging them along the pig's flesh and taking off its hair.

Once they'd finished, they pushed the pulley into place at the end of the trough. One of them took his knife and cut through the pig's rear legs by the tendons, sliding an axe handle through then and finally knotting a rope from the pulley against the wood.

Nobody spoke. No need; they all knew their parts. Now it was down to strength. Two men turned the handle, grunting with effort as the pig rose, upside down, dripping a pale pink mix of blood and water on to the ground.

The rope was tied off, the pig secure, swinging slightly as it hung. A final scrape to remove the remaining hair. The skin underneath was so pale it seemed to glimmer in the light. One of the labourers took out a long, thin knife and ran the blade across a whetstone.

Another dragged over an empty wooden tub until it sat directly under the body. Then the butcher began his work. A quick, assured cut to the back of the pig's head, a second across the gullet so the head dropped, barely held in place. Practised, deft. Not a moment's hesitation. More swift work until the head tumbled away entirely, staring up at them from the bottom of the tub.

The man plunged his knife into the pig's body near the belly and drew the blade down. Another stroke to where the neck had been. Then finally one more, starting between the hind legs and cutting steadily until the animal was completely opened up to the air, steaming in the cold.

How often had the labourer done this through the years? Simon watched as the man reached inside, tugging at the organs, tying off some of the entrails with string before he sliced them away and tossed them down into the tub. He didn't even need to think about what he was doing.

'Only the details left now,' Seaton said, his voice filling the silence. 'After that we'll cut it up and salt everything for winter. We use everything bar the tail. Once this one's done we'll clean up and move to the next. We have three more to do this morning. Hawkins,' he called over his shoulder, 'show Mrs Westow around the farm.'

'Yes, sir.'

A man hurried across. He pulled off his battered straw hat and asked Rosie to follow him. She looked at Simon, unsure.

'You go,' he told her. 'I'll be fine.'

He watched until Rosie and the man disappeared around the barn. Then he turned, facing Seaton and Arden. The autumn slaughter was a ritual that happened every year in farms and houses across England. It had drawn him in, like a dark, bloody dream. A lesson for him to learn.

But that was what they wanted. To show him how easily life could end. This time it had been a pig. A man would be no different. He glanced at the butcher steadily working on the animal, more of the innards dropping into the tub.

Seaton began to walk. Arden followed, Simon beside him.

'I know that girl of yours is outside, Westow. She probably thinks she's being clever, but the gamekeeper here spotted her before she came anywhere close.' Before Simon could say a word, he continued: 'She's safe enough unless she does something stupid.'

By the time Seaton stopped, they were out of earshot of the men who were working. He couldn't see Rosie anywhere, and for a moment he felt a surge of panic. Then he caught a flicker of her dark cloak off near the horizon.

He needed to take the lead, to try and put Seaton and Arden on the back foot.

'You said you wanted to talk. That's why we're standing here, isn't it?' He glanced from one man to the other.

'I already told you, Westow, what you've been doing has caused us trouble,' Arden replied. 'First it was Riley, and now Perkins isn't worth a tinker's damn to me. I had the physician examine him a second time. He'll never be able to fight again.'

'You paid Riley to kill me,' Simon said. 'He's lucky to still be alive. And Perkins picked his battle. He lost to Jane.'

Arden shrugged. 'He lost, that's what's important. I don't pay men to lose. Now I have to find someone new. I don't need that aggravation. You're costing us good money. You scared off a pair of Mr Seaton's overseers. Now the rest of them are wondering what you might do to them.'

Were they, Simon thought? Good.

'There's another overseer who's dead,' Simon said, thinking of Warner. 'The constable seemed to think I was responsible, but we all know that had nothing to do with me.'

They didn't answer and that told him all he needed. The pair in front of him were behind Warner's murder. But something had gone wrong, something that stopped them blaming Simon.

'What do you propose?' he asked.

'That you stop.' Seaton had finally found his voice.

'Why should I?'

'It helps you stay alive,' Arden told him. Blunt, straightforward. Not a threat, a plain statement of fact. 'You and that wife of yours. Your two children. Richard and Amos, isn't it? A handsome pair of lads. It might also keep that lass away from prison.'

As soon as he heard his sons' names, Simon began to reach for his knife. He wouldn't take any threat against them. Arden began to smile, knowing he'd scored a blow.

'If you want me to stop, you need to make a few changes in your mill.' He turned to Seaton, waiting until the man was staring directly at him.

'What do you want?' His voice was raw and dusty.

'You give money to the families of Peter Hardy and Jacob Easby for what happened to them. A decent settlement, a foreman's wage for a year to each one.'

'I'm willing to do that.' He'd agreed too easily, Simon thought. The man had expected him to demand more. 'Anything else?'

'Your overseers stop beating children.'

Seaton shook his head. 'No. It's the way mills work. I thought you claimed you'd spent your childhood working in one.'

'I did. That's how I know. And someone has to take the first step to end it.'

'That won't be me.'

He wasn't going to give ground on it. At least Simon had tried to start a change. Still, the compensation would help those families a little.

'The money?'

A reluctant nod. 'I said yes. But nothing more than that.'

'Everything done quietly. No repercussions for the Easbys or the Hardys. No violence against my family or Jane.'

'Agreed,' Seaton said after a moment. 'As long as you stop.'

'I will.' What else could he achieve, anyway? He'd exhausted all the possibilities. This way he walked away with some small victory.

'I need to supervise the rest of the work.' Seaton stalked off.

'You'd make a fair businessman,' Arden said as the two of them ambled back to the killing ground. 'You strike a powerful bargain. But in case you ever get the urge to do anything else against me, remember what I said earlier, Westow. I'm a bad enemy to make. I'm not afraid of a little blood and I won't care whose it is.'

How could he forget?

'You and Seaton,' Simon said. 'You're friends from when you were in York?'

'Started out together.' A glance to make sure the meaning was understood. 'We've gone our separate ways here, but we still look out for each other. Always will.'

'You know each other's secrets.'

'We do, and we keep them well. Did you ever hear of a blood covenant?'

'What? Friendship, you mean?'

Arden shook his head. 'More than that. Closer than family. We protect each other. If someone attacks one of us, then both will come down on him. Today was your warning. Today we agreed peacefully. Anything more and you'll pay.'

'What about Riley?' Simon asked. 'That was more than a warning. You wanted me dead.'

Arden shrugged. 'We didn't succeed, so perhaps this is the better answer for everyone.' He glanced towards the two figures rounding the barn. 'There's your wife, she's had the full tour. Good timing, eh, Westow?'

'Very.' An empty word to fill the country quiet.

'You achieved something, and we've given you food for thought.' His face split into a grin. 'I'll send over some food for your belly later, too. Maybe a shoulder from that pig we just killed. You can have it all roasted up and tasty and remember what it was like alive.' A tip of his hat and he strode off.

Rosie was waiting by the chaise, the horse back in its traces. He helped her up, and they set off down the drive. On the road he watched for Jane. No sign. He had to believe that Arden wasn't lying when he said she was safe. They were a quarter of a mile down the turnpike, going back towards Leeds, before Rosie spoke.

'What did they want?'

'They wanted to call a halt without any more bloodshed. It seems we worried them.'

She raised an eyebrow. 'Did you agree?'

'With some conditions.' He explained, keeping a gentle hold on the reins and watching the horse.

'It all sounds reasonable,' Rosie said. 'If it wasn't for the men making the agreement, it would be almost civilized.'

'As long as they keep to it. Arden's lost a bodyguard he trusted. I can't see a man like that being happy without his revenge, can you?'

'We'd better hope he is.' She gathered the heavy blanket closer around herself to keep out the cold. 'You know, Seaton has a large farm. That man only had time to show me a small part of it. They keep plenty of sheep and sell the fleeces. A large piggery, too, by a stand of oak trees. The pigs like it there. They love acorns, he told me. But they'll eat anything at all. Animals, he said, even people if they're hungry enough.'

'I never knew that.' Simon grimaced at the thought.

'Did you notice Seaton never spoke directly to me?' Rosie asked.

'He's an odd man. Too used to having his own way in life, probably. What did you think of the killing?'

'It wasn't as awful as I expected,' she told him eventually, then smiled. 'Seeing it once was enough, though.'

'They wanted to use it as a lesson. How simple it is to kill.'

'They're certainly not subtle,' Rosie said with a smile. 'Do you feel schooled by your lesson?'

'I think it all ended as well as we could have hoped.'

EIGHTEEN

Morning, and Jane sat across the kitchen table from Rosie and Simon at the house on Swinegate.

'I waited in case Seaton sent anyone after you.'

'Nothing?'

'No one left the farm.'

She knew someone had spotted her near Seaton's. A figure that moved silently through the autumn undergrowth and kept watch on her. But he never came close, didn't threaten. After the chaise left, she glanced across and he'd vanished.

She listened as Simon told her everything he'd agreed with Arden and Seaton.

'He confirmed that he turned out Perkins the bodyguard.'

Jane nodded. She'd wanted to cripple him, to make him pay for everything he'd done to soldiers over the years. This was payment of a sort.

'I want you to find him,' Simon told her.

'Find him?' she asked, scarcely able to believe what she'd heard. 'Why?'

'He might be able to answer some questions for me about Sebastian Ramsey, that body they pulled out of the river.'

'All right,' she agreed reluctantly.

'Once you know where he is, then we'll visit together. He'll probably be terrified to see you again.'

'He should be.' She rose and put on her old green cloak, buttoning it at the neck before raising the shawl over her head. 'Are we safe?'

'Yes,' Simon answered. As long as he did nothing more, Arden and Seaton had no reason to send anyone else after them. But how long would their promise last? 'For now, at least.'

As she walked along the streets, she was grateful for the hobnails on the soles of her boots. The cold meant the pavements were icy, slick and dangerous. People tumbled. She heard the snap of a bone and the cry of pain as a man slipped. People rushed to help him.

Jane asked questions. In shops and taverns, at a couple of the inns and at the stables, where the warmth from the horses heated the buildings. She found children desperate for food, gave them a little money and told them to hunt for Perkins then tell her if they discovered him.

A morning of moving around Leeds drove the cold from her bones. No more feeling that anyone was following her. Still, nobody with a scrap of sense would wander around in this weather if they had a choice. Especially someone with a long wound to his face and a bandaged hand.

It took a little while to find Dodson the beggar, the man who'd lost a leg just before Waterloo. He smiled as she put coins in his tin cup.

'I hear someone hurt Perkins,' he said.

'That's what people say.'

'Someone who knew about his weak right knee.'

'So I heard.'

Dodson cocked his head. 'Why didn't you finish him?'

'I did,' she told him. 'Everything he was is over now.'

Jane took out more coins and let them rattle into the metal.

'Thank you,' she said.

A little after noon she stood at the corner of Briggate and Boar Lane, buying hot food from Kate the pie-seller. The big woman was wrapped up warm, a long cloak and fingerless wool mittens, chattering nineteen to the dozen about nothing at all.

From the corner of her eye, Jane noticed a boy running along Duncan Street. He began to slide and flail his arms as he tried to keep his balance. For a fraction of a second she thought he'd crash headlong on to the ice, but he managed to keep his balance and hurried on towards her.

'That man.' He was breathless, red in the face but beaming with pride. 'I know where he is.'

She handed him the uneaten pie.

'Where?'

He told her, voice as quiet and serious as someone revealing a grave secret.

'If you're lying—' Jane began.

He shook his head. 'It's the truth. I'll take you there right now if you want.'

'No need.' She took coins from her pocket, enough to feed the lad and find him somewhere to sleep during this cold snap. He was already thin as a twig. Another night or two out in this and he might never wake up again.

She had the information. Time to tell Simon.

He'd had a quiet morning, staying in the kitchen to rest and enjoy the warmth from the range. He went over everything that Seaton and Arden had said, trying to divine if there was a deeper meaning to their words than he might have heard.

The day before had drained him. The concentration and effort of driving the chaise on those roads, then the confrontation itself. Not too long ago he'd have shrugged it all off. Now it seemed to settle about him and drag him down with weariness. He needed a little time to recover.

Simon let the day happen around him. Rosie at her work,

baking bread, preparing the dinner. The sound of the boys and their tutor from the parlour. Everything ordered and ordinary, a comfort around him.

He dozed at one point, like an old man, an invalid, coming awake with a snort and a guilty start.

As soon as Jane arrived, he knew she was bringing information; her face betrayed little, but he could read the excitement in her eyes. He eased his feet into the boots and buttoned the heavy coat. Out of sight, he slipped something into his pocket, then adjusted his hat in the mirror.

There was no hurry; a man with a ruined knee wouldn't risk going anywhere when the streets were like this. They took their time, walking carefully, no need to exchange any wasted talk. Out beyond Fearn's Island, with the River Aire on their right hand, they turned and followed the road as it began to climb up Cavalier Hill.

'There,' Jane said, pointing to a stone house that stood on its own. 'That's what I was told.'

'Let's find out if it's true.' He took the knife from his belt. Perkins was injured, but he was an old soldier. He'd survived battles and campaigns; he could still be deadly.

A blade eased between the lock and the door and they were inside. Two rooms downstairs. Empty now, but somebody lived here. A fire had burned to ashes in the grate and coal sat in the scuttle. A pair of dirty plates were on the table in the kitchen.

Simon heard someone shift above, followed by a short cough. He eased his way up the stairs, Jane behind him. A single door. He kicked it open.

A small blaze glowed in the hearth, throwing out just enough heat to take the edge off the cold. Perkins was sitting in a chair, covered in a blanket, his bad leg resting on a stool. A glass and bottle stood on the floor by his side.

The man raised dull eyes towards them and smiled. He'd taken something; laudanum, perhaps, some drug to dull his pain and push the world away. He had the look of a man who'd given up on his life.

'Well, well, it's the girl who beat me.' He spoke slowly, taking his time to make sure each word arrived clearly. 'Come to finish the job, have you?' He spread his arms. 'You might as well. There's nothing worth keeping.'

'Arden dropped you,' Simon said.

The man shifted his gaze. 'All thanks to what she did.' He pointed a dirty finger at Jane.

'You'd have killed her if you'd had the chance,' Simon reminded him.

'True,' Perkins agreed with a thoughtful nod. 'What about it, girl? Going to repay the favour? Or would you rather leave me crippled and no use to man nor beast?'

Simon tossed a coin on the floor, letting the sound ring around the room.

'If you want to talk about killing, I have a question or two for you. There's money for honest answers.'

'Pay your pennies.' Perkins appeared amused. 'I've no need to lie.'

'Sebastian Ramsey. Do you know the name?'

A slow series of nods. 'In the water and missing a hand.'

'Your work?'

'It was an easy job. I can't recall one that was simpler. The only problem was they'd told me to go after the wrong man.'

'They?' Simon asked. 'Who?'

'Arden and Seaton. They thought he was stealing from the mill. Afterwards they realized they were wrong.' He shrugged.

'Who was the right man?'

Perkins gave a slow, exaggerated shake of his head. 'I don't know. They didn't ask me to punish anyone else for it.'

'The hand – that was to show he was a thief?' Simon asked.

The man nodded. 'Arden told me to do it that way.'

'You'd used it once before, hadn't you?'

Perkins raised an eyebrow. 'Not me. That was Arden. A long time ago. In York, he said. Before I worked for him.'

'What about George Collins?'

'That one was the Arden boy,' he continued. 'He even came and asked me the best way to do it.'

Perkins reached down, hand groping for the bottle, and raised it to his lips. No need for the glass. A tiny sip, but enough to dull the surface of the pain. Simon threw down two more coins. One span on its edge before landing, face side towards the ceiling.

'What will you do now?'

'I don't know.' He didn't seem to care. 'Sit here until I die, maybe. Or perhaps I'll goad her into giving me an ending.' He jutted his head towards Jane. 'God knows there have been plenty who've tried in the past.'

Simon reached into his pocket and brought out the bayonet. The sight of it made Perkins go pale. Was that what he imagined, killed with his own blade?

A flick of the wrist and it sailed through the air to land on the bed.

'For whatever it's worth, you might as well have it back.' Behind him, Simon could sense Jane's anger.

He turned and left. They'd been walking for two minutes before she asked the question raging in her mind.

'Why? Why did you do that?'

It was the first time he'd ever felt her full fury. She had a right to it, he knew. It had been her life at risk to beat him.

'You saw him,' Simon said. 'The only person he's likely to hurt now is himself. At the moment he's no danger to anyone else. He doesn't even look as if he can stand up.'

'We fought. He lost. I took his weapon.'

'Believe me, he knows that. That's what's causing most of his pain. He was beaten by a woman. For all the damage he can do, he might as well have it back. It gives him a little of his self-respect. Men like him need that.'

She was silent. Still unhappy and not hiding it. They were close to town, smoke hanging below the clouds, when Simon spoke again.

'There's always going to be someone who's better,' he told her. 'Always. It doesn't matter who you are. Perkins forgot that. He never expected it could be you. Riley would have defeated me if you hadn't been there. Sooner or later there's always someone.'

Charles Ramsey lit a cheroot and stared at the tip.

'There was no need for my brother to have died at all?'

'None,' Simon said. 'I'm sorry.'

They were standing on Pitfall, staring out over the river. It was late in the afternoon, the air growing colder against their faces as night loomed.

'What about the men who ordered his killing?' Ramsey asked.

'Both alive. Both rich.'

Ramsey nodded. 'Of course. That's always the way with the wealthy. Nothing touches them.'

'Maybe it will one day.'

'I don't expect it, sir. But I thank you for finding the truth. What do I owe you for your time?'

'Nothing.'

'I must. This is your work.'

Simon quoted him a low amount, ridiculously small.

'I'll send it to your house, sir. Tomorrow I might as well start back to Boston.' He looked around with sad eyes that seemed on the verge of tears. 'There's nothing to keep me here now.'

He stuck out his hand and Simon shook it.

'I wish you well.' One mystery solved, even if the solution was a plague of sorrow.

NINETEEN

Saturday morning. Simon dressed and walked to the coffee cart outside the Bull and Mouth. The early morning didn't feel quite as brittle as the last couple of days; the air had mellowed a little overnight. But a sense of snow hung over the town, as if the clouds were pillowing, just waiting to let it fall.

According to the gossip he heard, the weather had already closed the Great North Road south of Darlington, and going west was impossible, no chance of moving beyond Halifax or Skipton. Only a matter of time before it arrived in Leeds, he thought.

A visit to George Mudie; the man was busy producing posters to advertise a new milliner's shop on Vicar Lane.

'It all helps pay the bills, Simon,' he said with a gentle sigh. 'Has your life been more interesting?'

'More agricultural.'

That was enough to make Mudie stop and listen. By the time he finished, the man was shaking his head.

'Arden likes to hammer his point home, doesn't he?'

Not just that, but to finish the job completely. The evening before, a man had delivered a sticky, bloody parcel. The shoulder of pork that he'd promised. It would be roasting this morning, dinner for them all today and tomorrow. He'd been hesitant about accepting it, but Rosie had insisted.

'I'm not going to turn down good meat. We've both known what it's like to be hungry.'

She was right; of course she was. Now the thought of hot roast pork made his belly rumble.

'What are you going do about Arden and Seaton?' Mudie asked.

Simon shrugged. 'There's nothing more I can do. I have to trust they'll keep their side of the bargain.'

'Good luck to you, then. You're done with work just in time for the snow.' He nodded towards the window. The first flakes were drifting down. 'Go and enjoy yourself, Simon.' He tapped the pile of posters. 'Just be glad you're not the one who has to go round and paste these up.'

At home he settled to read in a quiet corner of the kitchen, grateful that the snow might mean a break and another chance to regain his full strength. Going through the articles in the *Mercury* and the *Leeds Intelligencer*. Letting the smells of food rise around him. Roasting meat, potatoes, cabbage cut and waiting to go in the pot.

The knock on the door came as a surprise. He and Rosie looked at each other.

'It's going to be for you,' she said.

He wasn't expecting anyone. This was hardly the kind of weather to drag out new clients.

He certainly didn't recognize the man facing him. Snow had gathered on the shoulders of his greatcoat and the wide brim of his hat. A face that had spent most of its time outdoors and in the weather, ruddy cheeks and steady eyes.

'You're the thief-taker?'

'I am,' Simon told him. The boys were with their tutor in the parlour, Rosie was busy in the kitchen and not about to be shifted. Where could he take the man? An inn was the only solution. 'Might I ask your name?'

'Collins,' he answered. 'George Collins was my son.'

They settled in a private room upstairs at the Rose and Crown. The man had taken off his coat and shaken snow across the floorboards. He had a countryman's body, muscled and used to work.

'My son is in the ground at home,' Collins began.

'You do know that someone thought I might have killed him?' Simon asked. It was better to address it now, directly. From the look in the man's eyes, he hadn't heard that.

'Did you?'

'No. I only ever saw your son in his rooms. That was just for a few seconds. Do you know what happened?'

'I do.' He took a long drink of the beer in front of him. 'I was up here before, to collect the coffin and take everything from his rooms. Your constable told me what he'd discovered. It didn't seem to be much. He hasn't been able to find the man who killed my son.'

'That's what I heard. I'm sorry.'

'Do you know who's responsible?'

Simon waited too long to answer as he weighed his reply.

'You do, don't you?' Collins said.

'All I can say is what someone told me. That's not the kind of evidence for any courtroom.'

'I don't care about that. Who was it?' The man leaned forward, elbows on the table, pressing in his grief.

Simon held back for a moment. If the man decided to do anything with the information, he could be placing his family in danger. But Collins's eyes were filled with pleading.

'A man named Franklin Arden,' Simon said finally. 'Your son had stolen some silver from him.'

'I see.' His eyes glittered with fury. 'I thought they were supposed to be friends.' Another small silence. 'You said someone told you. Do you believe it?'

'I do. It came from a good source,' Simon said after another brief hesitation. He wasn't going to reveal Perkins's name.

'What about the constable? Does he know? Any of the authorities?'

'I have no idea. I don't think so. I just told you: there's no evidence at all.'

'Could you find some?'

'No. Quite honestly, I don't believe I can.' He took a breath, wondering if he should say more. First Ramsey, now Collins wanting him to investigate murders. But this time he knew with certainty that there was nothing else to learn. 'You should understand something, Mr Collins. Franklin Arden's father is a power in Leeds.'

'What about it? Even if his son's a murderer? Doesn't that matter?' He was raising his voice. Soon the landlord would be hurrying up the stairs to see what was wrong.

Simon spoke quietly and calmly. 'I know it's wrong, but no one called Arden would ever be arrested and convicted of anything in Leeds. Especially not murder.'

Telling a stranger the bald truth hurt. It made the town seem corrupt. Good and bad, Simon had spent his life here. He still loved it. But it wasn't a fair place. Honesty had little value.

'That's it? That's all?'

'Yes,' he said. 'I'm afraid it is.'

'Then you're as bad as these Ardens and everyone who helps them.' He stood, pushing back the chair. Fire flamed behind his eyes 'You've not got an ounce of courage, the lot of you.'

Collins stormed down the stairs. Maybe the man was right, Simon thought. Some people had too much power. Men like Arden and Seaton. People were scared of them. Scared for their jobs, scared for their lives.

Was he any better? He'd given Collins the name, but he wouldn't do more than that. Even that might be one step too many. In Leeds, justice and the law were two different things.

He left the inn. The snow was still falling, covering the ground and giving a strange stillness to everything. By the time he arrived home, the meal would be almost ready. But he'd lost his appetite for Seaton's pork.

*   *   *

The snow kept coming, silent, relentless. Simon was content to watch it through the window.

An afternoon rest felt like a weakness, but he did it anyway, curled up in his bed; only an hour, but it felt like a restorative. No dreams he could recall, just a deep plunge into sleep.

Alongside Rosie, he took the boys out in the fading light so they could throw snowballs with the other children. He watched, content, as they ran and shouted and played, warming themselves with a bag of hot chestnuts bought from a seller.

Simon had put Collins's father from his mind. The man had endured a bitter loss, but there was nothing Simon could do. He'd told the truth of the matter. If the man had any sense, he'd take a coach straight back to Chesterfield before the roads became impassable.

A quiet evening. They tried to play a game the twins invented, the boys making up the rules as they went along and collapsing into fits of giggles. Hearing them so happy and carefree was all Simon had ever wanted. His family was healthy, he had a solid home and there was food on the table. What more could he desire?

The next morning he woke early, feeling rested. The snow had stopped, but a good six inches of it had stuck to the ground and the clouds seemed pregnant with more. No matter the weather, even on the Sabbath the coffee cart would still be on Briggate outside the Bull and Mouth, to serve those who had to work.

The air was thick with conversation. Another body discovered on Leeds Bridge. A sickening fear rose from his belly.

'Who?' he asked. 'Do they know?'

The man telling the tale grinned and showed off the gaps in his teeth. 'Oh aye, the constable's men knew straight off. Hard not to when it was Franklin Arden.' He gave a harsh, thick laugh. 'They'll have their hands full looking for the killer. Never been any shortage of people who wanted him dead.'

Maybe not, but Simon knew exactly who'd done it, and why he'd been left in the same spot as George Collins. Simon had set him on the trail. He'd given him the name. But dear Christ, he hadn't imagined the man would be stupid enough to do this.

And now Collins was trapped in Leeds. No escape back to Derbyshire with the roads closed. Thomas Arden would be searching for the man who killed his son. Simon finished the coffee, listening for any other fragments of the story. What else was there to say?

All through the morning he tried to settle to the newspapers. But his eyes skipped over words until he realized he hadn't taken in a single thing he'd read and tried to start over. It was close to half past ten when a fist hammered against the front door. Later than he'd expected.

Constable Porter and a pair of men from the watch. He showed them through to the kitchen. Rosie and the children were off visiting a neighbour. Porter would be gone before they returned.

'Someone told me you were at the coffee cart this morning.'

'I was.'

'You'll have heard, then.'

'I'm sure the whole town has by now,' Simon told him.

'Where were you last night, Westow?'

'Upstairs, asleep in my bed like every honest man.'

He wasn't worried. If Porter truly believed Simon was the killer, he'd have turned up as soon as the body was identified. All this meant was he didn't know a thing; he had no idea that George Collins's father was in Leeds. Simon wasn't about to tell him; maybe the man would be able to perform some trick and vanish. Franklin Arden was no loss. Women in town would breathe a little easier with him gone. For a brief second he'd wondered if it might have been Jane's work, but no. She would never have been so blatant.

Five minutes and the constable had left. The man looked worried. Well he might; Arden would be putting on the pressure. He'd be desperate for revenge. How long before he came calling, wanting to ask Simon some questions? Or perhaps he'd find another route to the truth. A few coins and his reputation would loosen men's tongues.

Someone would die for this. That was obvious. Anything less and people would wonder if Thomas Arden was no longer the man he claimed to be.

He was walking down Trinity Street in the shank of the afternoon when he felt someone fall in beside him. Her footsteps made no sound in the snow and she seemed to have come from nowhere. But that was her talent, to be invisible.

'Did Porter come and see you?' she asked.

'Came and went. He knew I hadn't done anything. What about you?'

She shook her head. 'Who was it?' she asked.

He told her about Collins's father coming to see him and what he'd told the man.

'What now?' Jane said.

'We wait and see.' It wasn't their fight. Getting involved would be reckless, begging for danger. Collins had arrived in Leeds with one aim and he'd achieved it.

'Shouldn't we help him?'

'We already did.' The name had been enough. He hoped it wouldn't end up being too much.

That didn't stop a broken night, shards of guilt cutting him in his dreams. Once again, Simon was up early, walking through the end of the night to wait on Briggate for the coffee cart to begin serving. A few men milled around, chilled to the marrow and still groggy from sleep.

A woman hurried up Briggate, limping as she tried to run.

'There's a body on Pitfall.' Her eyes were wide and glittering. She looked as though she relished being the first to bring the news.

Simon didn't need to ask. Didn't need to listen. He drank the coffee in a single gulp and walked away.

Mudie listened, standing close to the stove in the printing shop.

'What do you want me to say?' he asked when Simon had finished. 'If you want absolution, you'd better go and see if you can find yourself a Catholic priest. It's not my business. You can't even be certain it's Collins lying there.'

'True.' He stood, sliding the wooden chair back across the rough broads. But he knew full well that the corpse couldn't be anybody else.

He took his time going home, trying to come to some peace with his thoughts. All around he heard snippets of conversation about the killing. How frenzied it had been, how brutal. All the injuries. More than twenty wounds.

If Simon had kept his mouth shut, a man might still be alive. But if he hadn't said a word, someone else might have conjured up a name, maybe not even the right one. Collins had deserved to know the truth. The feeling of guilt would fade to the dullness of history.

Rosie put bowls of porridge in front of the boys. Simon watched his sons eat. If someone hurt one of them, he'd want to know who was responsible. He'd make them pay, whatever happened after that.

'Are you listening?' Rosie asked.

'I'm sorry,' he answered. 'I was thinking about work.'

She gave him a curious look but said nothing.

No more questions during the day. He dozed in the afternoon; Rosie had to shake his shoulder to rouse him.

'Arden's at the door,' she hissed.

Simon stretched and studied himself in the mirror. Presentable. Not that Arden would notice. He'd come to vent his fury.

'Not inside, Westow.'

'Where?'

'We'll walk.' He turned and moved away. A moment and Simon joined him. The snow had begun again, light, fluttering, as if it was hardly there at all. Arden strode out quickly, with a purpose, along Swinegate to Leeds Bridge and over to the other side. He stopped, looking back at the town.

'What do you see there, Westow?'

Simon took his time. He stared at the skyline, the sharp angles of roofs and chimneys blurred by smoke and snow. 'People who are hoping. People who've been hurt.'

'I see money,' Arden told him. 'It's there to be made if you try. But there's a price, isn't there?' It wasn't a question that demanded an answer. 'Right there.' He pointed to the centre of the bridge, in the middle of the road. 'That's where they found Franklin. I wanted them to show me.'

People passed, boys on their way back to businesses or homes, pushing empty handcarts and giving them curious looks. Of course, two men standing without speaking, looking at something no one else could see.

'It took me a little while to find out who'd done it.' His voice had become quieter, a memory. Long gaps between the thoughts

that became words. 'He sat there like he knew I'd come for him.
I think he was relieved.'

'Why did you bring me out here to tell me?' Simon asked.

'You know the reason as well as I do, Westow. You gave him
Franklin's name. Collins told me before I killed him.'

The man knew, there was no need to say more about that. The
question was what he would do.

'They're saying you made it last.'

'Of course I bloody did.' The words exploded out of him.
'What else was I likely to do? He killed my son. He knew I was
going to make him suffer. I don't think he cared.'

Arden could admit it. It didn't matter if half a hundred people
heard, he knew he'd never be tried for the murder.

'Why are you telling me?' Simon asked.

'Because I want you to know. You gave him Franklin's name.
You're as guilty as he is. I'm not going to forget that. You've
been warned.' He took two paces across the bridge.

'Before you go,' Simon said, 'remember that all this killing
began when your son murdered George Collins. The son you
assured me wouldn't be stupid enough to do anything like that.'

'Maybe it did. And *you* remember that it might not be over yet.'

Too many deaths. Far too many.

Jane stood in the snow on the other side of Briggate from the
Pack Horse. All around her, it kept swirling and falling. People
who passed looked faint, ghostly in the pearly light. None of
them noticed her, caught in the shadows, her shawl covering her
hair.

Simon had come to Mrs Shields's cottage in the afternoon,
asking her to follow and explaining why. Now she was here,
waiting for the glee club to end. No feeling of danger. No sign
of anyone lurking, but it was impossible to see much in this
weather. Instead, she had to rely on her senses.

No more hint that her father was still in Leeds. She'd let
him off lightly, she knew that; a scar and a finger were hardly
payment for all he'd caused her. But she'd made certain he
wouldn't forget her.

She began to stir as men emerged from the passage that led
to the inn. A few moments and she picked out a familiar shape.

He was talking to someone. They shook hands and Simon strode off down Briggate. Jane drifted along the other side of the street, staying several yards behind. She kept one hand on her dagger, eyes watching for sudden movements.

They were on Swinegate, just a few paces from Simon's house when the men came quietly from a gateway. A pair of them, both with knives. Simon acted as if he hadn't noticed them. She let out a low whistle and began to run. The hobnails on the soles of her boots crunched down in the snow.

One of the attackers turned. Too late. She was already on him, slicing open his arm so he dropped his blade before he could strike a single blow. A second swift cut to the muscle at the back of his thigh and all he could do was hobble away. It would be easy to finish him, but she remembered Simon's advice: only kill if you have no other choice. It saved questions and lies and a hangman's rope.

The other man was on his knees, staring up hopelessly as Simon held the point of his weapon to his throat.

'Go back and tell Arden that it all ends now. Do you understand that?' The man tried to swallow as he nodded. 'Go.'

He scurried off, glancing over his shoulder as he tried to make sure it wasn't a trick.

All done in seconds. Barely any noise. No one had pulled back the shutters to stare. Maybe they felt it was safer not to know.

'Do you think he'll stop?'

'No.' Simon shook his head. 'If they'd killed me here they could have had my keys and been inside the house in a moment.' He rubbed his temples. 'Thank you.'

'Did you know they were there?'

'Yes, but two against one . . .' He gave a wan smile. 'You made it easier.'

'Do you need me tomorrow?' Jane asked.

He shook his head. 'I should be fine. There's nowhere important I need to be.'

Simon watched as she wandered off. A few seconds, then he blinked and couldn't see her any more. Her talent. One of them, at least. He might have been able to beat both the men. But they could easily have overwhelmed him; he was still too slow. He was angry at himself; he should have recovered by now. He was furious at his body for letting him down and failing him. But he might as well have been howling at the moon for all the good it would do.

Safe, with all the doors bolted and the shutters closed, he drank a tot of brandy. The blood was still roaring through his body. He was exhausted, but until he calmed, he knew he wouldn't sleep. No sense in waking Rosie to tell her what had happened; morning would be soon enough.

At least there was one small piece of goodness from the evening. He'd seen Jeb Easby at the glee club and the man told him that Seaton had kept his word. A handsome sum to him and the Hardys. It could never replace their dead children, but it would make life a little easier.

Simon rubbed his fingertips across the grain of the table. Arden had followed through on his warning. This one had failed. But he'd keep trying. Sooner or later he was bound to succeed.

TWENTY

'We need to keep the doors locked,' he told Rosie. A chilly morning as the fire began to take hold in the range. He'd laid out everything that had happened the night before. 'If you answer it, keep a knife in your hand.'

'All right.' She agreed immediately, mouth hard.

'When you go anywhere with the boys, keep them close.'

'They'll hate that. You know how they like to run around.'

'I do.' He covered her hand with his own. 'But we need to do this. Until things are resolved. Arden's son is dead and he's going to take his revenge on everyone involved. What better way than on our boys?'

'He'll have to kill me first,' she said.

That was the truth.

* * *

Jane checked on Mrs Shields. The woman was in her bed, sound asleep. Breathing steadily and evenly, none of the rasping and wheezing that had troubled her during the wet spell. The dry cold of this snow might not be good for much, but it helped her.

The house was secure, the fire banked. As she settled under the blankets, Jane thought about tonight's attack. Well placed, so close to Simon's house; he'd been right about that. But the ones who tried were amateurs. The kind of hard men who were four a penny, strutting around in the beershops, muscled and boasting, ready for a fight after a few drinks. No skills and little courage, only strength and brutality.

If Arden was using men like that it meant he hadn't found anyone to replace Perkins. No one with the ability of Riley the knife man. Sooner or later, though, he'd come up with someone quick and talented. A fighter who could think. After that . . .

No. She pushed it from her mind. So much could happen.

Slowly, the warmth of the bed crept through her body. She felt cosy, safe. Nothing bad could touch her here, Jane thought as she drifted into sleep.

She was out early. The snow had finally stopped, a good eight inches of it covering the ground now. It was impossible to judge where pavement ended and road began. Not that it mattered; beyond a few handcarts, there was no traffic. Precious few people braving the cold, either. A pair who'd struggled in through the countryside drifts with baskets on their backs set up at the market. High prices to make the trip worthwhile. But they were busy. All they'd have to carry home would be empty sacks.

The butcher on Timble Bridge always gave her good measure for the money, sometimes throwing in a little extra: a kidney, or a scrap of calf's liver. Keeping his steady customers sweet.

She'd just come out, arm weighed down with her purchases, when the feeling arrived again. Moving up her spine, making her draw in her breath. Jane moved the bag to her left hand, reached under her cloak to the pocket of her dress and took firm hold of the knife handle.

Someone was there. Her father? Possibly. Or a man sent by Arden? Whoever it was, she needed to be ready. Jane walked as if she was unaware, stopping to glance in shop windows or give a coin to a beggar or a street child. Charity, but more than that. She'd add a whispered word to look if anyone was following her.

Near the top of Lands Lane, a girl appeared. Dirty hand outstretched, face staring up hopefully. Woollen stockings that were more hole than yarn, a cotton dress and worn clogs.

'Charlie said to tell you there was a man following you. Older, got a bandage round his hand.'

Jane nodded, counting out coins. Probably more than the girl had seen in her life.

'Share it with him,' she said. 'Get yourself something hot and a place indoors for tonight.' She glanced at the ragged figure and added another sixpence. 'Some new stockings and a coat.'

'Thank you, Miss.' The girl stared at the money in disbelief, then closed her small fist and ran off in case Jane changed her mind.

Her father was still in Leeds. She'd deal with that later. Maybe he already knew where she lived. If not, she couldn't risk leading him to Mrs Shields's house. Instead, she cut through the ginnels and courts until she was certain she'd shaken him off. The only person who could have followed her was one who'd used the streets to stay alive.

Joseph Truscott didn't seem to believe that Leeds might yet be the death of him.

Jane cooked. Strange to imagine that she'd ever do simple, ordinary things like this. Cleaning, washing. All the things girls learned but she'd barely been taught by her mother. Mrs Shields had tried to teach her to sew, but her fingers fumbled with a needle as she tried to darn a stocking. It made no sense; with a knife, Jane was precise and deadly. Try to mend a seam, though, and the thread caught or the point wouldn't push through the fabric.

Soon enough she'd need to decide what to do about her father. For today she was determined to enjoy an afternoon of peace.

Simon walked. He felt safe enough in the daytime, armed and alert. The snow was still crisp and the air held a brisk freshness. Even with the manufactories working, churning smoke into the sky, Leeds felt oddly calm and peaceful.

Very few people were around. No traffic in or out of town,

the roads blocked, too dangerous for coaches and wagons. Up at the Talbot, Barnabas Wade was trying to part travellers from their money. As soon as he saw Simon, he gave a tiny shake of his head. Not now.

Mudie sat in his printing shop, making changes to a sheet in front of him.

'I might as well not have bothered opening today,' he said as Simon entered. 'No trade, unless you want something printed.'

'Go home, then.'

'We don't all have the luxury of being thief-takers,' Mudie told him. 'Someone might come through that door offering the kind of business to keep me afloat for a year.' He sighed, picked up a small glass of brandy and drank it off. 'Then again, I could stop dreaming.'

'Heard much gossip?' He didn't think anyone had mentioned last night's attack; Mudie would already have been asking about it. But there might be vague words floating out there.

A shake of the head. 'Who from? There's hardly a soul to be seen.' His eyes twinkled. 'Unless you know some, of course.'

'No. My life is calm. I want to keep it that way for now.'

'Still recovering, Simon?'

'Getting there,' he replied. It was largely true, at least. Getting there.

The days passed, close to a week. Two small jobs, both completed in a morning. Simple thefts, everything returned. All the time he was outside, Simon kept glancing over his shoulder, wary of an attack that never happened. His nerves hung on edge.

He was worried for himself, but even more for Rosie and Richard and Amos.

Life drifted by. Cold clung to the town and the snow stayed on the ground. Smoke turned it black and gritty and feet wore it smooth and slick.

He went to the glee club again, with Jane waiting outside.

Jeb Easby came and sat on the bench beside him.

'How are things at Seaton's mill?' he asked him.

'From all I hear, much the same. New overseers, same discipline. That won't change.'

'What about you?'

'Took that money Seaton paid us and we're going to open a small shop.' He grinned; the smile made him look ten years younger. 'Be our own bosses. Maybe I can give the children something to inherit, who knows? It's not like having Jacob, but . . .'

His death had given the family a chance. A future.

'What's Mr Hardy doing?'

'Already packing up to go back to Ripon. As soon as the roads clear, they'll be gone. He's going to buy a smallholding and make his money that way. You did a little good, Mr Westow.'

It gave him some heart. But it didn't stop the fear rising as he walked home. Jane was there, he knew it, even though she stayed out of sight. But all it took was one swift blow and he'd be dead.

No trouble, not even a whiff of it. At the door he turned. For a second, just long enough for him to spot her, Jane emerged from the shadows before melting away again.

A little good, he thought as he sat at the kitchen table. The singing at the club still rang in his ears. But he couldn't do enough, he couldn't help everyone in the factory. The price the Hardys and the Easbys had paid for their fortune was far too high.

Simon couldn't change things. What he'd wrung from Seaton wouldn't be repeated. The man would likely be overjoyed if Thomas Arden succeeded in having Simon killed.

A blood covenant; he remembered the words Arden had used. Hurt one and you hurt the other. He had two opponents. If he defeated one, the other would be waiting for him. At the moment Arden was sitting back, waiting for Simon to lower his guard. He couldn't afford to do that and it was wearing him down.

He felt frayed. When he looked at Rosie, he could see the tension on her face. The boys were chafing at all the restrictions. They wanted to be off with their friends, throwing snowballs or shooting downhill on a sledge, all the things children did in weather like this. The children from families with money, at least. For far too many, every daylight hour was spent working.

At least his body was healing. Rest helped, good food and early nights. Simon felt stronger, more alert. But still he tired easily, appreciated a rest during the day. It was as if the illness couldn't bear to completely loosen its grip and let him go.

*   *   *

The knock on the door roused him. Mid-morning, the reflection of grubby snow-light through the window gave a strange brightness. Simon had read his way through the *Mercury* and the *Intelligencer*. Now he was going back through the advertisements in case he'd missed someone offering a reward for missing items. Nothing. This weather kept honest folk at home and thieves closer to their own hearths.

He was wary as he turned the key, standing back so he wouldn't be thrown to the ground in case someone rushed the door. Knife in his hand. In front of him stood a meek man who flinched at the sight of the blade.

'Forgive me,' Simon said. 'Sometimes I need to be careful.'

The man nodded, then asked, 'You're a thief-taker?'

'I am.'

'I've had something stolen and I need it returned. I'll pay well.' There was a desperate edge to his voice that sounded genuine.

'You'd better come in and tell me.'

Simon locked the door again and guided him through to the kitchen.

'What's been taken, Mr . . .?'

'Harding, sir. My name's Gideon Harding. It's a bundle of letters. I employed a maid for a few weeks and she took them. I suspect she's going to try and sell them back to me.' He looked down at the table and reddened.

'I see.'

Harding shook his head briskly. 'No, you don't. They're extremely sensitive.'

Simon studied the man. He had a plain, open face, hardly handsome, with a pale complexion and dark hair. Well-cut clothes, but no air of real money. A man who could manage to do no more than bob along in the current without working.

'What's in them isn't my business.'

Harding explained that he lived on the road towards Woodhouse Moor. Simon knew the house, he'd passed it dozens of times. A month before, Harding had taken on a new girl after the last one left to marry. She'd vanished just the day before, taking a silver salt and pepper set, along with the bundle of letters, carefully tied with string.

'I'd just paid her wages for the month, so she has some money.'

'Can she read?' Simon asked.

Harding frowned. 'I've no idea. Does it matter?'

'Maybe not,' Simon told him. 'Is there any reason the servant should believe the letters were important?'

'They were in a drawer with other papers.'

'How many letters in the bundle?'

'Twelve . . . perhaps fifteen.'

Curious. They were important, he kept them close and wanted them back, but for some reason Harding was unsure how many there might be.

'What's the servant's name?'

'Clarissa Lumley. She told me that her family lives on Quarry Hill.'

'Do you know whereabouts?'

Harding shook his head. 'I never asked. It didn't matter.'

'My fee depends on the value of the items,' Simon told him.

'I understand that. The salt and pepper have a little worth. But it's the letters that are important to me. I'll pay you well for the letters if you return them all.'

All? The man had just said he didn't know how many there were. It made him cautious. Simon wanted to be working, to be doing something instead of being stuck at home behind a locked door. But this seemed too convenient, too suspicious. His instincts told him to walk away. If this was a real job, there would be others in Leeds who'd take it.

'I'm sorry, Mr Harding, I don't think I can serve you well on this.'

'Why not?' He sounded affronted at the rejection. 'You were recommended to me.'

'I don't have time at the moment,' Simon said and dared the man to call him a liar.

'In this weather?'

'Even in this weather.' Simon rose. 'Now, if you'll forgive me. You might have more luck with Will Oughton. He has rooms on Vicar Lane.'

Simon watched from the bedroom window as Harding trudged along Swinegate. No one was waiting for him, and he still seemed to be a sad, retiring man.

As soon as Rosie returned, he left. Careful, aware of everyone around him as he hurried up towards the Head Row and Green Dragon Yard. The little cottage hidden behind the wall was another world.

Jane in an apron, her hair up in a mob cap; it wasn't a sight he ever expected to see. Her cheeks were flushed and pink from washing and wringing out the linen. As she worked, Simon explained what he needed.

'You go, child,' Mrs Shields said. 'I can finish this.'

Each time he saw the old woman she looked less substantial, as if a heavy gust might blow her over. But there was warmth on her face, and real caring for Jane in her eyes. They made a good pair, each looking after the other in different ways.

Ten minutes and they were moving. A few more people out today, taking their chances in the snow. Heavy wagons lumbered along the roads. The air stank from smoke and soot.

'See what you can find out about this Gideon Harding. Keep watch on his home for a few hours. I'll look into the servant. We'll meet back at the house at dusk.'

A nod and she'd gone. Harding knew Simon's face, but not hers. Maybe he was wrong; perhaps the man was all he claimed. But something inside kept tugging at him, telling him no.

Two hours on Quarry Hill established one thing: no family named Lumley lived there. Never had, according to the old women with long memories and wicked minds. Still, the servant could have lied to her master, planned a theft from the very start. She wouldn't have been the first.

He went further, out along Mabgate and down in the other direction towards Fearn's Island and the river, but it was all guesswork. By the time he walked home in the gloom, he was convinced that none of Harding's story had been true.

The shadows were long, the temperature falling rapidly. He was weary. But careful. Arden wanted him away from the safety of the house. Outside, he became a target. His hands were hidden away in the pockets of his greatcoat, each one gripping the hilt of a knife. He was listening for any noise that seemed out of the ordinary; difficult with this snow packed down on the ground. His eyes flickered from side to side, watching, assessing.

But there was no threat. Simon looked around once again as

he unlocked the door. The only thing to see was the first few flakes of fresh snow beginning to fall.

Jane was already there, sitting at the table watching the boys eat. They attacked their food like animals, always hungry and wanting more. Growing lads, he thought, and didn't begrudge them a bite. He, Rosie, Jane, they'd all known empty bellies and gnawing hunger. It didn't build character, it didn't make you stronger.

He was grateful to finally sit down and pour himself a mug of beer from the jug.

'Did you give me the right address?' Jane asked.

'Yes,' Simon replied. 'He was quite specific about the house.'

'He doesn't live there. It belongs to a family called Ogden. No one's ever heard of Harding.'

At least his senses had been right. 'It was the same with the servant on Quarry Hill.'

'What do we do now?'

For a moment, Simon was tempted not to do anything. Arden's trick had failed, he wasn't going to be able to trap them. Then he gave a grim smile.

'Let's find out who this man called Harding really is. It struck me that he might be an actor. I don't know why, he seemed to be used to pretence.'

Rosie stood. 'Simon . . .' she began, but he shook his head.

'Don't worry, I'm not going to hurt him. Just send him back to Arden with a message.' He spread his arms. 'We can't spend the rest of our lives in here. We have to take the fight to him.'

'That isn't a battle you can win,' she warned. 'Not going against him and Seaton together.'

'Then we'll have to arrange things so we can.'

TWENTY-ONE

There was only one theatre in Leeds. It lay south of the river, an old building on Hunslet Lane. Jane had passed it often, but never gone inside. She had no desire to hand over money to watch people being someone else; she saw enough of that in her work. She couldn't read the playbills, found no pleasure in words.

Now she stood across from the entrance, watching men come and go, carrying supplies. Simon had given her the description of the man who called himself Harding. If he really was an actor, she'd spot him here.

She found a small, sheltered space, out of the cold wind and under an overhang of roof, free of trampled snow. More was falling. It had begun as she arrived at Simon's house. Slowly, lazy flakes at first, but heavier now, lying and gathering, turning the world white again. It was growing harder to remember when it had been any other way.

Jane ran her fingers up and down the ladder of scars on her forearms. Reminders of all her failures and frustrations. Her own history.

Lights outside the building broke the dusk. She watched people arrive for the performance, all on foot. Not so many tonight.

She was still there in the same place as the audience left, and when the actors emerged a little later. He was easy to pick out from Simon's description. But the meekness had gone, replaced by an arrogant manner, waving away company to walk back alone to his lodgings.

Simple to follow him. He didn't suspect a thing. Back into Leeds and a house on Kirkgate. She waited until a light glowed in the attic and a hand closed the shutters against the night.

'Tomorrow,' Simon told her, when she reported to him. 'In the morning. He's an actor, he won't be up too early.'

A check on Mrs Shields after she arrived home. Home. The word still made her smile with gratitude. The old woman was comfortable in her bed. Jane locked and bolted the door, made sure the windows were secure, then settled down. It had been a long evening, her legs were aching from standing so long in the cold. But no more sign of her father. He'd appear, she was certain of that. And she would be decisive next time.

'We won't go in,' Simon said. 'No fuss, no landlady who would remember us.'

They stood in the opening to a court, watching the house

across the street. The snow had stopped again during the night, pillowed thick and soft on the ground. Leeds was gloriously hushed. Even the sound of the factories was muffled. Simon had watched men struggling along the pavements on their way to work. The weather didn't offer ordinary folk any rest.

He raised his head, then quickly ducked back as the shutters in the attic were pulled open.

'Not long now.'

'What are we going to do?' Jane asked

'Stop him before he can reach the theatre. Then we'll have a word. Give him the message to pass on.'

They were ready. Not following as soon as the man left, but slipping through the courts, over the bridge well ahead of him, and waiting round a corner as he passed.

'Mr Harding,' Simon called. The man hesitated and turned his head, suddenly worried as he noticed Simon. 'Quite a surprise to see you again. Do you have business over here?'

He looked ready to run, but Jane stood a few yards ahead of him.

'Full credit to you. You gave a good performance. Just not convincing enough.'

After a small moment of indecision, the man gave a nod of defeat.

'Who paid you?' Simon asked in a genial voice. He took a pace forward, close enough to be menacing, as Jane approached from the other side.

'Someone at the theatre asked if I wanted to earn a little extra.' The words came reluctantly. 'No actor would turn that down. He said it would be easy.'

'Who?'

Another hesitation, then: 'His name's Martin Vaughan. He runs the place. He gave me an address.'

'In Park Square?'

'Yes.'

'Did the man there give his name?'

'I never asked him. He told me what to do, what I had to say, and told me to come back when it was done.' He looked up at Simon, his face filled with regret. 'All I wanted was to have a little more in my pocket.'

Simon brought out a gold sovereign. He'd taken it from the secret drawer in the stairs this morning. Now he held it up, the colour glowing in the light to catch the actor's attention.

'You're going to make a little more.' Not an offer. An order.

The man stared at the coin with greedy eyes. 'What do you need me to do?'

'Go back to Park Square, to the same house. I have a speech for you to deliver. It's only short, it should be easy enough for an actor. When you come out, the money will be waiting. What's your name? Your real name?'

He stood a little taller, 'Ralph Willoughby. I—'

'You'd do well to listen as we walk, Mr Willoughby. The only part to concern you now is the one you're about to play.'

Away from view, they watched as Willoughby left Arden's house, looked around nervously, then picked the coin from the cleft of a tree before hunching his shoulders and hurrying away like a nervous animal.

'Will it help us?' Jane asked.

'I don't know,' Simon replied. 'But it puts a little more pressure on Arden.' He pursed his lips. 'Have you heard if he has a new bodyguard yet?'

'Nobody's mentioned one.'

'Good. I'm going to follow him for a while.'

Jane studied his face. 'Why?'

'To keep him unsettled. I won't come close. I'll only do it long enough for him to know. So he'll be aware that we can be there whenever we choose.'

'He can hire men easily enough.'

'I've no doubt he will,' Simon grinned. 'But before he does we'll remind him that he can be a target, too.'

Doubtfully, she nodded. 'What did you have that actor tell him?'

'It wasn't much. Just that each play has its ending and every day its sunset.'

She frowned. 'Do you think Arden listened?'

Simon shrugged. 'Probably not. But he'll have heard, and maybe he'll remember.'

* * *

It was simple enough to talk about following Arden, but harder to accomplish. Simon waited and watched until dark, but the man never emerged from his front door. Hard to blame him in this weather. No carriages and coaches on the roads and he probably had little need to walk anywhere.

As evening fell, Simon stirred at a noise. The knife was ready in his hand as Jane appeared.

'I thought I could follow you home,' she said. 'Just in case.'

'He hasn't shown his face today. I'll try again tomorrow.'

Only a few straggling figures on the streets around them. After standing for so long, walking warmed him, but not as much as the heat from the range in his kitchen.

Tomorrow he'd do things differently. No hiding; he'd stand where Arden couldn't help but see him. Make it blatant. A day or two of that should have an effect.

He picked a spot where Arden would notice him every time he looked out of his window. He'd be a burr in the man's side. Today, then tomorrow. After that . . . let him wonder and worry for a little while.

By the time the light began to fade he was chilled through to the marrow. Earlier, Jane had brought him some food from Kate the pie-seller, still wrapped, its warmth so welcome. She stayed for ten minutes, long enough for him to enjoy the company, then drifted away again.

Simon straightened as the door to Arden's house opened. He reached for his knife, fingers stiff and cold as he grasped the handle.

Arden wore a heavy coachman's caped greatcoat that reached almost to his ankles, leather gloves and a tall hat. He marched directly across the square, glaring, arms swinging by his sides.

'What the hell do you think you're doing, Westow? Every time I glance up I see you staring at my house.'

'I gave your friend, Mr – what was his name, Harding? Willoughby? – a message for you.'

Arden shrugged. 'Words.'

'I'm here so you know they have a meaning.' Simon tilted his head towards the western horizon. 'Sunset. The end of the day.'

A small bow and he walked away, listening closely in case Arden rushed after him. Simon smiled to himself. He'd burrowed under the man's skin. He'd be in Arden's mind now. Tomorrow he'd take up his position again. Stay for an hour or two then leave. Return at different times during the day. Arden would be there, watching and waiting for him to appear; he wouldn't be able to help himself.

'It's all well and good,' Rosie said. 'But what does it *achieve*? For all you know, he could be out right now, hiring more men to kill us. All you're offering him is a bigger reason to do it.' She exhaled and shook her head. 'Why, Simon? What's the point of it? You're acting more like Richard or Amos than someone who's supposed to be grown up.'

The boys raised their heads for a moment as they heard their names, then returned to their game.

'Why? We've reached a stalemate with him. You know that. He's after revenge for his son. He'd see you and the boys dead without a single regret.'

'I hadn't forgotten.' Her voice was dry. 'Believe me.'

'He's not going to have the chance.'

'Isn't he? We're not just going up against him, though, are we? It's Seaton as well. What was that pact they talked about?'

'A blood covenant.'

'That's it.'

'Seaton's hidden away on his farm. I can reach Arden. He's here in town.'

'Fine. Even if you somehow manage to deal with one, the other will still be waiting.'

He smiled, trying to give her some reassurance. 'We'll face that when it happens.' Simon turned towards the boys. 'Right, it's past your bedtime. Upstairs. Now!' he added as they didn't move.

The woman lost her balance in the snow, her foot sliding from under her. As she passed, Jane reached across and grabbed her above the elbow to steady her.

'Thank you, pet.' The woman's expression was a mix of gratitude and relief. 'I don't know what would have happened if I'd taken a tumble. I might have broken something and never got up again.'

But Jane was barely listening. It was there again, the feeling that someone was behind her. She turned her head quickly, hoping to catch a face, a shape, but all she saw was the gloom of dusk.

'I'll be right now, pet,' the woman told her. 'Thank you again.'

She let go, moving off into the growing darkness. It was him, she thought. Her father. Already the sense was fading, growing softer. He'd passed close; he might not have even realized she was there.

Simon was in Park Square before dawn. A stop at the coffee cart on Briggate had warmed him inside, and a slice of bread and dripping put a lining on his belly. Now he stood in Park Square. Simon would be the first thing Arden saw after his servant pulled back the shutters.

He was certain to look. Simon knew that all the way to his core. The man would probably have had disquieting dreams about him. That was a start. It was time to do more. After an hour, he left. Maybe Arden would believe he'd had enough of the cold. The bitterness had eaten into his bones, but Simon was here to protect his family. He'd return.

A stop at Beckett's Bank, then a brisk stroll out past Fearn's Island and up Cavalier Hill to force the blood through his body. By the time he reached the house he could feel the sweat starting to trickle down his back. Stopping for a moment, he felt drained. He'd pushed himself. His health still wasn't quite back.

Perkins was in his chair, bad leg raised on a stool, the ruined knee firmly bandaged. He had a fresh bottle of laudanum at his side, but this time his eyes were clear and his face was alert. The bayonet had gone from the bed, back in the scabbard that hung from his belt.

'You don't look like you're here to gloat and you don't have the girl, so you haven't come to finish me off.' He snorted. 'That means you must want something.'

Simon nodded. 'Very perceptive. How much do you hate Arden?'

'Enough. He dropped me without a penny and I'd served him well for years.'

'Can you walk?'

Perkins raised an eyebrow. 'A little more than I could last

week. I can drag myself around if needs be. But not far and not fast, and I have to take care.' He stared at Simon. 'Why do you want to know?'

Simon reached into his waistcoat pocket. He brought out a piece of paper and unfolded it with a flourish, holding it so the other man could see. Beautifully handwritten and signed, a banknote in the sum of ten pounds. A small fortune.

'This would keep you for quite a while. Do you want to earn it?'

'That depends.' His voice was full of suspicion. 'What do you expect me to do?'

'No killing. No violence. I promise you that.'

Perkins's eyes were fixed on the money. He ran his tongue around his lips. 'Go on.'

'Then listen . . .'

Simon stood, looking across Park Square at Arden's house. Beside him was Perkins the bodyguard, resting his weight on a crutch. The man's mouth was a straight line, set firm against the pain. This was their agreement: for the next three days, Perkins would spend three hours a day here; in return he'd earn his money.

Even ruined and hobbling, Perkins looked fierce; with the bayonet dangling from his belt, he was dangerous, deadly.

The sight of Simon would have worried Arden. Having Perkins here, too – even in this condition – should leave him fearful. That was the gamble.

It didn't work that evening. He saw the silhouette in the window, standing and watching for two full minutes before the shutters closed. Nothing the next morning, either. They stood, wind-scoured and bitterly cold, breath clouding as soon as they exhaled. Simon's face felt as if someone had scrubbed it with ice.

'You learn to ignore the weather,' Perkins told him. 'Just keep going. You don't have any choice in the army. I had to keep others moving. Marching, always ready to fight.' Still, he grimaced as he shifted his weight and rested heavily on the crutch.

In the late afternoon they arrived again. Simon could smell the rum on Perkins's breath, the contented glaze of laudanum in his eye. What did it matter if it helped to keep the man warm? The snow was still clinging hard to the ground, no sign of a thaw in the air.

They'd been standing for ten minutes. Perkins had taken out his pipe and was attempting to light it.

'He's coming out of the house.'

Warmly dressed, with a pair of polished riding boots, Arden strode out, quickly covering the ground across the square until he was just five yards from them. Far enough away to be safe.

'What do you want, Westow?'

'Want?' Simon asked.

'Want. The neighbours have been talking. They're not happy with you being here all the time.'

'Blaming you, are they?' Perkins said. 'Too scared to come over here and ask for themselves?'

Arden tried to ignore him, shifting to face Simon. 'I'm going to ask again: what do you want?'

'An end to things. You're the one with revenge on his mind.'

'You told Collins that my Franklin had killed his son.'

'Why wouldn't he?' Perkins answered, his voice raw, loud enough to carry a good distance. 'Your boy came and asked me the best way to do it.' He stared at Arden, lips curling as he saw the surprise on the man's face. 'Perhaps your precious lad forgot to tell you that.'

'Why should I believe you?'

But his question was too late. Simon could see it in his expression: Arden knew he was hearing the truth.

'You've given yourself the answer.' Perkins waited for a heartbeat. 'Found a new bodyguard yet?'

'That stopped being your business a while ago.'

Perkins grinned. 'A good fighter with a brain is difficult to find. Remember that. And if you send someone after me, he'll need to be the best. Even crippled I'm better than most you're going to find.'

Arden snorted. 'You were beaten by a girl.'

'I was. She did something no man has managed. If she sets her sights on you, you'd do well to keep that in mind.'

Simon took a breath. It was time to step between the pair of them before the insults grew into something more dangerous.

'Do we have an end to things?'

'No,' Arden told him. His eyes flickered across to Perkins. 'There's only going to be one end.'

No more words. He turned on his heel and walked away.

'We've got a war,' Perkins said.

'We?' Simon raised an eyebrow.

'We. If he can, he'll kill me, too.' He gave a wry smile. 'You'd best warn that girl of yours that we're on the same side now.'

TWENTY-TWO

One day a man was your enemy. The next time you looked, he was your friend. Things turned and twisted and she didn't understand them. Jane had listened as Simon told her, but all she could think of was Perkins wanting to kill her. Battling him had been life or death, and now she was supposed to stand shoulder to shoulder with him. The world was a strange, ugly place and none of it made sense.

She left the house, pacing off her anger along Swinegate. The length of Briggate, all the way to the Head Row, then beyond, into the small cluster of new streets where Ann Carr had her religious mission to help poor children.

The dirty snow on the pavements had been pounded down by boots of men trailing to work then home again.

A hundred yards farther and she was among fields when the snowfall lay unbroken, as if she'd somehow crossed into another world. She glanced over her shoulder to make sure Leeds was still there, that she hadn't dreamed the place.

A few people had come along here, but looking out ahead, there was no one to be seen. Just emptiness. A breeze lifted a few flakes of snow into the air, scattering them. She breathed deep. The air was clean and sharp in her lungs.

At least being out here took her thoughts away from enemies and new friends for a few minutes.

Jane turned to go home. The cold had burrowed under her cloak and into her flesh. But as she tightened her shawl around her head, she felt something. No mistaking it. Someone was watching her. By habit, she turned the gold ring on her finger.

Her eyes flickered as she walked, trying to spot him. It wasn't her father; this sensation was different, raising the hair on her arms. A warning. She gripped her knife, keeping it ready. Out here there were no streets or buildings to hide her. Everything was open. She was exposed. Run? Maybe, but that was dangerous. Who knew what lay under the snow? It was all too easy to slip and fall. Once she was down, she was a target, easy to kill.

Where was he?

Still there. She could feel him, the sense was growing stronger.

Then he appeared, sliding out from behind the trunk of a tree. A dark shape silhouetted against the white all around.

He wasn't a big man. She didn't recognize his face. Worn clothes, the brim of his hat pulled down to hide his eyes. No knife in his hand.

He was here to rape, not sent to kill. He'd probably seen her wandering on her own and decided she was a defenceless girl.

Jane took a breath. She'd hurt men like this before and never felt a twinge of regret.

He ambled towards her, smiling and showing brown teeth with plenty of gaps.

'It's not a day to be out on your own. This is the type of weather when you need a cuddle to keep you warm.'

Jane showed the hilt of her knife. He had the good sense to hesitate and hold up his hands.

'Now, now, you don't need that.' His mouth made a thin line. 'I'm not going to hurt you.'

She took a step closer. His eyes glittered and he licked his lips. Maybe he truly believed no woman could resist him. That he was God's gift. Jane could smell the brandy on his breath. The false courage.

'That's right, girl, just come here. Keep on coming. You and me, we can have some fun.'

'Go,' she told him. A single word, the only warning she was going to give.

'Don't be like that.' He opened his hand. Suddenly he lunged forward to grab her.

She could see everything; it was right there on his face. All the lust and anticipation. She'd spotted what he was going to do long before he started to move. Her blade flashed towards his head. He tried to duck away but Jane was too quick.

For a moment he stood, mouth gaping, eyes wide in horror. Then his left hand slowly reached towards his face, fingers groping for the missing ear and coming away covered in blood. He stared at his hand in disbelief.

She took another pace forward. The man backed off as his right hand fumbled for his knife. But he was too slow, in pain, uncertain. She sliced all the way down his forearm, cutting through his coat, his shirt, his skin as if they were nothing. Blood began to flow, dripping down to turn the snow red by his feet.

Jane raised the knife again. This time he flinched.

'If I use it again, I'll kill you,' she said. Her voice was calm, utterly matter of fact.

He ran, stumbling, falling, looking back in fear as he scrambled to his feet then dashed away. His left hand was still clamped tight against the hole in his head, right arm hanging useless.

Jane waited until he was out of sight, then rubbed her knife clean. His ear still lay in the snow. She kicked it away. He'd never be able to forget what happened today. It would be there, facing him each time he looked in the mirror. With luck, from now on every woman he saw would scare him, afraid of the damage she might do.

She walked, not letting herself think about it; the whole thing had barely lasted a few seconds. There was always some man who saw a woman alone as a chance to show his power. Then there were those who'd been given money to kill. She needed to stay alert.

Home was warm. Mrs Shields was in the kitchen, making stew from a rabbit Jane had bought at the butcher. The old woman was talkative, plenty of colour in her cheeks, gliding easily around the house.

Later, after they'd eaten and the dishes were washed and scoured, Jane took out her knife and began to run it across the whetstone. Stroke after stroke after stroke in a regular, lulling rhythm that let her thoughts drift.

Eventually they came back to her father. Each time it was the same. Jane knew there was only one way that would end things and let her push it all into a room in her mind and lock the door forever. She knew every place in Leeds where she could make it happen without being seen. Then why was she reluctant to do it? Twice she'd had the chance and let him walk off, wounded and warned, but still alive.

Next time . . . easy to say, but hard to do.

'Child?'

She realized Mrs Shields was speaking to her. Jane stopped working the knife and lifted her head. The old woman gave a soft smile. 'Your hands started moving so fast I was worried you might hurt yourself.'

'I must have got carried away.' She ran her thumb along the edge of the blade. Sharp enough to slice the air. Exactly the way she needed it to be.

Whatever she did, the past would stay with her. All the pain, the hurt. Even when she'd told Mrs Shields everything that had happened when she was young, it hadn't taken away what she felt inside. There was no magic for that.

'Simon, can you really trust this man Perkins?' Rosie asked as they sat and ate hot porridge for breakfast.

'Yes,' he replied. 'I think I can, anyway.'

He hoped so, at least. Strange allies, perhaps, but the man's offer had seemed genuine. He was mercenary, but who was likely to hire a crippled bodyguard? If he was true to his word, Perkins would be in Park Square now, standing and watching Arden's house, worrying the man and angering all the neighbours. But Simon would wager good money that none of them would dare to come out and tell him to move.

It had given him the welcome chance to sleep later. He felt stronger, his limbs looser, his muscles more elastic. His mind was sharp. Once all this was done, perhaps he'd allow himself a break to heal fully.

When it was over.

If it ever ended.

He finished the last mouthful of porridge and pushed the bowl away.

'I need to work,' he said as he rose. A kiss for Rosie, tousling the boys' hair. 'Remember, door locked at all times,' he said.

'I haven't forgotten.' She moved her hand just enough to let him see the knife in her pocket. 'And if we go out, I won't let this pair out of my sight.'

Satisfied, he put on his heavy boots with the long hobnails. They gripped well on hard snow and ice. A thick greatcoat, gloves, hat. He was ready.

A check at Park Square. Exactly as they'd agreed, Perkins stood like a sentinel. On to the cottage behind Green Dragon Yard, where Jane was waiting.

They strolled out to Woodhouse Moor, the same clearing they'd used before, settling for an hour of knife practice. She seemed especially quick today, he thought. Eager. Even more dangerous than usual.

He had to be fast to counter her, never mind start an attack of his own. Her eyes drilled through him. Every move was exact. Pity anyone she faced with real anger in her heart, he thought.

After an hour he called time. Simon was panting, exhausted, his body damp with sweat.

'You were different,' he said as he slid his knife back into its sheath and wiped his face. 'What happened?'

She gazed down at the ground and shrugged. Maybe nothing, maybe something vital; whatever it was, Jane lived inside her secrets.

Later, not long before the parish church clock struck noon, Simon felt the first hint of a thaw. A change in the air, shifting to come up from the south, soft, not quite as raw against his skin. Perhaps the weather was beginning to turn. That would be welcome. If it didn't, winter in Leeds was going to be long and hard indeed.

There were only a few souls gathered around the old market cross at the top of Briggate. Men huddled deep into their coats, stamping around as they tried to keep warm. The corn market. But several farmers had been able to make it into Leeds to try and sell what they had in their stores.

Simon knew a few of them by sight, but he had to wait for the one he wanted. Cuthbert Young was deep in conversation with another man, nodding as he listened, then waving a finger to make a point of his own. Another two minutes and they'd finished. Young wore a broad smile.

'A profitable exchange?' Simon asked.

'With a little luck.' He was young for this business, still eager and hungry for success. The son of a farmer who owned land near Wetherby, Young had lived his life around crops and animals, and he possessed a useful talent for turning one penny into two, on his way to becoming a successful corn factor. 'In the market, are you, Simon? A hundredweight of wheat?'

Simon grinned. 'Only if it's made into loaves first. I want to ask you a few questions.'

Young held up his hands. 'I haven't stolen anything, Simon. Not even any hearts, more's the pity.'

'How about some hot food? You look like you could use it.'

For a moment, the man considered: the profit he might lose by not being here against a fully belly and time in a warm room.

'Go on, then. You can have a little of my wisdom in exchange for a meal.'

Young shook his head. 'I've never met the man, so all I know is what people tell me and the gossip.'

'But?' Simon asked. He'd seen the flicker of doubt cross the other man's face when he mentioned Seaton's name. The meal was eaten, pint pots emptied, a jug of coffee on the table. Just the two of them in a private parlour at the Rose and Crown. Young lit his pipe.

'He's not a natural farmer. He employs good people and that helps. They can tell him what needs doing. The thing is, Simon, you either have a feel for the soil or you don't.' His face turned serious. 'All the good farmers I know have that, on top of the desire to grow things.'

'Seaton doesn't possess it?'

'As I say, this is only what I've heard. He has the land, he has money and he wants to do it, but . . . he's a gentleman farmer. Strides around and dresses the part, gives his orders and believes he's important.'

Simon thought about his visit to Seaton's farm. That all fitted. The instructions, the careful way he clothed himself, how he kept himself apart from the real work.

'Is he married? I don't know a thing about him.'

'He was,' Young replied. 'I think his wife died in childbirth. The baby went out to a wet nurse but only survived a few weeks. You have to understand, Simon, that was a long time ago. I wasn't even born then.'

Death was everywhere. Bringing a new life into the world could put a woman in the grave. All the joy turned to sorrow in an instant.

'I don't think he makes much profit on the farm,' Young said. 'Very likely the lambs and the fleeces from his sheep keep it going. He doesn't have much growing, and by all accounts he doesn't keep many cattle. Someone could take that land and make much more of it.' He cocked his head. 'Why are you interested in him, anyway? Has he been stealing?'

'I was invited out to his farm.'

'Why?' Young's eyes narrowed with curiosity.

'To see a pig being slaughtered.'

'I don't under—'

'I won't try to explain. But it made me realize I know nothing at all about him.'

'I'm not sure anyone *knows* him,' Young said. 'Most farmers are social, they relish company, whether it's a drink or going to local balls. Seaton has a reputation for keeping to himself.'

That seemed to chime with the man he'd met. Reticent, uneasy around strangers, not addressing Rosie at all.

As they left the inn, Simon turned his head towards the soft breeze. Definitely a little warmer. If it lasted, maybe they really would see the end of this snow.

'The more I think about it,' Young said slowly, 'I don't understand how Seaton can make *any* profit on that farm. He'll be lucky to cover his costs. It's not a cheap business, no matter what you townsmen think.'

'I'll take your word for that.' Simon laughed. 'Mind you, you all seem well fed. It can't be that harsh.'

As he walked down Briggate, he heard the first hesitant drips of melting snow from the roofs.

He went out along Commercial Street, following it all the way to Park Square and spent an hour watching Arden's house. It gave him time to think about the things Cuthbert Young had told him. There wasn't too much. He didn't understand Seaton much more than when they'd sat down to eat. No obvious weaknesses, other than his farm. That was his life. The mill simply gave him the money to indulge his passion.

An hour and Simon vanished, to return a while before dusk. Perkins was already in the Square, leaning heavily on his crutch, his face creased with pain.

'I'm doing what I promised for your damned money.'

He needed to complain; it was a soldier's way, after all, and he'd never stop being one.

'Any sign of him today?'

'Nothing in the times I've been here. This cold weather is killing me.' He coughed, a heavy, throaty sound, and spat phlegm.

'It's starting to change. Another day or two and the world will look different.'

'How long do you intend to keep coming out here, Westow?'

'No more after today,' Simon answered. He'd mulled it over as he strolled from home. This had served its purpose. They'd unsettled Arden. When they stopped appearing, he'd wonder where they'd gone and what they were planning.

'What will you do if he sends someone after you?' Simon asked Perkins.

'Kill him,' the man answered. Not a scrap of feeling in his voice. 'Or he'll put an end to me. Either way, someone will die. Have you told that lass that I'm working with you?'

'She knows.'

Perkins inclined his head to the house across the square. 'What are you going to do next?'

'I don't know. Give me some ideas,' Simon said. 'You worked for him. How's he likely to act?'

'He'll be in a rage. We've been humiliating him in front of all the rich neighbours he likes to impress. He'll be planning something.' Perkins stared at him. 'Whatever it is, you'd better watch out.'

Simon nodded. 'What about you?'

'I've been looking out for myself since before you were born.'

How many had died because of Arden, he wondered as he walked home? George Collins, his father, Franklin Arden, Sebastian Ramsey. Four bodies in less than a month. Those were just the names he knew. Go back further and how high would the count reach? Maybe the preachers were right and God would have His reckoning. But in Leeds, Thomas Arden remained untouchable.

TWENTY-THREE

There was little choice at the market. Only two sellers had managed to struggle in. With the roads not yet open for carts, all they had was what they'd been able to load on the back of a packhorse. Jane selected a turnip, carrots, onions, a few potatoes and a cabbage and felt lucky to find that much. Another half-hour and customers would be going away empty-handed.

As she walked down Briggate she felt the change in the air and heard the drip of melting snow.

Jane turned on to Kirkgate. Her eyes searched for danger, taking in all the people. She kept her free hand in the pocket of her dress, ready to snatch out the knife. Arden was still a threat. Simon had come to the cottage the evening before with the warning. But she was always alert. For too many years she'd had to be aware of everything and ready to fight to stay alive.

She spotted the man but didn't think much about it as he walked towards her; just someone else on his way to work or home. Two yards from her he stopped, holding up a pair of empty hands with thick calluses on the palms.

'Miss . . .' he began. A quiet voice. Not a beggar; his clothes were worn, but far from ragged. He looked to be in his early thirties, wearing a deep frown. Something about the man's features seemed faintly familiar, although she knew she'd never spoken to him in her life.

'No,' she said and started to move around him.

'Please,' he said, careful to keep his hands where she could see them. He seemed innocuous, but Jane remained cautious. He might have an accomplice ready to steal her purse. 'A minute, that's all.'

'No charity,' she told him as she carried on walking.

He shook his head, keeping pace with her. 'I don't want any.' A gentle smile. 'Do you know me?'

'No,' she replied. 'Should I?'

'I'm your brother.'

The world stopped. She stood absolutely still, gazing hard into his face. Not believing, yet believing at the same time. He had no guile. As Jane looked, she could see it. The man was telling the truth. No wonder she'd imagined she might know him. But there was no trace of her mother, only a sense of her father in the eyes, the jut of his chin.

'But—' she began, and halted, unable to find words.

'Your half-brother. My mother died a year after I was born. Her sister and her husband raised me. Then your father met your mother . . .' He took a breath and shrugged. 'He used to come and visit me as much as he could when I was growing up. I was almost grown when he stopped. I didn't know why. He vanished. I didn't see him again until he came back to Leeds a few weeks ago. He found me and told me why he'd had to leave.'

His voice trailed away and he looked at her. He had an open face, she thought. Honest, hopeful. Whatever her father had told him, he'd believed it.

'Did he give you the truth?'

'Yes.' The man looked down at the floor. 'He admitted it all. Everything he did. But he said—'

She wasn't going to let him finish. No excuses; there weren't any. 'What do you want?'

'I saw what you did to him with the knife—'

Her anger rose. 'You never saw what he did to *me*. Him and my mother together.'

'He's sorry,' the man told her. His voice was calm and reasoned. 'I believe he means it. He didn't come to Leeds just to look for me. He wanted to ask you to forgive him.'

'He said that.' Her voice was ice. 'I told him to leave. There's no forgiveness for what he did. What my mother did.'

'But—'

'Did he send you?'

A short nod was his reply.

'Then go back and tell him nothing's changed. If he wants to live, he'd better leave Leeds.'

'He's my father, too,' the man said.

Jane looked at him, seeing something in his eyes. His need. 'Then I feel sorry for you.'

She began to walk away from him.

'You have two nieces and a nephew,' he called. 'Don't you want to know them?'

She kept on going, back straight, staring ahead. No, the only family she had was Mrs Shields. The old woman was all she needed. All she wanted. Catherine Shields was her harbour, her home.

Jane shopped at the butcher and made her way home, wary in case the man reappeared. She didn't doubt who he was, she believed he was telling her the truth. His truth. But they were words she didn't want to hear. She had no desire to know who the man was, to hear about his wife and children. He was nothing to her. A stranger, someone she'd never met before this morning. A face she'd never see again. Yet she knew that was a lie. He'd be there when she closed her eyes tonight.

He was blood, but he wasn't kin. He was Joe Truscott's son, sent out as her father's messenger. But there was no peace in her heart for the man who'd raped her and let her be thrown out to die on the streets. She'd survived by her own will, by the strength inside her.

She stood in the yard outside Mrs Shields's cottage, breathing deeply. The air was heavy with the stink of the town but it still cleansed her.

Simon slept and woke refreshed to the smell of dinner. Through the window he could hear the low trickle of water melting under the covering of snow. The weather was definitely changing.

He glanced up and down the street, his gaze stopping at an unfamiliar shadow. He knew every inch of Swinegate, each gate and roof and opening. This was new. Simon pulled back a little, out of sight but able to keep watch. A few seconds later and the shape shifted.

Someone was spying on his house.

In the kitchen he gave quick instructions to Rosie, then left through the back door, out of the yard, cutting through the courts and ginnels and yards until he came up behind the figure. A man. Wiry, fair hair that hung lank on to his shoulders. A long knife in a sheath on his leg. The kind of blade that would intimidate if he knew how to use it properly.

Simon waited. Then the man began to strain forward. Rosie must have opened the door and looked out, exactly as he'd asked.

Silently, he took three steps forward and laid the edge of his knife against the man's throat.

'If you don't want to die here, you'd better not move.'

Two movements and he'd disarmed the man, tossing the long knife behind him and feeling for others. Only one, tucked into the top of the boot. Gone.

'Arden's man?' Simon asked.

'Yes.' The word came out choked as the man tried to keep his head still.

'Are you here to kill me?' No response and Simon pushed the edge of the blade just deep enough to draw a tiny bead of blood from the man's neck. 'Well?'

'Any of you. Whoever I could hurt if I got the chance.' He closed his eyes. 'That's what he said. He'd pay me for whoever died.'

'Then you're in the wrong line of work,' Simon said. 'You're not good enough.' He brought his face close enough to smell the fear and see the whites of the man's eyes. 'Tell me: do you think you deserve to live? Should I let you go or drag you where no one goes and kill you?'

'Let me live.' He seemed to barely breathe the words, uttering them like a prayer. 'Please.'

Simon kept the knife against his throat. This man had just admitted he'd have killed Rosie or Amos or Richard. His family. And now he was begging to be allowed to walk away unhurt. As if murder was nothing.

He looked down. A dark patch on the man's trousers. He'd pissed himself with terror.

Simon could feel the man shaking and trying to hide it. Very slowly he eased his knife back from the man's neck. He had to stop himself from slicing through the man's skin. Putting an end to him. But he couldn't do it like this. He'd only killed once, and that had been when there was no other way to stay alive. Even for this . . . he couldn't.

Simon stepped back and the man crumpled to the floor as if someone had dropped him. Tears were running down his cheeks. Curled up, crying.

Jane would have been ruthless. She wouldn't have let him live. He wished he could be the same. Instead, he squatted and pulled the man's head back.

'Go and see Arden. I don't care if you have to crawl there. Tell him you failed.'

The man's eyes widened. 'I can't do that.'

'Then you'd better run. Far and fast. Make sure he doesn't catch you.' Simon turned away, then back again. 'I'm never going to see you here again.'

It was a command.

'Who was he?' Rosie asked.

'Arden's man.' He paused, pressing his lips together. 'Hunting all of us.'

'What did you do?'

'Sent him back.'

'Simon.' Her voice was a warning. Just like Jane, she'd have killed the man with no hesitation, no regrets. Left him for the rats and all the other creatures. Maybe it would have been for the best. But it was too late now.

Still, Arden had made his choice very clear.

It was going to end in blood.

Jane watched Simon pace around the parlour of Mrs Shields's house. He told her what happened, the bare, smooth bones of it. His body was tight and tense. Trying to control his anger, she thought.

'He'll send someone after you, too. Sooner or later, it's bound to happen,' Simon warned her and lowered his voice. 'Maybe both of you.'

'I'll be ready.' The old woman was in the bedroom, door tightly closed. 'I'll make sure I look after her.'

She didn't mention the man who'd tried to rape her. No need.

That was different, it didn't matter now. She'd already locked it away, just as she was trying to cram the news of a half-brother and his children into another of the rooms in her mind. But that refused to vanish so easily. It had overwhelmed her.

Until she moved into this house, she'd been alone for so long. No thought of any family. She didn't doubt the man was telling the truth. But he'd been poisoned by her father's words. He believed the lies and promises.

She couldn't.

'What about Perkins?' Jane asked.

'He's expecting something. He'll look after himself,' Simon answered after a moment's thought. 'I'm not sure he'd mind too much if he lost, as long as he did some damage on the way.'

Jane glanced at the bedroom door. Whatever happened, she'd make sure it didn't touch Catherine Shields. The woman had done so much; she couldn't repay her by bringing violence into this house.

'How are we going to stop Arden?' she asked.

Simon shook his head. 'I don't know.'

But she did. The man would have to die. It was the only answer.

By the time he came out into Green Dragon Yard, Simon felt drained. The surge that had carried him was ebbing to nothing. His body ached with tiredness. He wanted to go home, to close his eyes and rest. But there was still one more place he needed to visit. Always one more, he thought wryly. Always.

As he walked, he was aware of the flow of water. The drip had become a trickle. Bit by bit, the snow was vanishing.

George Mudie was reading a sheet he'd just printed, circling mistakes in the type. He put down the pen, took a sip of brandy and looked at Simon.

'What's happened?'

'Why? Have you heard something?'

'No. But I can see it in your face. It's either that or the sickness has caught up with you again.'

'I want you to do something.'

Mudie chuckled. 'Always the favour, eh, Simon?'

'Pass the word around that Arden sent someone to kill me and my family and I sent him crawling away.'

'Is it true?' All the humour had gone from his words. He took another small drink.

'Every word.'

'Did he hurt any of you?'

'No. But a lot of that was luck. I was glancing out of the window at the right time and crept up without the man noticing. I had an opponent with no skill. If I'd been up against someone better . . .

'Arden truly wants you and your family killed?'

'He's after whoever he can get. Me, Rosie, the boys. It doesn't matter to him.'

Mudie exhaled slowly. 'Attacking you is one thing. It comes with your work. But your wife and sons . . . people won't like that.'

Simon was banking on it. It was a weapon he could use. It might keep his family a little safer. Something to make people look at Thomas Arden in a different way, maybe even turn a few against him. Money could buy a great deal, but it couldn't overcome revulsion.

Mudie didn't waste time; Simon heard a version of it the next morning as he waited by the coffee cart. According to the gossip, Arden had arranged to have the twins snatched, but Simon had thwarted it. Then the speaker turned, saw him and reddened before moving on to another topic.

It was out there, moving around Leeds. The story had taken on a life of its own and nothing could stop it now. He smiled.

A long, deep sleep had restored him. If he dreamed, he didn't remember it. He'd been warm and cosy in the bed, Rosie beside him. Up early and ready for whatever Arden was preparing.

The air felt like autumn, not winter. As it should, he thought; they were still only in November. He felt the snow and ice crunch and give under his boots as he walked. Water had made runnels and streams that twisted and snaked down the road. Wet, glistening slates shone up on the roofs where the snow had slipped down. Another few days and there would only be memories of this around town. Very soon the coaches would be running again, bringing people and goods, news in the London papers. It was strange how quiet Leeds seemed without them and the other carts on the roads, how quickly they'd become used to it. Yet always there was the sound of the machines in the factories and the mills.

By midday the story had circulated all across Leeds. Arden would hear it and start hunting for the man he'd employed. Very likely he'd make the next move tomorrow. That offered one day of peace, at least. A chance to prepare.

He spent the morning going around the inns, standing quietly and listening as people talked. A little after ten, Simon found Barnabas Wade in the Talbot. He was showing a man figures scrawled on a piece of paper. But the customer kept shaking his head, finally walking away and leaving Wade to order a glass of rum.

'No luck?'

'A few have bought.' He downed the liquid in a single gulp. 'The trouble is, there are never quite enough, Simon.'

'You'll survive,' Simon said. It was a precarious life, but it seemed to suit him.

'It gets harder.'

Simon signalled for another drink and placed a coin on the table. 'You've managed all this time. If the thaw continues, you'll have fresh customers inside a week.'

'All show.' He gave a wan smile. 'I thought you'd seen through me years ago. I've been living on credit and luck. The problem is that both run out eventually.'

'How much do you need?'

Wade shook his head. 'More than I can repay, but I wouldn't take it from a friend.'

'Things will change.'

'Maybe.' He turned as a fresh face entered the inn. 'Maybe they will.'

He adjusted his stock and ran a hand through his hair. As he walked, he altered, exuding confidence, back straighter, frown turning to a smile. He greeted the stranger, took him by the arm and guided him to a table in the far corner, talking all the while.

Simon watched for a minute, then left, out into the fresher air. He'd always taken Wade as he presented himself. It went to show you could never really know another person. But there was nothing he could do to change things. Barnabas would struggle by with his lies. If not, there were jobs he could do. He'd been a lawyer until he was disbarred; others would employ him to work for them.

No matter, he thought. Time to go home and eat his dinner. After that, he and Rosie could take the boys out to enjoy the snow while it remained. They'd enjoy a little freedom, breathing space before Arden tried his next move.

Jane watched, curious, as Mrs Shields read a book. The old woman did it most evenings, sitting silent and turning the pages, as if she'd somehow lost herself in the story.

'Why do you like it?' she asked. Jane hadn't meant to speak, but the words seemed to arrive of their own accord. Anything to distract herself from thoughts of her father and the man who called himself her half-brother.

'Like what, child?' She closed the book, marking her place with a thumb as she held it on her lap.

'Doing that. Reading.'

Catherine Shields gave her gentle smile. 'I've always enjoyed it, ever since I was a girl. You've seen me doing it often enough.'

'I know, but . . .' She searched through her mind to find what she needed to ask. 'What does it do?'

The woman weighed her answer. 'Almost anything I want. With some books, I can learn things. Or there are others, like this.' She held it up. 'They tell stories to entertain and amuse. They can take me far away. And it's not just men who write. This one says by "a lady". Books can bring me different kinds of pleasure.'

'You can hear a storyteller on Briggate.'

'Oh, I know that, child. I've heard plenty of them in my time. Do you like them?'

'Sometimes,' Jane admitted. When she was younger, without a home, a few of the tales carried her away from the desperation of trying to live. They offered a brief taste of freedom.

'Books can do the same thing. But instead of hearing them once, you can read them over and over again.'

'Do they change each time?'

'No.' She laughed. 'No, child. Once they're printed, they always stay the same. In a book you can hear about places and people you'd never know otherwise.'

'Like that one?'

'Yes.'

'And you enjoy reading them again and again?' Jane asked.

'I do.' Mrs Shields sighed. 'It can feel like visiting an old friend.'

'But you have to know how to read.'

'Yes,' she agreed. 'You do. I could teach you, if you like.'

'How?' She didn't understand.

'The same way I was taught when I was small.'

'Is it hard?' Now the idea was there in front of her, Jane was scared by the thought of learning. What if she failed, if she couldn't do it? Without thinking, her fingertips ran over the line of scars going up her forearm.

'You already know words,' Mrs Shields told her. 'You can call things by their names. All you'd need to do is recognize those on a page. Here, I'll show you.' She flicked through the pages until she found what she sought. 'Here, where we live, what do we call it?'

Jane glanced around at the walls, the windows. 'A house?'

'Yes. Now look here, that word. It's house.'

She stared, but she couldn't connect those letters to the building. Mrs Shields placed a bony finger on the page, sliding it along as she sounded out the different parts of the word.

'You'd pick it up quickly.'

'I don't know.' What if she didn't? What would the woman think of her then? Maybe she'd feel Jane was a disappointment.

'It's your choice, child. It always will be. But if you ever decide you want to learn, I'll teach you.'

TWENTY-FOUR

S imon watched his sons rough and tumble with the other boys at the bottom end of Woodhouse Moor. The snowballs they made were mostly ice, but they relished the fresh air and the chance to laugh and run and slide.

It felt close to a normal life. But neither he nor Rosie could enjoy it. Instead, they watched, assessing every face to see if it meant harm. Aware of where the twins were each second, and of everyone moving around. Simon kept one hand close to the hilt of his knife, ready to act immediately if anything happened. His body was tight and tense. He glanced at his wife. She stood ten yards away. For all the world she appeared like any other mother with her children playing in the last of the snow. She was wrapped up in a heavy cloak, a dark blue hat standing high on her head, topped by a peacock feather. Her hands stayed warm in a fur muff. But Simon knew she had a blade in there, and another in the pocket of her dress.

After an hour, he felt his concentration starting to slip. Time to go home. But the danger remained until they were inside and the door locked behind them. Only then could he let out a long breath, close his eyes with relief and feel safe.

A day passed, and then two. Arden did nothing. The word that he'd paid someone to kill Simon's family had spread all across Leeds. At the coffee cart and in the beershops, people claimed he'd gone to ground in his house on Park Square.

Arden would emerge when he was ready; Simon had no illusions that the threats had disappeared. In the afternoons he practised with the knives, sparring with Jane. Large areas of green grass and dark, damp earth showed through the snow now, and his boots slipped and slithered in the mud and slush. Twice she took advantage; if she'd been a real opponent, he'd have been dead.

'What do you think he's going to do?' Jane asked as they strolled down from the moor.

'I don't know.' His heart was still beating hard from the exercise, muscles warm from constant movement. He'd sleep well later. 'Maybe he's hoping we'll lower our guard. We'll think we're safe and then he'll strike.'

She shook her head. 'We can't. Not while he's alive.'

'No.' That was the problem. Arden would never let go of his grudge. Not until someone was dead.

Jane woke early and peered through the shutters at the dark outside. She'd had a broken night, disturbed by dreams of her father and her half-brother together, pursuing her for mile after mile when she had no weapon. All she could do was run, glancing over her shoulder to see them just behind, always there, never giving up.

She dressed, pulled the shawl over her hair, and let herself out of the house, turning the key in the lock. Still a couple of hours before dawn, and a stark chill in the air. Only a few dirty patches of snow still clung in the shadows. The rumour was that the roads would soon be passable, coaches expected the day after tomorrow, maybe even sooner. Already, men were delivering goods around the town with carts, the streets as muddy as bogs.

Leeds was ghostly. A Sunday, very few workers on their way to labour. Here and there she smelled the perfume of fresh bread. Jane drifted, sensing no one who meant harm. No pursuers, just the freedom to walk where she wanted.

She knew every inch of Leeds. Didn't even have to look. Places she'd hidden when she was young, trying to stay warm and alive for a night. The spot where she'd killed a man who'd attempted to rape her. She'd only been on the street for a year, surviving, growing a shell to protect herself.

That was the first time. She'd had no choice. As he tightened his arm around her throat, he told her what he was going to do. He expected her to be helpless, easy prey. She was young, small, living without enough to eat. But Jane intended to stay alive. Afterwards, as she sat staring at his body, she felt no guilt. Before she left, she emptied his pockets, took the money and anything she could sell. There'd been no remorse for any of the others since then, either. They'd all been men without compassion, men who'd forfeited their souls.

She drifted, out and around on either side of the river. The town stirred around her, the first light glowing on the horizon. Down by the water again, close to where Sheepscar Beck met the Aire.

A slight movement in the tree caught her eye, a darker shape against the blackness. Her fingers grasped her knife and she stood still, scarcely breathing. She became a part of the surroundings.

It was there again, a gentle sway to and fro. She heard the small creak of a branch. A few more seconds and she eased herself closer. Cautious, aware of everything. But she was the only living person around here.

The day was just beginning to lighten. It was enough for her to make out the corpse hanging from a rope. Wrists tied behind his back, an old army bayonet plunged deep into his belly. A grubby bandage tied awkwardly around his knee. A crutch tossed against the tree trunk.

Simon was walking along Swinegate, on his way to the coffee cart outside the Bull and Mouth, when he heard someone in the distance, running, coming closer. He tensed, ready, as the soles of their boots clattered against the paving stones.

It was Jane, head down, pelting along. Simon took out his knife in case someone was chasing her. But she slowed as she neared him, catching her breath.

'Perkins,' she said. 'Dead.'

'Where?'

Without a word, she turned and walked away. He hurried to follow her along the streets, across Timble Bridge and down towards the river. It was light enough now to make out the man from a distance, dangling, barely swinging.

He came close enough to see the battering to the face, the blade in his stomach, the way the hands had been tied. It hadn't been a quick death. Arden had made sure Perkins suffered first.

Simon cleared his throat. 'We need the constable here.'

His voice sounded raw and cracked.

'We both know who did it,' Jane said.

'He's not trying to hide it. He wants everyone to know who's responsible. We need to report it before Constable Porter tries to accuse us of murder.'

The inspector was comfortable in the gaol. Sitting and smoking his pipe as the fire burned and kept him warm. He listened and reluctantly pulled on his coat and hat.

'If it turns out he killed himself, Westow . . .'

'Then it would be the strangest suicide I've ever seen.'

The man turned silent as he saw the corpse.

'Perkins,' Simon said. 'He used to be Arden's bodyguard.'

'I know who he is. Was. I'm wondering who did this.'

'Why don't you ask the man who used to employ him?'

The inspector turned a bland face towards him. 'If Perkins didn't work for him any more, why would he want to kill him?'

'I'm sure you'll find a reason when you start to investigate.'

'You could have done this. You and the girl.' He nodded towards Jane. 'I've been hearing things.'

'Then you'll have heard that Perkins and I were together in Park Square and Arden came out in a rage.'

'The constable will look into it all.' He turned and started to walk away.

'Is that it?' Simon called. 'Are you going to leave him dangling there for everyone to see?'

'I'll send men to cut him down and take him away.' He stalked off.

'This wasn't just revenge,' Simon said, glancing up at the body. 'It was a message for us. He's pushing us to act, to try and hurt him.'

She said nothing, just stayed by his side as they crossed back over Timble Bridge. The town had grown busy as people hurried to work.

Mud clung to their boots as they walked. Around the coffee cart they already seemed to know about Perkins. Some details, some gruesome exaggerations. A couple of the men waiting gave Simon cautious looks and moved away.

He heard little he didn't already know. Most people seemed to think Arden was responsible for the killing.

But Simon knew there would never be any proof. If anyone had seen it, Arden would make sure they were paid off or threatened. He'd never end up in court for the murder. The man was flaunting that.

He walked out along Commercial Street, past the grand new shops and the lending library. Out to Park Square. No need to stay long. Just enough time for Arden to be aware he was there. Maybe it was a small way of paying respect to Perkins.

As he stood, Arden's front door opened and a figure armed with a sword slipped out to stand guard. Simon knew the face. Jane would know it even better. Joe Truscott. Her father. Smirking, the man put a hand round his throat.

But Simon wasn't about to be tempted. He needed to prepare and to warn Jane.

'What did she say?' Rosie asked.

'Nothing. She nodded once when I told her. That's all.'

Not even a twitch of her mouth. Mrs Shields had given a small gasp and placed her hand over the girl's for comfort. He'd made his excuses and come home.

'He's going to come for us, isn't he?'

'Yes,' Simon said. No point in saying anything else. Arden was going to have his full revenge. And he intended to use his power to make sure he never paid a price for it. 'Be careful.'

'I am.' The knife was there in her hand.

A new morning, a thick, damp mist clinging to the ground. It softened every sound, made it impossible to see more than a dozen yards. Shapes ghosted through the gloom, and precious few of those so early.

She'd need to rely on her other senses to judge if there was a threat. But she'd felt nothing in the hour she'd been walking. If her father was Arden's bodyguard, he wouldn't stray far from his master's side.

For now, she felt safe enough. But she still pulled her shawl closer around her hair and kept a hand on the hilt of her knife. It was easier to be out here than sitting at home, brooding as she waited for daybreak to come. Sleep had left her, but she wasn't weary.

It would all end in blood, Simon had said, and she believed him. Last night she'd sat by the fire, running her blade over the whetstone. Over and over, until it couldn't be any sharper. It was a ritual that brought her comfort and left her feeling prepared.

Mrs Shields had looked up from her book, smiled and said, 'You'll wear the metal away if you keep doing that, child.'

'If I do, I'll buy a new one.' A good knife was one of the tools of her trade, like a stout pair of boots that fitted well. She had the money to afford them. There had been little paying work for thief-takers lately, but she had plenty saved. So did Simon, she was certain, tucked away in that bank account he had.

It made no sense to her. If he didn't have the money right there, where he could touch it, how could it be his? It wasn't safe; it was too easy to steal, for someone else simply to declare that it belonged to them. But he seemed content; he trusted it. She kept hers hidden behind a brick in the wall. If anything happened to her, Catherine Shields knew where to find it.

She'd checked on the old woman before she left, gliding silently into the bedroom and watching for a moment, hearing the soft, even breathing. Locking the door behind her, out through the gap in the wall, and Leeds was there, waiting.

Jane wasn't looking for anything, not searching for anyone. Restlessness kept her moving; it was easier to walk than to think.

No bodies today.

Closer to the river, the mist became dense fog. It was dangerous, all too easy for someone to lurk, but she didn't hesitate, plunging on by the warehouses towards the bottom of Briggate.

Standing by the bridge, she could make out a noise in the murk. Rhythmic, pounding against the ground, then a shout. In a rush of speed, the London coach rushed by, slowing quickly before the entrance to the Bull and Mouth.

The wheels sent up spurts of mud and water as it roared past. Jane caught a glimpse of the terrified passengers inside as they peered out. At least their journey was done. All those waiting at the inn to go south would feel relieved. Soon enough they'd be on their way.

The coffee cart was doing brisk business. She hung back in the shadows, listening to the gossip. A few were still talking about Perkins. They all knew Arden was responsible for the murder. The only one denying it was the constable. There was another undercurrent, too: disgust that Arden would go after Simon's family. At least people hadn't forgotten.

Jane was close to home when she sensed it. Someone waiting. Jane neared the peak of the hill on the Head Row, no more than a few dozen paces from Green Dragon Yard when he appeared out of the gloom.

Her half-brother.

He extended his arms, palms forward to show he intended no harm.

'What do you want?'

'To see you,' he said. 'To ask if you've changed your mind.'

'I haven't.' She moved to the side, ready to go past him. But he shifted, blocking her way.

'He's repented.'

'No,' she told him again and showed her knife. He backed away, arms still out. She passed him and turned. One question had nagged her since their first meeting. 'You hadn't seen him for years. Why would you believe a word he says?'

'Because he's my father,' the man replied. 'It's my duty.' He pressed his lips together, stared at the ground for a moment, then at her. 'It's yours, too.'

Duty? What kind of a word was that? She didn't owe her father a thing. The debt was his for all those years she'd spent after he raped her. And the man hadn't repented. If he had, he wouldn't be working as Arden's bodyguard. Maybe he was the one who'd put the noose around Perkins's neck and stabbed him in the belly.

'Don't waste your words,' she said and strode away. Not directly home; she didn't want to risk him following. Jane clenched her hands into fists and opened them, time and again, as the anger surged through her. She walked out past Drony Laith and the huge Bean Ing mill, only returning once she felt calmer.

Her father was still the curse in her life.

TWENTY-FIVE

'Small? This is what you need,' the gunsmith said as he brought the weapon from its case. The polished wood, gleaming brass and steel reflected the light as he held it up. 'This is the smallest you can buy. We call them overcoat pistols.'

Simon weighed it in his palm. Not too heavy, easy to grip.

'It's just eleven inches long,' the man continued. 'It will comfortably fit inside the pocket of a gentleman's overcoat.'

No doubt it would. But this was for a lady, protection for Rosie; Simon had his own pistol hidden away in the drawer in the stairs at home. One way or another, she'd be able to manage it, he decided.

'How accurate is it?'

The gunsmith gave a dubious smile. 'I'm sure you know, sir, it can only ever be as good as the man taking aim,' he said. Cautious words, but they were true. In Rosie's hands it would be luck as much as anything. She'd never practised with a gun. But it was one more way to try to keep them safe.

Rosie stared at it. She reached out to touch it, running her fingertips over the barrel.

'I'll load it and prime it,' Simon said, 'and show you how to fire.'

She was reluctant; she didn't hide the doubt in her eyes. The boys were in bed, fast asleep. The only sounds from upstairs were them quietly shifting in bed.

'Try it,' he said. 'See how it feels.'

It appeared larger than he'd believed as she held it. She extended one finger, resting it on the trigger. Rosie raised it once, lowered it, hefted it once more.

He waited, hoping she'd accept it. He wanted every advantage they could have.

A nod. 'Show me how to use it,' she said.

He demonstrated, then let her do it as he watched. Once through and she was perfect. There wouldn't be chance for more than a single shot and the odds were that she'd miss. But the sight of a pistol should make any attacker hesitate. It would buy her a second or two; that would be all she'd need to start using the knife.

He cleaned and loaded his own gun and placed it in the deep pocket of his greatcoat. If he wanted Rosie to carry one then he should, too.

When he began asking about the deaths of two children at the mill, he'd never imagined things would come to this. He believed the issue had been settled when Seaton paid the families. Arden was the problem. He'd refused to let things rest after the death of his son.

Or was there more?

What about Seaton? He was the quiet man, keeping tucked

out of sight and tending to business on his farm. How much was he involved in any of this? He was Arden's friend; they had their damned blood covenant. He had to approve of what the other man was doing, but how far would he go to help? What might he do? It was one more thing to consider.

For now, though, he was exhausted. Staying on his guard the whole time, trudging through thick mud on the streets had left him drained. A good night's rest and he'd wake renewed and ready.

Dreamless. A heavy, solid sleep with nothing to disturb it. He stirred, sliding out from the blankets into the chilly air of the bedroom. Simon dressed hurriedly, standing in front of the mirror in the hall to tie his stock.

The pistol weighed down his greatcoat. His knives were close to hand, on his belt, in his boot, and the last up his sleeve. He was as prepared as he could be. With a deep breath he closed the door behind him and set off down Swinegate.

The faces by the coffee cart were mostly familiar, scattering in a hurry as a coach rushed out of the Bull and Mouth. The driver was grinning, relishing his power, the passengers inside and up on the top looking resigned to a long, uncomfortable journey. More roads were opening as the snow vanished from the hills and countryside. Another day or two and it would all fade into cold memory.

Simon spooned sugar into the hot coffee and sipped, feeling it warm him inside. He was glancing around, careful, listening for any useful gossip. Half-watching, he saw a man looking towards him, eyes wide, mouth opening in horror.

As he threw himself to the side, Simon felt a searing pain in his left shoulder. He rolled as his body landed, pulling out the pistol and one of the knives as he came swiftly to his feet.

The man was caught with his arm raised, blood still on his knife. He was young, believing he'd be fast enough to strike and run before anyone could pursue him. A good, quick killing. Now he was utterly still, his terror rising as he looked down the barrel of a gun.

'Put it down,' Simon ordered. Without a word, no complaint or hesitation, the man opened his hand and let the blade fall into the mud.

The whole thing had barely taken more than a pair of heart-beats. Anyone not watching would have missed it. He heard the buzz of noise as conversation began to grow.

'Rope,' Simon called. As he waited, he stared at the man who'd been paid to assassinate him. Thin, dirty, the uppers of his boots scuffed, a hole at one toe, and a lean face that looked hungry enough to risk his life for the promise of a reward. He had his head lowered. Soft tears ran down his cheeks.

He knew what lay ahead. A trial, prison, then either the noose or a voyage to the other side of the world, transported to Van Diemen's Land. If he lived long enough to set foot on land, he'd have years of hard labour before him.

Christ, his shoulder hurt. He could feel the blood inside his shirt, sliding down his back. He moved his arm and a jolt of pain shot through his body. But nothing seemed to be too badly damaged.

Simon knew just how lucky he'd been. Half a second later and he could have been lying lifeless on the ground. Instead, the man who'd wanted him dead was helpless in front of him.

Someone put another cup of coffee in his hands, thick and sweet, and he gulped it down. His heart was pounding and he had to force his hands to stop trembling.

Then the ostler appeared with lengths of rope. He bound the man's wrists then put more about the man's neck, with a length to lead him.

By the time he'd finished, Simon's breathing had steadied and his pulse beat more slowly. The pain in his shoulder had turned to a strong ache. His shirt stuck to his back as the blood dried. At least he hadn't lost pints of it. He exhaled slowly. He'd survive.

'Let's take him to the gaol,' Simon said. He started to walk, although his limbs felt so weary that all he wanted to do was sleep.

The inspector listened, then took testimony from the few who'd been quick enough to witness it all. He lit his pipe and looked at the prisoner.

'Who paid you?'

The man tried to gulp down his fear. 'Nobody. He looked like he had money. I thought I could rob him and escape.'

Simon turned away in disgust. What had Arden promised him? Or had he been given a grim warning about what would happen if he revealed the truth?

'Put him in the cell,' the inspector told the man from the watch. 'The constable will want to question him later.'

'Nothing more you want to ask him now?' Simon asked.

'He already said he wasn't working for anyone, Westow.' The inspector blew smoke towards the ceiling. 'What else do you want me to do?'

'Find out the truth.'

'Maybe that *was* the truth.'

Simon stormed out of the building, letting the door slam behind him and striding away.

Constable Porter wouldn't pursue it. He'd gladly take the attacker at his word. The man would go to his fate, probably with a little money to ease his way. Or Arden might pull the strings and his puppets in the court would dismiss the case.

Justice? It didn't happen in Leeds if you had the right name.

'Simon,' Rosie said when she saw him. 'What's happened? Your coat's all dirty. Take it off.'

He unbuttoned it, but he couldn't remove it. The pain was intense as he tried to raise his left arm.

Simon knew she wouldn't panic at the sight of blood. Instead, she gently eased the shirt away from his back, sharply drawing in breath as she saw the wound.

'There's plenty of blood,' she told him. 'At least the cut doesn't look too deep.' She poked around it.

He gritted his teeth.

'Water's heating on the range to clean it,' Rosie said. 'Mrs Shields gave me some ointment she made. I'll put that on and bandage it up.'

She started her work. He closed his eyes, breathing slow and shallow as he went through it all again in his mind. If he hadn't noticed the expression on that man's face . . . But he had, and he'd acted fast enough to save his own life. Maybe he'd recovered more than he imagined.

The ointment stung as she rubbed it on the wound. But after a few seconds, it eased to a lulling, comforting warmth that gradually spread through his body as Rosie wound the bandage around his shoulder. By the time she'd finished, the urge to sleep was irresistible.

'How do you feel?' she asked when he came downstairs. It was later in the afternoon. The light was beginning to dull and fade; he'd rested for hours.

'Better,' he replied with a smile, and meant it. He leaned over and kissed her forehead. The boys were playing in the parlour, trying to put together a wooden jigsaw of the world. It was enough to keep them engaged, at least for now.

'The arm?'

'Stiff,' Simon said. 'Very sore.' He'd had to contort himself to put on his shirt. But whatever was in the ointment had helped; he'd have her apply more before bed. For a few days, though, his left arm wouldn't be much good. The last thing he needed when Arden wanted him dead.

'You had a parade of callers,' Rosie told him. 'George Mudie and Barnabas Wade this morning. As soon as they knew you were fine, they wanted the details of what had happened.' She pursed her lips. 'Jane came an hour ago.'

A silence, as if she was reluctant to say more.

'Go on. What's happened?'

'The man who tried to kill you escaped from gaol.'

So that was how Arden had decided to play this game. Simpler than a rigged trial. The constable would mount a feeble search, fail to find him and express his regrets. Then everything would fade away.

'I see,' he said.

'She's hunting him.'

Then God help the man, Simon thought.

The coffee cart was busy when he arrived. He'd slept a little later, lulled to a deep rest by the ointment, then struggling to dress. His shoulder still ached and his arm refused to move easily. But he was whole, he'd mend soon enough. Above all, he was still alive.

Simon felt safe here. His attacker wouldn't dare return. But he kept the pistol primed and ready and the knife up his sleeve ready to fall into his palm.

'Have you heard the news?' the man serving the coffee asked.
'What's that?'

'The night watch found another body. Word is it's that one who went for you yesterday.'

'If it's true, I won't shed any tears over him.'

'Funny, isn't it, the way he managed to escape from gaol just like that.' He raised an eyebrow. 'Next. Come on, I don't have all day.'

Simon turned away. The coffee scalded his tongue. Jane had found her target, and she'd done it quickly.

It had been simple. Three conversations, a few pence spent, and she had his name. James Cartmel. From there it had only taken a matter of hours until she tracked him down.

He'd been walking in the darkness with his hands in his pockets, softly whistling a merry air when Jane confronted him. He didn't try to reach for his knife. Backed away two paces, glancing over his shoulder as if he might try to run.

She never gave him the chance. He'd have been happy to kill Simon and take whatever Arden was paying for the job. Instead, the bill had come due.

No one saw her. Not a soul around in the night. She left his body there and vanished through the streets with the shawl over her hair, just another woman.

She thought about it as she stared out of the window at the yard. The earth glistened with damp under heavy grey skies. Jane tensed, starting to reach for her knife, as someone stepped through the gap in the wall.

Simon. He must have heard the news.

'Thank you,' he said as they stood outside. Jane had been careful to close the door of the house behind her. No need for Mrs Shields to hear their conversation.

She shrugged.

'Did he put up a fight?'

'No,' she answered. 'He didn't even look surprised.'

'Arden will be coming again. He has to. Either that or lose his reputation.'

'Yes.'

'Be ready.'

'How's your arm?' Jane inclined her head towards his shoulder.

'Hurts like the devil,' he told her with a grimace. 'I can't really raise it. A few days should see it right.' He put his right hand on her arm. 'Thank you again. I don't imagine the constable will come sniffing around.'

She hadn't even given that a thought. If he did, she'd simply deny it. There was no proof, no witness.

'Be ready,' Simon said again. 'Every single minute.'

'How much longer will we have to live like this?' Rosie asked. They were in the bedroom; Simon stood by the window, staring down at Swinegate and trying to spot anyone watching the house.

'I don't know,' he answered. 'That depends on Arden.'

She sighed, came up behind him and put her arms around his waist. 'The boys are chafing. You must have noticed.'

Of course; it was impossible to miss. They were used to having their freedom, to being able to go outside to play and run wild. Now they were cooped up with their mother, and if they went out, she stood guard over them, never letting them stray more than a few yards from her side. In return, they misbehaved at home, leaving half the food on their plates and a wilful mess wherever they went. He knew he should discipline them. The rules were for their own safety. But they were young, they couldn't imagine that death might touch them, and whatever punishment he gave would only bring more resentment. They had too much of him in their souls for anything else.

'We'll take them out later,' he promised. It wouldn't be much, but at least it was something. He flexed his arm, rolling his shoulder a little and feeling the pain.

'Do you want more ointment?'

He was about to say no, but this was a good time. The twins were downstairs with the tutor, there was nothing else for him to do. A rest would help. Who cared if he seemed like an old man, dozing during daylight?

He woke to the smell of hot food. A thick soup with vegetables and small pieces of meat, the bread still warm from the oven.

Two helpings and still he was hungry. It was good to feel this way once more. A small return to the way he'd been before the illness.

'Right,' Simon announced to Richard and Amos, 'I'll give you half an hour to do the work your teacher set. If it's good enough, and I do mean *if*, we'll all go up to Woodhouse Moor.'

They were eager, dashing off. Simon used his spoon to scrape the bowl and took a final swallow of beer.

'What's Arden likely to do next?' Rosie asked.

'I wish I knew. But after Jane took care of his assassin, he'll want it to be final.'

'We ought to look out for her and Mrs Shields.'

'She'd never let us,' Simon said. Rosie knew it as well as he did. Jane would never allow them close enough to guard her that way. Come to that, she was deadlier against any threat than he was. Ruthless. Last night she'd proved it again. There'd been no sign of regret on her face when he talked to her this morning.

But he understood something else: if there hadn't been others around the day before, he'd have killed James Cartmel himself. The guilt would have come, but he'd have taken that burden.

Enough. There was life, and an afternoon with his family ahead. A time for joy.

TWENTY-SIX

The knock on the door took him by surprise. Simon took the knife in his right hand, then drew back the bolts, wincing as pain shot down his arm when he gripped the handle and turned it with his left hand.

He peered out, then stepped back. At first he could scarcely believe his eyes. He was gazing at a face he believed had left Leeds forever.

'Come in,' he said, stepping aside and locking the latch behind them.

'Thank you, sir.' He took off his hat and followed Simon into the kitchen.

'What are you doing here? I thought you'd be on your way back to Boston by now, Mr Ramsey.'

Storms over the Atlantic meant there was no ship waiting in Liverpool. Instead, Charles Ramsey had had time to brood over his brother's death as he idled away time in a hotel room.

'I simply can't let it rest this way, sir. Not when he was murdered for nothing. I think I was too stunned earlier. I've had a chance to think. Sebastian should be alive; he should have been travelling with me. Instead . . . there's only injustice.' He gave a small, solemn nod. 'I had to wait for the roads to clear enough for a coach to bring me back here.'

'What do you think you can do?' Simon asked him. 'Legally, there's nothing at all. You won't have heard, but Perkins, the man who killed your brother, is dead. A few things have changed. Sit down, I'll explain.'

Ramsey frowned. 'What about this man Seaton?' he asked when Simon had finished.

'He's out at his farm. And he has plenty of men around, in case you're thinking of going out there.'

'The order for my brother's death must have come from him. He employed Sebastian.'

'Yes.' No doubt about that. 'But Thomas Arden helped to execute it.'

'You said his bodyguard is dead.'

'He has a new one.'

Ramsey sighed. 'I suppose men like that always do.'

He stood and shook Simon's hand. 'Thank you. When I left before, I wanted to go back to America and grieve for my brother. Having some time made me realize that revenge would allow me to go home a more satisfied man.'

'Do you think your brother would have wanted that?' He didn't need anyone else drawn into this battle.

'Honestly, I don't know, Mr Westow. Quite probably not. As you know, I only had a little time with him, but he didn't seem to have a violent bone in his body.'

'Do you?' The man looked like what he was, a respectable merchant who'd done quite well for himself. Not a fighter.

'A little under ten years ago, there was a war between England and the United States,' Ramsey said.

Simon struggled to recall it. The newspapers had been full of the fight against Bonaparte as the tide turned and Wellington's troops started to surge through Portugal and Spain.

'I don't remember.'

'I fought for the Americans, led a troop of men.' He gave a weary smile. 'Not too loyal to my homeland, I'm afraid. But yes, I've experienced fighting. I've seen men die next to me.'

'That's not the same as killing,' Simon told him.

'I've done some of that, too.' A brief nod. 'I'll wish you good day, sir. I've taken enough of your time.'

'What are you going to do?'

'I plan on attempting to restore a balance.'

After Simon locked the door behind him, he sat at the kitchen table. He'd never even asked Ramsey where he was staying in Leeds; he'd been too stunned that the man had come back. Even more when he learned what he intended to do. Who would have guessed that the man had been a soldier? He appeared too meek and polite. There was more steel to him than Simon had imagined. Perhaps Arden and Seaton would underestimate him, too. It might help him stay alive.

'Who was that?' Rosie asked when she came downstairs with the twins. They were bundled up against the weather: heavy coats that were becoming too small for them, caps on their heads, trousers tucked into boots.

'Ramsey,' he replied. 'The American brother of the man who they pulled from the river, the one with the hand cut off. I thought he'd gone home, but he turned back at Liverpool. He has something different in mind.'

She raised her eyebrows in a silent question, but he shook his head. He'd tell her later, while they watched the boys playing.

The roads were still thick with mud that stuck to his soles, the air heavy and damp. Patches of mist clung near trees as they reached the moor. He couldn't feel a breath of wind. This was the kind of November he knew, dank and dreary, not filled with snow.

Hardly a soul around, just faint, disembodied sounds in the distance. Simon kept wary eyes on his sons as they ran. Rosie listened carefully as he recounted Ramsey's visit.

'Do you think he'll try to kill Seaton and Arden?'

'Probably.'

'If he succeeds, that would take care of our problem,' she said.

'If.' Simon let the word hang in the air. 'Come back here,' he shouted at Richard as the boy started to run too far. 'He said he'd been a soldier, but he won't be used to this kind of fighting.'

'He could work with us,' Rosie said. 'We need more help.'

'I don't think he'd be interested. He seems to want to do it on his own.'

'Pity.' She spotted Amos dodging into a small copse. 'Come back here.' When he didn't immediately reappear, she said: 'I'll fetch him.'

Hurrying off, she pulled the knife from her pocket. He watched Richard kick up leaves, a broad smile on his face.

A few seconds and Simon felt panic climbing in his chest. They should have been back.

'Come here, now,' he called to Richard. 'Right this moment.'

With the boy at his side, he dodged between the trees. His heart was wild, head jerking round as he tried to spot Rosie and Amos. At first he saw no sign of anyone. Then a flash of colour in the grey.

She was lying on the ground. Bile rose in his throat at the fear she might be dead. He forced himself to touch her neck. The flesh was warm, the pulse strong. He tapped her cheek and her eyes fluttered as she began to stir.

'Papa, where's Amos?' Richard asked. 'Do you want me to find him?'

'No.' The word came out too sharply and he felt the boy withdraw, fearful. 'No, I'll take care of it.'

Rosie opened her eyes, looking around as if she wasn't certain where she was. Then the truth fell hard.

'He's got Amos. My God, Simon, he's got Amos.' She opened her eyes wide and tried to sit up. 'He hit me.' She reached a hand to her head, wincing as her fingers touched the tenderness. 'He hit me as soon as he saw me.' She tried to struggle to her feet, unsteady and frantic.

'Who was it?' Simon asked.

'I don't know. I've never seen him before. He had a scar

running down his cheek.' Without thinking, her fingertips traced the line on her own skin. He knew the man: Joe Truscott. Arden's bodyguard. Jane's father. 'We have to find him, Simon. We've got to.'

'We will.' He was trying to sound calm, even as his gaze flickered desperately across the ground, hunting for any type of clue. Grasping at every kind of hope and feeling the panic rise in his belly. Maybe his son had managed to escape, squirmed away and was looking for them now. He yelled the boy's name at the top of his voice, but it was swallowed by the mist as soon as it left his mouth.

Inside, he was frantic, trying to conjure up a plan, terrified of what Arden intended for Amos. He needed to start searching, but he couldn't begin with Rosie and Richard here. She seemed steadier on her feet, but utterly lost.

'Go to Mrs Shields's house,' he told her. 'Tell them what happened and say I need Jane. He put his arm through hers as she held Richard by the hand. 'Come on. I'll walk with you to the road. Nobody will attack you there.'

'But—' she began, and he could barely begin to imagine all the thoughts and feelings raging in her head. With every step she kept looking back over her shoulder, tears rolling down her cheeks.

'Please.' He nodded towards the boy. 'Someone has to look after him.'

'I couldn't keep Amos safe.' She sounded bleak, hopeless.

'We'll find him. I'll bring him back safe and sound. I promise.'

Even as he spoke the words, all he could do was hope they were true.

Jane listened as Rosie stumbled and tripped over her words. Mrs Shields mixed a cordial and placed it in her hands. Then she found a puzzle for the boy at the back of her desk, but he was too distracted by his mother's anguish to pay it any attention.

'The man who took Amos, what did he look like?' Jane asked. She was certain she knew who it was; she simply wanted it confirmed.

'He had a scar on his face.'

'Yes, of course.'

'Please go and help Simon. He needs you.'

Catherine Shields took light hold of Rosie's hand. 'They'll find him,' she said with gentle certainty. 'You sit here with me.'

Jane fastened her old green cloak and checked the pocket of her dress. Her knife was there. She knew it would be, but she wanted the reassurance of the handle. A final glance at Rosie, who was bending forward while Mrs Shields examined the wound on her scalp, and she left, locking the door behind her.

She pulled her shawl over her head and hurried up towards the moor.

This was her fault. If she hadn't listened to Simon, if she'd killed her father when she had the opportunity instead of just hurting him, he wouldn't have been able to do this. But she'd given him chances, and the wounds had put fuel on the fire inside him. Now, whatever happened to Simon's son, the guilt was hers.

She heard him long before she found him. He was bellowing out Amos's name, then pausing, hoping against hope for any sound as an answer.

'Where have you looked?' she asked.

Simon spun around, blade ready, filled with panic.

'All over.' His voice cracked, and he pointed off into the mist. 'Up there, down that way. Every place I can think of.'

'No sign of him?'

'Nothing at all.'

'He's alive,' Jane said.

'Do you think so?' He was clutching for any shred to keep him going.

'Yes.' Whatever Arden had planned, it wouldn't happen in a place like this. He'd want his moment of perfect pleasure. He'd need Simon there to witness his son's murder.

'Then where is he?' He looked all around, as if the trees and dripping branches might be able to tell him.

'Arden's house,' Jane said.

She watched as Simon narrowed his eyes. Now he had a place, a target.

TWENTY-SEVEN

They hurried along the street, side by side. Simon's face was hard as iron. From the corner of his eye he saw Jane's gaze flickering around, alert for the slightest hint of danger. But nothing as they reached Park Square. Simon hammered on the door of Arden's house, then stepped back to stare at the windows. He tensed as he heard footsteps in the hall, then the maid cautiously opened the door.

'Arden.'

She shook her head. 'He left an hour or so ago, sir. Ordered the coach. He didn't say when he'd return.'

He listened, staring at her. 'He's taken my son. I don't know if your master ordered you to say he's not here, but I'm coming in to see for myself. I don't want to hurt you, but if you try to stop me I'll have no choice. Do you understand?'

Without a word, she stood aside.

'Upstairs,' he told Jane, then started on the rest of the house. No need for order, they tossed over furniture, swept papers off the desk. Inside, he burned with desperation. The door to the cellar was locked. He stepped back, raised his leg and kicked. It flew back, crashing against the brick wall.

A candle and holder sat at the top of the stairs. He lit it and walked down, watching for movement in the shadows.

The room was empty. No one hiding, no indication that Amos had ever been here.

He was panting hard, pulling at his hair in frustration. Fear coursed through him. Jane stood in the hall. She shook her head.

Christ. Where was Amos? What had Arden done to him? Any harm and he'd take the man apart, make him beg for a mercy that was never going to come.

'Where?' he asked. He was lost, no more ideas. 'Where can we go?'

'Mrs Shields,' Jane told him, and he nodded his agreement. Rosie would be there. She needed to know.

As they crossed the square, a figure approached. Jane started to reach for her knife.

'No,' Simon told her. 'That's the American. Ramsey. He came back.'

'What does he want?' she asked.

'Revenge.'

The man approached. 'I saw you go into Arden's house—'

'Mr Ramsey, I'm sorry, I don't have time. His bodyguard has snatched one of my sons.'

'I see.' The man stiffened and pursed his lips. 'I saw Arden leave. He was on his own in the coach.'

'Which way?' Simon asked. Anything, any scrap might help.

'Towards the Head Row.'

That told him nothing at all.

'Thank you. We have to go.'

'Sir, if I can help you I'd be glad to be of service. Perhaps you can use an extra hand,' Ramsey said. 'I was a soldier, I told you that. We both want to find the same man.'

Help? They needed anything they could get. So many places in Leeds they could have taken Amos. Simon had to hold on to his faith that the boy was still alive.

'Yes,' he agreed. 'Thank you. Come with us.'

As they walked, moving swiftly along the streets, he recounted everything that had happened. Maybe there was a nugget in there that he'd overlooked. Any kind of hint to help.

No. There was so little. Truscott had knocked Rosie out and snatched Amos. They'd vanished; he must have had something, a horse or a cart of some kind waiting. He wasn't even sure how long it had all taken. Seconds? A minute or more? Time had turned upside down.

As they passed through the gap in the wall to the yard of Mrs Shields's cottage, Simon saw surprise on Ramsey's face to find a place like this in the heart of Leeds. Rosie dashed out, the hope on her face fading to nothing as she saw them.

'Where . . .?' she began.

'I don't know.' Simon wrapped her in his arms. She clung to him, shaking, trying to swallow. 'We'll find him.'

They felt like empty words, spun out of air. He didn't know where to go next.

Jane disappeared. She removed the stone from the wall in the bedroom and took out some coins, then came back and talked to the old woman. Just two sentences, waiting until Mrs Shields nodded. Then she vanished, out past the safety of the wall.

Someone had to know where to find Arden and her father. For enough money, they'd give up the information.

Darkness was falling, and the creatures of the night would soon be coming out. Those were the people she wanted, the ones who heard things, learned things.

An hour of searching out faces. A few pennies here, sixpence there, always dangling the reward of a guinea for anything that helped her find Arden or her father.

Nobody could help. Shaking their heads or telling lies as they hoped for the reward. She pushed people harder, asked the children in the abandoned buildings, but Thomas Arden seemed to have fallen off the earth.

She was close to giving up when one of the whores on Briggate beckoned her over. The woman had a face scarred by smallpox and sour breath, but her eyes were clear and sorrowful.

'You looking for Truscott?'

'Yes.' Suddenly she felt a glimmer of hope. 'Do you know where he is?'

'I know where he was last night.'

'Where?' She brought a guinea from the pocket of her dress. 'If he's still there, this is for you.'

The woman tilted her head so the light hanging over the entrance to the yard caught her face and picked out the dark bruise around her eye and cheekbone. 'He did that. Never paid me, either. You find him and hurt him for me.' She whispered an address.

'I will. I promise.' She pressed the coin into the woman's hand. She'd told the truth. Jane was convinced; she could feel the pain of honesty in the woman's voice.

The rooming house stood on the far side of Quarry Hill, part of a long terrace where fragile beauty had faded to age and ugliness. She found a place to watch the front door and tried to come up with a plan.

She could rush back, bring Simon and the other man. But she

didn't even know if her father was still here. They could do more
good hunting in other places for Arden.

For an hour she stood as the mist thickened. By then, she
could barely see to the bottom of the street. Men came and
went from the rooming house. Half of them looked as if
they'd scraped together every farthing they could find to afford
a bed for the night. Others possessed a little more, still in
clothes that weren't worn out. Saving money, perhaps, at the
expense of their pride.

She considered going in and asking for Joe Truscott. No, safer
to stay her hand, leave nothing to associate her with him. No
description to reach the night watch later.

Another hour and Jane began to wonder if her father was still
here. He might have gone off with Arden. She'd stay until the
clock struck again, then give up for the night.

Five minutes and her patience paid its dividend. The door
opened and light leaked out as a figure emerged. She could pick
out the scar running down his face.

It was time, she thought. But she'd choose her spot. A place
where no one could hear if he called for help.

If he knew she was following him, he gave no indication of it.
He went to a beershop near Mabgate. Even better, Jane thought.
With some drink in him, her father would be slow.

It took time. One hour edged towards two. Finally he came
through the door and turned to walk back to the rooming house.

She caught up to him where there was no pavement, a long,
empty gap between houses. He was lost in his thoughts. He never
heard as she came close and drove her knife into the muscle of
his right arm.

He bellowed and turned, fumbling for his own weapon. She'd
already skipped back out of range. Her father pressed his right
arm tight against his body, grimacing from the pain as he held
the blade with his left.

But his grip was awkward and unnatural. She possessed the
advantage; he knew it as well as she did. He lunged forward.
Jane saw it coming and slipped to the side, darting in to jab at
his wounded arm again. The point went through his coat and
shirt, piercing his flesh just below the elbow. Another cry of pain.

But he wasn't done yet. Nowhere near. Her father wouldn't

surrender. She'd have to grind him down and force whatever he knew from him.

His left foot edged forward. He tightened the grip on his knife. Jane waited until he committed himself to the move, trying to come under her, bring up the blade and gut her. She was younger, lighter, quicker, aiming for his eyes and forcing him to duck away. Her knife touched his face, sharp enough to slice open his right cheek. The blood began to flow; he tried to paw it away with his wounded arm.

He was distracted. For a second, he left himself open. She darted in, stinging him in the side with the tip of her blade, then forcing it deep. She moved back before he could strike at her.

Jane was going to beat him. He must have realized it by now. But she couldn't let herself taste victory just yet. She needed information from him before he died.

She saw him alter his hold on the knife hilt and heard him swallow. Jane was ready as he charged, moving aside, extending her leg.

He tumbled hard. His knife skittered away. Before he could move, she was on him, straddling his back. She grabbed his hair, smashing his face into the ground before pulling it up and placing her blade against his throat.

'You don't have to kill me.' His voice was a desperate croak. 'I'll go.'

Jane ignored him. 'Where's the boy?' He didn't answer immediately. She tugged harder on his hair and edged the knife into his flesh. He squealed.

'You took him. Where is he?'

He flinched. 'Will you let me go if I tell you?'

'Tell me.' She lifted the blade, bringing it close to his face. For a moment he tried to struggle, but his strength was ebbing. Too many wounds. 'Maybe I'll start by taking out your eyes.'

He twisted his head but she kept a firm grip, holding the knife steady.

'You'd better keep still and pray my hand doesn't slip. Where's the boy?'

'If you don't kill me, I'll tell you.'

She was silent, listening as he breathed. He'd pissed himself with fear; the acrid smell filled the air.

'Go on,' she told him.

'I want to know you'll let me go.'

'I'll let you go,' she agreed.

'The farm. Seaton's farm. They've taken him out there. Sent all the labourers away for a few days. Arden's sent a note to your precious Simon. You've been wasting your time with me. He already knows.'

Her hand remained perfectly still, the tip of the blade not half an inch from his eyes.

'I told you. Now you can let me go.'

'I lied,' Jane told him. 'You've deserved this for years.'

She ran the knife across his throat. His hands flailed for a second then stopped and he was still. Blood pooled around him.

The debt was paid.

She ran through the streets. Briggate, the Head Row, Green Dragon Yard, then home, unlocking the door to find everyone crowded into the parlour. Richard was curled up, sleeping on his mother's lap. Absently, Rosie stroked his hair and stared into the distance.

Simon and Ramsey were talking in low voices. Everyone turned as Jane entered.

'They've taken him to the farm.'

'Farm?' Rosie asked. She looked as if she was coming out of a fog.

'Seaton's farm,' Simon said.

He glanced out of the window. Full night. He wanted to gallop out along the Harrogate Road, to be there, to bring his son home. But he didn't know the land. It would be pitch-black out there. They'd all be stumbling around, easy targets for anyone who wanted to kill him.

The farm. Simon exhaled. For Christ's sake, it was so obvious. He should have thought of it straight away. He'd been too intent on Arden to think of Seaton. The damned blood covenant. They'd even had him out there to watch the pig being slaughtered. Now the lesson was coming to life.

He stood.

'We'll be out there as soon as it's light and we can see what we're doing. We need to go home and make a plan.'

He picked Richard up. The boy hardly stirred. Growing, but still so young, he thought. So innocent. Tomorrow he'd make sure his brother was back with him.

'Why not leave him here?' Mrs Shields asked. She'd been sitting so silently in the corner that he'd forgotten she was there. 'That way you won't disturb him if you're making an early start.' She gave a gentle smile. 'He's a sweet boy. I can look after him until you come back.'

She understood, he thought. She knew Rosie would be going to the farm with them. He looked at his wife. She stared at her son, then reluctantly nodded.

'Child, can he sleep in your bed?'

'Yes. Of course.' The question took Jane by surprise. She wouldn't even be here.

'Don't worry, I'll be close when he wakes,' Mrs Shields told Rosie. A few whispered words in her ear and she gave a faint smile.

'He said there would be a note at the house for you,' Jane said. She walked next to Simon. Ramsey was escorting Rosie, telling her about Boston, anything to keep her mind off all this. 'Nobody else is going to be there. Seaton's sent his workers away.'

'Did he say anything more?' No need to say who.

'No.'

'Is he still alive?'

She didn't reply, just stared straight ahead and kept on walking. It was enough of an answer. Joe Truscott deserved to die for all he'd done over the years. To her, to all the other children he'd hurt. Jane had earned the right to put an end to it all. Now she could tuck it away, hide it somewhere in her mind. Exactly as she did with everything else.

The house was cold. Rosie busied herself building a new fire in the range. Anything at all to keep herself occupied, her mind away from what was happening to Amos.

They'd bring him back, alive and well. He daren't believe anything else. No room for doubts. If he let those creep in, he was lost.

Simon opened the folded paper that had been pushed under the front door.

Farm. Nine o'clock tomorrow morning.

Unsigned, but it hardly needed a name.

'How do we beat them?' he asked.

'I'm coming with you,' Rosie said.

'Of course.' He'd seen the look in her eyes. She was ready to kill. 'You were taken round the farm. Can you draw a map of it?'

She blinked. 'I can try.' She took the paper with the note, turned it over and picked up a pencil.

'What can I do?' Ramsey asked.

'They're not going to expect you,' Simon said. 'They don't even know you're in Leeds. They have no idea how dangerous my wife can be, either. The pair of you are our surprise.'

Only Seaton and Arden out there, facing four of them. But they had Amos. That gave them the whip hand.

'Do you have a rifle of any kind, sir?' Ramsey asked.

Simon shook his head. 'Two pistols. Why?'

'I'm hardly a marksman, but I'm a fair shot. I hunt regularly in the country outside Boston.'

'John Napier,' Jane said. 'Remember, he boasted that he had that Baker rifle.'

He recalled that now. Another weapon would help.

'See if you can find him at home,' Simon said and she rose to slip away. 'Tell him I'll pay to borrow it. Stop at the ostler, too. Tell him I'll want a carriage first thing tomorrow.'

It was so easy to make plans, to put everything together. He didn't have to think about what could go wrong, or that they could arrive too late.

No. Arden had given him time. He wanted Simon to see every gruesome little detail.

For two hours they studied Rosie's map, trying to come up with possibilities. One thing was certain: Simon and Rosie would drive up together. Ramsey would be with them along the Harrogate Road, then slip away unseen to the far side of the farm.

He prayed to God that the American was everything he claimed to be. If he wasn't, he'd end up more of a liability than an asset. Still, he had his own spur for revenge against Arden and Seaton.

Simon glanced at Jane, sitting at the far end of the table, looking as if she was barely listening. A few hours ago she'd killed her own father. It was a long time coming, years and years, but she didn't show anything, no regret or satisfaction. Nothing at all.

The longclock was quietly striking three by the time they had everything in place. Simon was bone-weary, body heavy with exhaustion, but he knew he wouldn't sleep. Ramsey stared down at the grain of the wood on the table. The Baker rifle was propped against the wall behind him.

Rosie looked on the edge of tears. But she wouldn't allow herself to fall apart, he knew that. She'd go up against the devil himself to get her son back. Jane ran the edge of her knife over a small whetstone. Again and again and again, completely absorbed in her task.

TWENTY-EIGHT

D awn was close. Through the window, Jane could make out a thin band of pale sky on the eastern horizon. She pulled her cloak over her shoulders and fastened it at the neck, then tucked her shawl over her hair.

'Where are you going?' Simon asked.

'I'll start walking to the farm.'

'There'll be enough room in the carriage for all of us.'

She shook her head. After a night crowded by people, she wanted time alone. A chance to let her thoughts roam and to make her own plans.

She heard the click of the lock as she started down Swinegate. The mist had cleared to bitter cold, stars shining. Not a soul on the streets, just the emptiness of the small hours. Soon people would be waking and dressing and heading to another day in the mills and the factories. For now, though, she seemed to have Leeds to herself.

Up Briggate, across the Head Row, seeing only a few scurrying shadows of men who didn't want their faces known. Out on the road towards Sheepscar Bridge and the turnpike on the far side of the toll booth.

Her father was dead. She'd watched the blood pump out of his body. Felt the last heartbeat before silence, seen the weak, final flutter of his eyelids. For so many years she'd dreamed of ending his life. Yet when it happened it didn't bring her the pleasure she'd expected.

No regrets, none at all. But no satisfaction in her soul. The anger inside her hadn't evaporated. She didn't feel as if his hold over her had suddenly vanished. It would fade in time; she was certain of that. Turn to ashes and dust and blow away in the wind. For now, though, everything remained the same.

When morning came, someone would find his body. Let them.

Off in the distance Jane heard the faint, slow rumble of a cart. The sound grew louder; heading towards Leeds, mostly likely going to sell the food they'd grown. Before it came too close she ducked off into the darkness and watched it pass.

In a house up on the hill a light winked alive, then another next to it. She began to make out some features in the landscape: a thicket of bushes, the snaking line of a drystone wall. The day was growing.

Simon's plan was good, but she knew it was nothing more than wishes and desires. He couldn't dictate a single thing. Seaton and Arden were in control. She hoped she'd have a chance to move around the farm, to see what she could use. With all the labourers gone, she should have the opportunity.

Jane kept her steps light as she walked through Chapel Allerton. Behind the shutters of one house she heard a man's racking cough.

She left the little straggle of dwellings behind her. The air was raw and cutting against her face. Darkness had faded enough to see a thin rime of frost sparkling on the grass and the leaves. A cacophony of birds called and sang up on the bare branches. Out here she felt small, exposed. In Leeds she could become invisible in a street or a ginnel. Here she could be seen far too easily.

But Jane had no sense of anyone watching her as she followed the rising road towards the milestone. She moved very cautiously, searching for just the right spot to disappear into a wood.

There was no silence in the countryside. Once her ears grew used to it, there was noise everywhere. Alive and busy. The rustle of birds' wings, animals snuffling through the undergrowth.

Each step was slow, considered. As she neared the farm she became more cautious, taking her time, looking around. She heard cows lowing and the crow of a rooster. Peering towards the buildings, she couldn't make out any lights.

Then, from somewhere inside the farmhouse, she heard a man shouting. Another answered, and she recognized Arden's voice. A few sharp sentences and quiet returned.

Silently, she edged forward. Her knife was out, gripped so tight that her knuckles showed white. Jane stayed out of sight of the building, exploring the land, comparing it to what she remembered of the map Rosie had drawn.

The creak of a door opening and she shrank behind a tree before carefully peering round. Arden, standing, glaring at the day, looking as if he expected someone to arrive. Not Simon; it was still too early for that. Someone else. Then she understood. He was waiting for his bodyguard. Her father.

He stood for a few minutes, pulling out a pocket watch, moving from foot to foot to try and keep warm, Finally he went back inside, slamming the door. Arden hadn't spotted her, but why would he?

Jane realized she'd been holding her breath. She exhaled slowly and picked a path back towards the road.

A few vehicles were moving, most heading towards Leeds. She glanced up at the sound of hooves pounding against the muddy ground and saw the red livery of the mail coach fly past as it rushed north.

It shouldn't be too long before Simon arrived, she thought. He'd want to be early, eager to prepare himself. She'd be able to show Ramsey the track that led to the back of the farmyard, bringing him out next to the house.

Whenever she heard a voice or the sharp crack of a twig, she tensed, keeping still. But there was nothing. She was alone here. No notion of anyone lurking, watching for her and waiting.

Jane didn't know how long she'd been standing when she heard the carriage rattling up the hill. She could see Simon holding the reins and guiding the horses. Rosie sat grim-faced beside him. A black cloak, rug pulled over her legs, a small dark hat on her head. Ramsey was behind them, the Baker rifle at port as his head moved around, scanning the undergrowth for any attackers.

A final glance around and Jane emerged, waving her hands above her head. Simon slowed the vehicle, stopping beside her.

'How does it look?'

'Only Arden and Seaton. They're both inside the farmhouse.'

'And Amos,' Rosie's voice trembled. 'Amos has to be there.'

'Yes,' Jane agreed. She hadn't seen him, hadn't heard him. But she was right. He must be in there, still alive. It was the only thing that made sense to her. 'There's a path that comes out behind the building . . .'

Ramsey began to climb down, stretching his legs as he stood on the grass.

'I want Arden,' he said. 'I trust you'll do me that favour, sir.'

'Do what you like with him. We're here to take Amos home.'

Jane studied Simon's face. Pure anger in his eyes. He took out his watch.

'Ten minutes until nine. I'll arrive just before the hour.' He looked at her. 'Will that give you enough time?'

'Yes.' She hurried away, Ramsey close behind her.

Her mind was cold and sharp. They'd need to be quick, but the man seemed willing. Not one to ask questions or needing to speak. He simply followed.

She paused, cocking her head to listen for ten seconds, just in case there was anyone else. Nothing. The track wound between trees, across a small clearing, until it brought them out no more than a dozen yards away from the farmhouse.

'What now?' Ramsey whispered.

'I'll go over by the barn.' She pointed. 'I'll signal as soon as they both come out.'

After that, it was up to him. He had the rifle. She'd noticed a knife hanging from his belt.

Jane touched her gold ring for luck, took a breath and darted off.

The horses rested, heads down as they nibbled the frosted grass at the side of the road. Their coats were flecked with sweat from the trip. Poor beasts, Simon thought. He wouldn't be able to offer them any kind of rubdown until they returned to the ostler.

Or if the worst happened . . . no, he wasn't going to let himself consider that.

Amos would be unharmed. They'd take him home and put an end to all this. He squeezed Rosie's hand.

'Almost time. We'll be fine.'

She didn't reply. Lost in her thoughts and sorrows, she didn't even seem to realize he'd spoken. He took out his watch once more and opened the cover. One more minute. Would it give Ramsey and Jane enough time to move into place? What were they going to do? What *could* they do?

He'd made his plans, tried to take account of every possibility. But now he was out here, it all vanished like smoke. They'd never been more than a way to pass the time. Something to occupy their minds.

One final glance at the dial as the hands moved. He clicked the lid shut and returned it to his waistcoat pocket.

'Ready?' he asked, but Rosie didn't even look at him.

He lifted the reins. The leather was worn, rough against his skin. A flick and a click of his tongue and the horses began to move. Simon guided them along the road, then turned right, following the track through the gates to the farm.

He swallowed hard, eyes shifting across the landscape. He heard the cows in the byre.

The wheels of the carriage rattled over the cobblestones in the yard. He stopped. The horses were old, well-trained and docile. They wouldn't try to bolt.

Simon eased himself down to the ground, taking a few paces as he looked around, listening. They were in the farmhouse, Jane had said, but he couldn't see any shape at the window. No sounds other than the animals and the birds.

A bench sat to the side, a bucket underneath it. He remembered them well from when they slaughtered the pig. Telling him what they intended to do with his boy.

He helped Rosie down. She stood, not speaking. Removed, he thought. But he knew she was simply waiting. At the first chance of saving Amos, her rage would take over. Arden and Seaton would have no idea what to expect.

Simon stared at the farmhouse. Amos was behind that door. All he could do was hope that they hadn't hurt him yet. If they had . . . without thinking he tightened his grip on the handle of the pistol in his pocket.

Arden was making them wait. He knew they were here. He was relishing his power, his hold over them. Would he make them beg for Amos? Probably, and they'd do it, he knew that. Anything at all.

But he was going to destroy this pair. If Ramsey didn't manage it, Simon would. And if he couldn't, Rosie would finish the task. If it was the last thing she did on this earth.

The creak of a hinge and the front door of the farmhouse cracked open. Arden peered out, his face half-hidden in the shadows.

'You're punctual, Westow. But you shouldn't have brought your wife. This won't be something for a woman to see. Not with your own son.'

Rosie started to take a step forward, but Simon placed his hand on her arm. The man wanted a response. Simon wasn't going to give him the joy of one.

'He's in here. We haven't hurt a hair on his head. Truscott did a good job. Snatched him from right under your wife's nose.'

'Truscott's dead. Last night.'

'Is he now?' Arden asked. 'Your work, Westow?'

'No.' But he didn't mention Jane's name. No need to put the thought of her in the man's head.

'Pity. He did what he was told and he liked the violence. But he didn't have Perkins's brain. Never mind. I'll find another like him. No shortage of them around.'

He was talking too much. Sooner or later it all had to stop. He and Seaton had to bring Amos outside. Until then, everything was wasted words.

From the corner of his eye, Simon was aware of Jane at the corner of the barn. Just a hint of her shawl. That meant Ramsey was in position.

He took a deep breath. 'Are you going to hide and talk all day?'

'Looking to the end already? I didn't think you'd be in such a hurry to see your son dead. A handsome little lad. Not as good-looking as my Franklin. But he won't live long enough to grow into it.'

He felt Rosie tense. The man was goading them.

A tug on the door. It opened wider and Arden stepped out. He had a knife in his hand. Behind him, Seaton dragged a bundle. It took a second for Simon to recognize Amos's clothes. Rosie drew in her breath and covered her mouth.

'Don't worry,' Arden told them. 'He's alive, and well enough for now. We had to give him a little tincture of opium, that's all.'

'Let me see his face,' Rosie said. 'Please, I want to see his face.'

Seaton had hold of Amos's collar. He pulled him to his feet, head lolling to one side.

'He's breathing. No injuries.' A small pause. 'Not yet.'

Arden pulled back his coat to show a knife and a pistol. 'In case you have any thoughts, we're both armed. Seaton's a better shot than me. He's had plenty of practice out here. He'll aim for your wife, and believe me, he won't miss. Think about that, Westow, losing your son and your wife together. It would be a terrible blow.'

'Do you think you'd survive?'

The man gave a thin smile. 'I've forgotten more about fighting than you'll ever learn. He might not look it, but Mr Seaton is deadly, too. You'd do best to stand and take your punishment. An eye for an eye, isn't that what the Old Testament says? A son for a son.' He paused then raised his voice. 'I daresay you brought that girl with you. As soon as she shows herself, your boy is dead. No hesitation.'

As Arden spoke, Seaton placed Amos on the bench. His drugged body was limp, head lolling over the end. The final touch was the scrape of the bucket being pulled into position. To catch the blood, Simon realized. As if his son was no better than a pig.

'Don't,' Rosie said. 'Please.'

Arden stared at her. 'Your husband should have thought of that before he arranged the murder of my son.'

She started to move forward. Arden and Seaton drew their pistols, both weapons aimed at her. Simon rested a hand on Rosie's shoulder.

Whatever Jane and Ramsey were going to do, it needed to happen soon.

'This started before Franklin,' Seaton said. It was a shock to hear him speak. 'It began when Westow decided to involve himself with those two children who died at the mill. You caused trouble and you cost me money.'

'Your overseers killed them.' Inside, Simon was shaking with terror for Amos. But he made sure his voice sounded strong.

Seaton shrugged. 'People die all the time. For all kinds of reasons.'

'Like Sebastian Ramsey?'

'Some are mistakes. Unfortunate, nothing more than that. Clerks are easy to replace. Just like mill hands.'

He drew a long, shining knife from the scabbard. The same one that had been used to slit the throat of the pig.

'Why don't you kill me instead?' Simon asked.

'There's more pleasure in giving you a lifetime of sorrow and pain,' Arden replied. 'If I'd wanted it to be easy, you'd have found him dead yesterday. This way I can enjoy your faces.'

'No.'

He took a pace forward. Seaton had put down his pistol to attend to the knife. Arden moved his hand, weapon pointing at Simon.

'If you fire that and miss, I'll have you dead in ten seconds.'

'No you won't.' He inclined his head towards Seaton, standing over Amos with the knife at the boy's neck. 'His life would be over before you ever touched me.'

Simon felt his heartbeat, the breath moving in and out of his chest.

The rifle shot split the morning sky.

TWENTY-NINE

The sound filled his ears. Arden's pistol spiralled into the air. Simon watched as it rose, three fingers still attached to the metal as it fell to the ground. The man tried to fumble for his knife with his left hand.

Ramsey was already on him, his blade out. A slash across the forehead that sent blood cascading into Arden's eyes, leaving him helpless and open.

The explosion had stopped Seaton. He stood, long knife in his hand, staring at the fight as if he wasn't sure what to do.

Rosie took three steps towards him, brought the gun from under her cloak and pulled the trigger. She was too close to miss. The lead ball caught him in the shoulder and made him reel backwards.

He stared at the wound, then at her, as if it was impossible to believe a woman could have done that. She didn't give him the chance to recover. Rosie had her knife in her hand, stabbing him, shouting. The words became a blur, one dissolved into another. By the time Simon reached Amos, Jane was next to Rosie, watching as she hacked at Seaton's flesh. No expression on her face, not a sound out of her mouth.

He lifted the boy. So light. Alive, drugged, no sign of any injury. Simon needed to make sure his son was clear of the killing ground. Gently, he put him down on the cracked leather seat of the carriage and covered him with the blanket. Safe. Soon he'd be going home.

A man's scream cut through the air. He kissed Amos's forehead and turned.

Ramsey was on his knees, hands trying to cover the long gash across his belly. Arden stood, ready to finish him. His eyes were filled with blood, he was badly wounded, but he was grinning. Cuts all over his body. Somehow he'd managed to pull out his own knife and use it.

Shouting, Simon launched himself at Arden, catching him around the waist and sending him sprawling in the dirt. He struggled, starting to roll away. Simon drew the gun and placed the barrel again Arden's forehead.

'Is that what you're going to do? Shoot me in the head?' He was panting hard, trying to keep the breath in his body. The man was dying. No question about it. This was his last defiance. Face covered in blood. His coat was sticky and dark, shirt rust red.

'You're not worth the powder.' He kicked Arden's knife across the farmyard. He'd never be able to crawl that far. Let the bastard suffer. Let him die, slowly, painfully. The man's pistol lay a few yards away. Simon picked it up and discharged it to the sky.

Seaton lay on the ground, curled up, trying to protect himself. He was in a lake of blood. Rosie hadn't stopped. Still blow after blow. No sign of slowing. Jane stayed back. She caught his eye and Simon shook his head. Rosie needed this. A way to purge her soul. In a little while she'd exhaust herself and it would be over. Seaton was probably already dead. His body didn't move as she stabbed it.

Ramsey was on his side. The day was cold, but he was sweating.

'I let down my guard.' He attempted a smile, then grimaced with pain. 'I was taught not to do that. My fault. He was better than I expected.' He could only manage shallow breaths. 'Your son?'

'Alive. He'll be fine.'

A flicker of the mouth. 'Did your wife kill Seaton?'

Simon glanced over. Rosie had finished. She was climbing to her feet as if she'd stumbled out of a dream. Blood all over her dress and her hands. Her face was spattered with it.

'Yes,' he replied.

'Good. If only it would bring back Sebastian. Go and look after your family, sir.' With an effort that made him clench his jaw, he raised his hand. Simon took it.

There was nothing to be done for him. Charles Ramsey was beyond the care of any doctor.

'Thank you.'

'My pleasure, sir. Truly it was.'

Simon rose to his feet. Everything was death. Seaton. Arden. As he stared down, Ramsey's eyes closed.

Rosie looked around. The knife hung from her hand. Very gently he slid it out of her fingers and wrapped his arms around her. She began to shiver and he hugged her closer. Trying to give her his warmth.

'It's done,' he whispered. 'We have Amos back.'

With slow, small steps he walked her over to the carriage. Amos had some colour in his cheeks and his eyelids were beginning to flutter.

'Why don't you stay here with him?' Simon said.

He helped her up into the carriage. Rosie cradled the boy's head in her lap, stroking his hair and cheek. Once he felt sure she was settled, Simon walked back and stood, hands on hips, surveying the scene.

It was like staring at a battlefield after the fighting had ended. Three bodies and a pool of blood soaking into the cold dirt.

'What are we going to do with them?' Jane asked.

He'd forgotten she was there.

Arden and Ramsey lay close together. It would be easy enough for someone to imagine they'd fought each other to the death. If there was no other story, people would accept it. Eventually, perhaps, someone might recognize a description of Ramsey. The night watch would never come anywhere close to the truth. Simon picked up the Baker rifle. That would go back to Leeds with him. There were only a few in town; it wouldn't be too difficult for the constable to track down its proper owner and start asking awkward questions.

Seaton was the problem.

They could simply leave him. But that would bring problems when the farm workers returned and discovered the scene.

Bury the man?

No. He'd never manage it. He was too drained to dig. All the tension and the fury that had fuelled him through the night was beginning to ebb. His body was heavy, legs feeling as if they were cast from lead, not made from flesh and blood.

Besides, the men who knew this land would spot any fresh hole quickly enough. No, it wasn't the answer.

Maybe there was nothing else he could do. There was nothing here that could touch him or his family. It could remain a mystery, an horrific slaughter that no one would ever solve. Let gossip and rumours fly all through the winter, maybe for years.

Tempting, he thought. Give people some meat to chew. But it was dangerous, too. Maybe someone would conjure up a tiny fragment, a connection that led to Simon. With Seaton and Arden dead, he couldn't afford that risk. Alive, they'd been too rich and influential. Even as corpses they were important.

He looked around one final time, hoping against hope for some kind of answer. A piece of magic to make Seaton's body disappear.

Nothing. Then he caught sight of the piggery around the oak tree. He remembered what Rosie had told him after they'd come out here before.

She was still cradling Amos, wetting a handkerchief in her mouth and using it to clean off his face. He looked much closer to stirring, his arms moving, thrashing around a little.

'Nothing's broken,' she said. 'I can't see any cuts.'

Thank God for that. They'd been saving him for Seaton's knife.

'The last time we were here, on the way home, you said something about the pigs.'

'What?' Blinking, she raised her eyes to look at him. Slowly, the memory surfaced on her face. 'Yes. The man who showed me round the farm said that pigs will eat everything.' Rosie frowned, suddenly alarmed. 'Why? Simon, what are you going to do?'

'I'm going to try and keep us safe.'

He stood over Seaton's body. The man's eyes stared up at the grey sky, but he'd never see it again.

'Can you help me with him?' Simon asked Jane as he took hold of Seaton's wrist. The flesh was still warm, but rapidly growing cooler than anything alive, the texture of the skin harder, waxier. Uncomfortable to touch. He forced himself to take a firmer grip.

Jane grabbed the other arm as if it was nothing.

'Where are we taking him?'

He gestured over his shoulder as he started to drag Seaton along. The long horse trader's coat snagged and ripped apart on roots and twigs.

Simon stopped. He was breathing hard, his back ached, and they weren't even halfway there yet. A few seconds of rest and he bent again. This time Seaton's flesh didn't feel so strange.

As they came closer, the pigs sensed something. They began to squeal and grunt with excitement. Their hooves scrabbled against the brick walls of the sty. Growls and snarls as the animals turned on each other.

'Are we putting him in there?' Jane asked. She glanced nervously over the wall.

'Yes.'

'Won't the workers find him when they come back?'

'No. The pigs will eat him.'

Her eyes widened, a mix of fear and disbelief. 'They eat people?'

'They do,' he told her. For the first time he could recall, Jane looked shocked.

Tipping the body over the wall took the last of his strength.

It was harder to manoeuvre a dead weight than he'd ever imagined. Especially with the pigs jumping up and snapping their jaws. They had sharp, eager teeth; twice he had to snatch his fingers away.

One final push and Seaton was gone. Tumbling down into a swirl of noise on the dirt and the straw. Simon looked. Only an instant had passed but he couldn't see the man any longer; he was lost as the beasts clambered over him, fighting each other for space. He heard the bites, the devouring of flesh. They'd turned him into a rare, delicious feast. Simon shuddered as he turned away.

He took out his watch. Barely twenty minutes past nine. He held it close to his ear to be certain it was working. Twenty minutes? He felt as if an entire lifetime had passed since he guided the carriage into the farmyard. How could it all have happened so quickly? Death should have stopped time.

The pigs were growing louder and angrier. It was time to leave. To go home.

Home.

It sounded like a word to wrap around himself. He'd come out here roaring with anger. With hope. But deep inside he hadn't been certain they'd be taking their son home. Or who would be returning to the house on Swinegate.

He pulled himself on to the bench of the carriage. It felt like scrambling up a mountain. Simon sat for a moment before he took the reins in his hand.

'Do you want to ride back with us?' he asked Jane.

She shook her head, exactly as he knew she would.

'Thank you,' he said to her. A final glance of gratitude to Ramsey. The man had died where he'd been born, not where his heart lay. But without him this might never have succeeded.

All the dead. What had happened to their souls? he wondered. Where had they gone? Heaven? Hell? Or was there nothing at all?

He wasn't the man to answer those questions. Not when weariness was creeping up his body. He needed to be away from this place, free of them all.

A flick of the wrist and the horses began to move. Out of the drive, along the track to the Harrogate Road. As they turned toward Leeds, Simon let out a long sigh of relief. It was over.

* * *

Jane watched them go and started to walk. No need to look back and see what remained. Another hour or two and the wild animals that lived out here would be sniffing at the corpses.

More vehicles on the roads now, so she kept her distance, tramping through the grass and the undergrowth. She knew the people in the carts and coaches would barely give her a glance. Those who did would likely forget her before they even looked away. Another girl, nothing more.

Once she'd passed through Chapel Allerton she could see Leeds on the horizon. Factory chimneys reaching to the sky.

She'd wanted to help Rosie with Seaton, but Simon's wife had been in a frenzy where nothing could reach her. She had to keep going until it was done. The man never had a chance against her.

It was Rosie's fight. Her need for revenge. No one had the right to take that from her. Exactly the way it had been with Jane and her father. She had to be the one to end his life, to prove beyond doubt that he could never hurt her again.

After she'd walked away from his body, she'd put him into an empty room in her mind with all the thoughts and memories and nightmares. Forced it all in there, closed the door and locked it. No more. Perhaps he was finally gone for good.

She smelled Leeds long before she reached it. After the clean air of the country, it caught in her throat and left her choking and retching, coughing to try and take the taste from her mouth.

Over the bridge and into Sheepscar, then along the hill that took her to town. By the time she'd came to the Head Row, Jane barely noticed the soot.

Through Green Dragon Yard and the hole in the wall, then unlocking the door of the cottage. Mrs Shields and Richard sat there, both turning, expectant and hopeful, as she entered.

She gave a small nod to the old woman. Catherine smiled, and all the tension left her face. They'd been playing a game of some kind, something she'd never seen before, a board with ladders and snakes on it, and small coins for counters.

'I'm sure your parents would probably like you to go home now,' she told Richard. 'Your brother will be there.' Mrs Shields turned to Jane. 'Isn't that right, child?'

For a moment she didn't know how to reply. Then she caught the eagerness in the boy's eyes.

'Yes, he's waiting for you. Come on, I'll take you.'

He knew her; she'd lived in the attic of Simon's house before she moved here. He'd seen her every day. But Richard was still hesitant around her, looking to Mrs Shields for reassurance. One night here and he trusted her. That was her gift.

'You go,' the woman told him. 'I'm glad you could spend the night. I hope you'll come and visit me again. Bring your brother next time.'

'I will. Thank you, ma'am.'

He stood and bowed like a young gentleman. At the door he looked back and waved shyly.

Simon pulled on the reins and the carriage halted outside his house. Waves of exhaustion shuddered through him. Amos was awake, but still bleary and groggy, with his head in Rosie's lap. She looked peaceful, glad to have her son back safe.

So was he. Too often since Amos was snatched he'd imagined finding the boy's corpse. For once the story had a happy ending.

He'd mourn Ramsey. A good, decent man who'd wanted to do right by his brother. Without him at the farm, who knew which way things might have gone? He'd been their surprise; he'd fought without fear. And the men responsible for his brother's murder were both dead. The blood covenant had been broken.

Simon climbed down, steadying himself as he stood and took a deep breath. He slid Amos off the seat and into his arms, sagging under the weight. An hour before the boy had felt as if he weighed nothing. How had he suddenly grown so heavy?

Rosie unlocked the door. Climbing each step to the bedroom was an effort. Finally he could lower the boy on to the bed and stretch his back.

Home. Secure, safe. No more threats. No glancing over his shoulder every time he went out. Simon gazed down at his son. In time, he hoped Amos would be able to put the last day to the back of his mind. There would be nightmares, he was certain of that, and his son would never completely forget. But children healed quickly; that was what people claimed. Let it be true.

He ached for his bed, to close his eyes and enjoy a few hours of oblivion. But he wasn't done yet. He still needed to return the carriage and trudge back here. That pleasure would have to wait a little longer.

'Where did you go?' the ostler asked as he examined the beasts. He lifted the hooves to inspect them.

'Kirkstall,' Simon answered. He had the lie ready. It was a completely different direction from Seaton's farm. Safer in case anyone ever grew suspicious. 'Had to deliver a few things to my wife's friends over there.' He shook his head. 'You know what women are like.'

The man chuckled. 'All too bloody well. They never stop going on until you do what they want. The horses look grand, Mr Westow. Come back next time you need something.'

Jane had brought Richard home. Now he was sitting upstairs with his brother, breathlessly reciting everything he'd done with Mrs Shields as if they'd been the greatest adventures in the world.

Rosie had changed her dress and scrubbed the blood from her face and hands. Her hair was gathered back. She stood and watched the twins, content, but looking as exhausted as he felt. No surprise. Just an hour before, she'd killed a man, stabbed time and again. Now that had ebbed away. He put his arms around her, smelled her skin.

'They can't ever hurt us again now.'

She nodded and rested her head against him. 'Tired?'

'Yes.'

'You go and sleep. I'll stay here with them.'

'Are you sure?'

But she didn't need to answer the question. They were her babies. After all that had happened, she needed to gather them close to her. He didn't argue. In their room, he closed the shutters, threw off his clothes and settled under the blankets. For a little while, at least, the world could go away.

THIRTY

Leeds, December 1823

The air was hazy with smoke, but if the wind picked up, they might see some blue skies and sun later, Simon thought as he strode across Leeds Bridge and back into town. It was a chilly morning and he moved briskly, easily, glad to feel his old self once again. Just a week before, he'd woken with all the aches and tiredness that had slowed him earlier in the year finally purged from his body.

His full recovery had come just as a pair of cases arrived, thefts of money and plate. Straightforward work; he was on his way home after returning the items from one of the robberies.

A week until Christmas. The shop windows were filled with goods tempting people to open their purses. He had money in his pocket; maybe he'd buy something for Rosie and the boys.

Close to the Moot Hall, someone called his name. He looked up and saw William Hey, the physician from the infirmary, hurrying towards him, walking stick thumping the pavement with every step. He stared at Simon's face with a clinical eye.

'You're looking in fine fettle, Westow.'

'I feel it,' he replied with a smile.

'Your colour's good, eyes clear. All the symptoms gone?'

'Everything back to normal.'

'Excellent news.'

'What did I have?'

Hey shook his head. 'Honestly, I'm damned if I know. We learn more about medicine every day, but with too many things . . .' He shrugged. 'We guess and hope for the best, unfortunately.' A small cough. 'Did you ever manage to do anything about those two children who died at Seaton's mill?'

'A settlement for their parents.'

'At least there was something.' He frowned. 'That was a strange business out at his farm, wasn't it?'

'Very.'

Word had buzzed around Leeds for weeks. Arden and an unknown man both dead, Seaton nowhere to be found. Gossip had been rife, overflowing into rumours and possibilities. Simon listened in the mornings at the coffee stall, amused by some of the stranger ideas he heard.

No one came close to the truth; he hoped they never would. The constable had come to ask him if he knew anything about it and gone away again when Simon said no. Seaton's bones had never been discovered; maybe the pigs had devoured those, too.

The whole thing would remain a mystery forever. It would end up as one of those tales that people enjoyed but never quite believed.

Amos had started with the nightmares on his first night at home. He woke screaming three times. Rosie soothed him, Simon sat and held him. It had been the same for a week. It hurt to see his son thrashing and hear him crying out. After that, it had eased a little. Only twice in the last month. During the day he seemed fine; Simon had watched him carefully. The boy appeared absolutely normal, playing and studying the way he always had. At night, though . . . that was when the demons came out to play in his head.

At the first cry, Rosie always hurried out of bed, as if she was never more than half-asleep. She'd been quieter since their return from the farm, more attentive to the twins. He'd catch her watching them, silent and brooding. If she wanted to say anything, she would.

'Do you think Seaton's gone off somewhere and he's still alive?' Hey asked.

'I don't know,' Simon told him.

'Curious.' The doctor lifted his hat. 'I'm glad to see you well again, Westow. A good Christmas to you and your family.'

The quick tap of stick on stone as he walked away.

Jane came out of the ginnel as the boy ran towards her. He was glancing back over his shoulder and didn't see her in his way. He swerved, trying to avoid her and crashed into a brick wall. She took hold of his collar, twisting it, and showed him the knife in her hand.

'You're going to take it back and apologize.'

It was an embroidered handkerchief, with careful lace work

on the edges. Expensive, an item for a lady. She'd been passing the mercer's shop when the boy dodged by, ducking inside the door. Not even a second and he was out, running off with the handkerchief balled in his fist.

He thought he was quick, but he wasn't clever enough. Now he was terrified, squirming and trying to hold back the tears brimming in his eyes. Clothes no better than a scarecrow, no shoes or stockings on his feet. Just bare, dirty flesh.

The woman behind the counter opened her mouth in disbelief as Jane forced the boy through the door ahead of her. 'Go on.'

He opened a grubby hand and dropped the handkerchief. 'I'm sorry.' His voice was weak, reedy, the words barely making it out of his mouth.

Jane let go of him. He slithered away, disappearing before she could catch him again. No matter, she knew his face; if she ever wanted to, she could find him.

'Are you his family?' It was an accusation. Understandable. She didn't dress like someone with money. Still the same old dress and cloak. The shawl covering her hair. Boots, not shoes.

'No. I was passing.' She nodded towards the handkerchief. 'How much?'

The woman wore a mocking smile as she named the price.

Jane brought coins from her pocket and counted out the money. 'I'd like it washed and ironed. I'll collect it tomorrow.'

'Yes, miss. Of course.' The shopkeeper was all sweetness now. She waited and took the receipt the woman wrote out. 'First thing in the morning. Thank you.'

The handkerchief would make a good gift for Mrs Shields. Christmas was close and the woman liked delicate, feminine things. It was the least she could do.

By evening she'd traced the boy. He was in an abandoned building across the river, sitting with the other strays around a fire made from old beams. Shadows leaped across the walls. At least they had some warmth for the night.

He didn't notice her until she was next to him, dropping a few coins into his lap. Enough to buy him shoes and socks. Enough for food to keep his belly from being empty for days.

It was probably stupid, a pointless gesture. But she didn't want his thanks. She recalled what it was like to live out here, to never know about tomorrow. Jane let the money trickle from her fingers and walked away.

'You were involved, weren't you, Simon?' George Mudie settled behind his desk at the printing shop and poured himself a small tot of rum.

'Involved in what?' As if he didn't know what the man meant. Since Arden had died and Seaton disappeared, Mudie had been peppering Simon with questions.

'Don't be coy. Up at the farm. Who was the man no one can identify?'

Simon held up his hand in surrender. 'I'm not the person to ask. You keep thinking I know, but I'm no wiser than anyone else.'

He and Rosie had discussed it one night after the boys had fallen asleep. They would carry it as a secret to their graves. It was much safer to keep quiet than risk word ever leaking out.

'Did you hear that Seaton's mill is going up for sale in the New Year?' Mudie asked. 'The lawyers can't find any heirs, so everything's on the block.'

'Someone will buy it. The place makes money. Nothing will change.'

'Of course not. Grow up, Simon. It's never going to change until the law gives them no option. Even then they'll try to find a way around it. The rich will grow richer and the poor will stay desperate.' The briefest of hesitations. 'I'd love to know what happened to Seaton, though. Didn't take anything with him when he left – no one's heard a word about him. It's almost as if he died, except there isn't a body.'

'I don't suppose we'll ever know.' Simon stood, smoothed down his coat and picked up his gloves. The morning was cold. Before dawn it had been clear enough to pick out the stars, thousands of them in the sky. Now the factories were churning out smoke, and Leeds was blanketed by its haze.

'Come on,' Mudie said as Simon reached for the door handle. 'Give me a clue. The third person.'

He turned back, smiling. 'At the coffee cart, someone suggested it might be a foreigner.'

It was a lie, but it would keep him busy for a while as he tried to dig and find the truth.

Fathers and sons, he thought as he cut along Commercial Street. Billy Hardy and his boy Peter, Jeb Easby and Jacob. Both boys dead before they really had lives. George Collins and his father. Thomas Arden and Franklin. From one generation to the next. Sin and blood covenants. All the fabric of lies. And finally Simon and Amos, the lucky ones, still alive.

When he was young, growing up in the workhouse, the master beat the vengeful words of the Old Testament into them every Sunday. He could still hear the voice, clear and angry, cutting through all the years: 'The Lord, the Lord, a God merciful and gracious, slow to anger, and abounding in steadfast love and faithfulness, keeping steadfast love for thousands, forgiving iniquity and transgression and sin, but who will by no means clear the guilty, visiting the iniquity of the fathers on the children and the children's children, to the third and the fourth generation.'

God help them all.

Jane walked down Briggate, taking the mercer's receipt from her pocket and unfolding it. Everything neatly written in an elegant, flowing hand. She'd watched the woman do it, so practised that she hardly paid attention to making the words.

And here she was, unable to read any of it.

In the shop, a girl younger than her, dressed in a pale frock and a heavily starched apron, glanced at the receipt and brought a package from under the counter. It was wrapped in paper and tied with red and green ribbon.

'Here you are, madam.' Her smile turned doubtful as she took in Jane's clothes, but she still sketched a curtsey, the way she'd been taught, and added something to the receipt. 'To show it's been collected,' she said with a smile.

'Thank you.'

Jane left, suddenly uncomfortable and awkward around these women who took things like reading and writing for granted. She pushed the packet into her pocket, out of sight, as if carrying it was embarrassing. Her fingers cradled the hilt of her knife and she smiled to herself. They might have skills that were beyond her, but there were things she could do that they could never imagine.

She slept well every night these days. The ghost of her father no longer haunted her dreams. The knife and the quiet gurgle of his last breath had exorcized him. She was free. She'd shaken off the past and she could make her own future.

She was still wrapped in her thoughts as she walked through the court, a short cut back to Mrs Shields's house. He appeared from around a corner in front of her, blocking the path.

Her half-brother. She hadn't sensed any threat. Yet here he was, trembling with anger and fear as he stood holding a knife.

'You killed him, didn't you?'

Jane stared. It must have cost him a lot to come and find her; she could read it on his face and hear it in the wavering voice.

'Yes,' she told him. No need to go into the reasons. He wouldn't care about Simon's son. That wasn't even the whole truth. 'I told you what he did to me.'

She closed her hand around her blade and produced it from under the cloak. He looked as if he'd scarcely ever handled a weapon, let alone used one.

'He'd only just come back and you took him from me again.'

'Did you say you have a wife and children?' she asked quietly.

'Two girls and a boy,' he replied, wrong-footed by her question.

'Go home to them,' Jane told him. 'If you try to use that knife on me, I'll have to kill you. Your wife will be a widow, and those children of yours might never remember their father. Is that what you want?'

He pushed his lips together, rocking back and forth. She moved forward, took the knife from his fingers and dropped it on the ground. Then she strode on, leaving him there.

She didn't want to know his name, didn't want to know his children. All that was behind her.

But as she entered the yard by the cottage, she knew she needed something more.

Mrs Shields was sitting by the fire, reading her book. She glanced up with her gentle smile.

'Did you mean what you said about teaching me to read?' Jane asked.

'Of course I did, child.'

'Can you teach me to write, too? Is it hard?'

AFTERWORD

In strange, unlikely ways, novels often refract the world the author sees every day. That's certainly true in this case. I started an earlier version of *The Blood Covenant*, which then had a working title of *The Blood Yard*, at the beginning of 2020. The Simon Westow novels have always been carried along on a wave of anger, and mine was certainly there. It was sparked by the excavation of bodies in the graveyard of the old Ebenezer Chapel. The dead factory children brought from the earth had been starving when alive, always hungry although they and their families worked twelve hours a day. Then the pandemic arrived, and the fury evaporated, replaced by sorrow and the sense of fragility and impermanence of life. In lockdown I put the book aside and began another, one for the Tom Harper series called *A Dark Steel Death*. By the time I'd finished that, in the autumn of 2020, my rage had returned tenfold at all the lives lost due to the incompetence of people in power almost everywhere around the globe. *The Blood Covenant* has similarities to the book I started at the top of the year, but it's definitely not the same. I hope I've used the feelings inside to better effect than before. After all, as the song lyric goes, anger is an energy.

There's no deliberate intention to have the novel resonate with any of the affairs of 2020. If that appears to be there, it's purely unconscious. This is fiction. Of course, the events of 1823 are there: the documented cruelty to children in the factories all around England that's the starting point here, the huge gap between rich and poor.

History is cruel. In the early part of the nineteenth century, the working classes often led short, hard lives. The men who built the combinations – trade unions – and fought the bosses found themselves facing wealthy, ruthless opponents. Change happened very slowly and it was hard won. People died, blood was shed, many were convicted of 'crimes' and transported to the other side of the world. For the lives we enjoy today, we all owe them a debt.

Each time I sit down to write, I try to make a book the best I've ever written. Ultimately, though, that judgement is down to you, the readers. I'm grateful to each and every one of you and I hope this book has satisfied. But while I put the words on the page, there are plenty of others to thank: Kate Lyall Grant, for commissioning this, Sara Porter, my editor at Severn House, and all the others in the office who do such a wonderful job, not only for me, but for all their writers. My agent, Tina Betts. My editor and friend, Lynne Patrick. Friends who've read versions of this on its way to becoming the finished article. And above all, my partner Penny, who has heard me talking about this all through the writing and revision process before reading it herself, then correcting typos and pointing out errors and contradictions.